I0763180

ECHOES OF INFAMY

Books by Shaina Steinberg

UNDER THE PAPER MOON

AN UNQUIET PEACE

ECHOES OF INFAMY

Published by Kensington Publishing Corp.

ECHOES OF INFAMY

SHAINA STEINBERG

kensingtonbooks.com

KENSINGTON BOOKS are published by

Kensington Publishing Corp.
900 Third Ave.
New York, NY 10022

All Kensington titles, imprints, and distributed lines are available at special quantity discounts for bulk purchases for sales promotion, premiums, fund-raising, educational, or institutional use. Special book excerpts or customized printings can also be created to fit specific needs. For details, write or phone the office of the Kensington Special Sales Manager: Attn. Special Sales Department. Kensington Publishing Corp., 900 Third Ave., New York, NY 10022. Phone: 1-800-221-2647.

Library of Congress Control Number: On file

KENSINGTON and the K with book logo Reg. US Pat. & TM Off.

ISBN: 978-1-4967-4784-6
First Kensington Hardcover Edition: June 2026

ISBN: 978-1-4967-4785-3 (ebook)

10 9 8 7 6 5 4 3 2 1

Printed in the United States of America

The authorized representative in the EU for product safety and compliance
is eucomply OU, Parnu mnt 139b-14, Apt 123
Tallinn, Berlin 11317, hello@eucompliancepartner.com

For Jason

Chapter 1

Los Angeles, June 1949

Evelyn Bishop's red suit stood out like a beacon against the dull gray sky. Her dark brown curls were pinned back neatly. She wore simple makeup and jewelry. As the female president of one of the largest companies in the world, she understood she was a novelty. Her usual instinct was to hide in the shadows, but that was a luxury she could no longer afford. Instead, she stood on a high, hastily constructed stage on the edge of an empty field that would soon become the new Bishop Aeronautics Factory. The podium was covered in red, white, and blue ribbons, while several American flags waved lazily in the breeze. Almost two hundred people were in attendance—mostly employees, politicians, and locals, who were all counting down the minutes until they popped the corks on the free champagne.

The mayor of Los Angeles, newly minted and unaware of the company's recent history, spoke of Bishop Aeronautics' outstanding commitment during World War Two when it came to manufacturing the airplanes that flew over Europe and the Pacific. The governor, playing to the crowd, talked about the company's service to the troops, both during the war and upon the veterans' returns. The U.S. senator, who knew better, simply spoke of the future.

In between each speech, the local high school's marching band struck up rousing renditions of national songs. They ranged from "America the Beautiful" to "My Country, 'Tis of Thee" to "You're a Grand Old Flag." It felt like overkill. As Evelyn waited for the last bars of "The Battle Hymn of the Republic" to fade, she wondered if this show of patriotism was meant to counteract the fact that her father was a traitor. For the last two weeks, Lewis Bryson, her vice president in charge of operations, had stopped by her office at least once a day to warn her against mentioning Logan Bishop. Each time, she nodded, wondering how to celebrate the expansion of her company without mentioning its founder. Evelyn had spent months working on her speech. It was hard to find the words to explain the significance of this project. It was the fulfillment of her father's dreams . . . and the last of the road map he left before ceasing to be one of the lodestars in her life.

Evelyn glanced down at her notes. The mischievous part of her wanted to deliver an epic poem. The pragmatic part knew she had to be done by four so the story could run in the evening edition of the *Los Angeles Times*.

"Bishop Aeronautics is a family company," Evelyn began. "Not just because my father built it from the ground up. Nor because I'm currently running it. It's our belief that everyone who works here is a vital part of this community and we take care of each other. We understand that every aircraft holds someone precious, whose loved ones are waiting at the end of a journey. New advancements, like those produced here, will shrink the world and open up new adventures. A journey from New York to London now takes seventeen hours. Soon that will be reduced to seven. As we step into the jet age, we have a commitment not only to the city of Los Angeles and the state of California, but to every single person who flies on our planes. We hold this mission sacred and promise to continue earning your trust every single day."

Polite applause and one loud wolf whistle from Evelyn's husband, Nick Gallagher, followed her speech. Even five months after their wedding, it still felt strange to use the word "husband." As Evelyn stepped off the stage, flashbulbs burst, recording the seventy-six-step journey to where a silver shovel waited for the official groundbreaking. Until recently, this was farmland and Evelyn's heels sank low into the loamy earth. She took the shovel and symbolically moved a scoop of dirt two feet from where it originated—a prelude to the excavators arriving the next morning. After another round of applause, she was swallowed by well-wishers and those wanting a photograph to commemorate their presence. The bureaucrats smiled broadly, sharing the glory of an event in which they took no part. It felt like ages, but realistically, it was approximately a half hour before she finished the obligatory handshakes.

Evelyn let out a deep sigh, relishing the stillness after the pomp and circumstance of the day. Nick pushed through the lingering crowd. He was tall, with dark hair and a nose that tilted at a slight angle from where it was broken years ago and never properly set. The look he gave her always made her feel like they were the only two people in the world. He grabbed her in a bear hug, swinging her off her feet and twirling her in a circle.

"Great speech," Nick said, then kissed her in a way that was not meant for public consumption.

"You liked it because it was short," Evelyn teased.

"I think you hit all of the high notes," he replied, not denying her statement.

Behind Nick was Carl Santos, one of her oldest and closest friends. Broad-shouldered, with sharp, intelligent eyes, he often looked stern and imposing, as befit his position at the FBI. Underneath was a warm, kind person who could make anyone feel at ease. Evelyn, Nick, and Carl met during the war when they worked for the OSS. The fear and the secrecy of their assignments cemented their bond, both behind the enemy lines and in the pubs of London. Now, years later, in the daylight of civilian life, they were still family.

Evelyn gave Carl a hug.

"Thanks for coming."

"For you, always," he replied with a broad smile. It wasn't the first time he showed up for her, but at least this time, no one was shooting at them. "This place is going to be incredible."

"You put together a nice shindig," said a voice from behind Evelyn. She turned to see LAPD Captain John Wharton, whom she had invited to represent the police onstage. Both Nick and Carl had served under him with varying degrees of success. He was a gruff man, utterly devoted to the job and the citizens he protected. Evelyn worked with him enough to develop a deep respect that almost bordered on friendship.

"I'm so glad you came," Evelyn said as she gave him a hug. He stood stiffly for a moment, before putting one arm around her and patting her back awkwardly.

"Hate to break it to you, but this isn't my jurisdiction."

"What? Who am I going to call when I get into trouble?" she asked.

"You could let things be boring for a while," Wharton suggested.

"If only," Carl sighed.

"Can't imagine it's easy with Gallagher around," Wharton agreed.

"Nice to know you care," Nick said, grinning.

A few other people, including Evelyn's close friends Colette and Lily, came by to offer their congratulations. Evelyn's aunt Taffy, who, along with Evelyn's secretary, Julia, had organized the event, approached to receive their well-deserved accolades.

" 'Battle Hymn of the Republic'?" Evelyn asked with a raised eyebrow.

"They went rogue," Taffy replied. "I told them two songs up front, but it seemed rude to call out fifteen-year-olds for showing off. This might be their only moment of glory."

Evelyn laughed, but her attention was caught by a soldier, wearing his dress uniform. He made a beeline toward them, his innate confidence not hiding his anxiety, nor his anger. As he approached, Evelyn deciphered his rank from the insignia on his uniform.

"How can I help you, Captain?" Evelyn asked, offering a guarded smile.

Carl looked over with surprised recognition. "Billy? What are you doing here?"

"I'm sorry I didn't tell you. I worried you might try to stop me," the man replied before turning to Evelyn. "My name is Billy Takemura from the 442nd. You're building this factory on stolen land."

Chapter 2

Twenty minutes later, Evelyn, Nick, Carl, and Billy Takemura were sitting in Evelyn's office. It was sparsely decorated with a desk, a few chairs, and an uncomfortable couch. The most prominent feature was a picture window that looked over the factory floor. It was quiet and dark, seeing everyone went home after the ceremony. Julia Martinez, Evelyn's secretary, arrived with two bottles of champagne, but when she saw their expressions, she changed her offer to coffee. Evelyn glanced toward those assembled, who shook their heads.

"No, thanks," Evelyn said. "But, please check if Lewis is still here. He would have been part of the land deal."

"Of course," Julia said, then left the office, closing the door behind her.

Billy's eyes warily surveyed the room, already on the defensive. Carl stepped closer and put his hand on Billy's shoulder reassuringly.

"Captain Takemura—" Evelyn began.

"I'm no longer in the Army," Billy corrected. "However, I find people are more willing to hear me out when I remind them that I am an American citizen who served my country. I was born in Long Beach and I deserve to be here as much as the next person."

Clearly, this was an argument he had fought more times than Evelyn could imagine.

"Billy and I met during the war," Carl explained. "In Bruyères."

"Didn't really catch me at my best," Billy agreed, with a faint smile.

Nick whistled under his breath. In late 1944, the 442nd, a unit made up entirely of Japanese American soldiers, was caught up in a brutal campaign to rescue Bioffontaine and Bruyères, in Northern France. It involved over twenty-four hours of intense combat. Before they could rest, however, they were tasked with breaking through German lines to rescue a battalion from Texas. It was almost a full week of fighting uphill, through mined fields, and suffering hundreds of casualties.

"You lost a lot of good people," Nick said. "Never seen a braver group of men."

"The Japanese American unit was the most decorated in the war," Billy replied.

"Which was even more impressive, considering the circumstances," Carl added.

Billy's face softened slightly as he looked at Carl in gratitude for his support.

"Why don't you start at the beginning," Evelyn suggested.

"My parents were born in Japan. They came to the States when they were young, thinking this was the land of opportunity, where they could build themselves a life." Billy shook his head at the irony. "My brother, Hanzo, is the oldest, then me, and last is my sister, Mary. Life wasn't perfect before the war, but we worked hard and my parents had a thriving restaurant, right on the corner of the land you're turning into your new factory. Dad managed the front of the house, serving meals, overseeing staff, and handling the money. My mother cooked in the back. My brother, sister, and I picked up whatever else needed to be done. It was the only place where we didn't quarrel. My father would have killed us."

"This place was the same for my brother and me," Evelyn remembered. "A family business is sacred."

Billy studied her for a moment, then nodded.

"I went to Occidental for college and studied history," he continued. "Back then, I wanted to be a professor."

"And now?" Nick asked.

"Who would hire me? There aren't a ton of opportunities for Japanese Americans. They'll let us work in the fields or clean homes, but they don't want us teaching their kids or performing surgery on their parents. Somehow, we're still the enemy."

"You and your family were interned in 1942," Carl said.

"No human should ever be rounded up by armed men and thrown into camps. My parents did everything right. They worked harder than you can imagine, never asked for handouts. They spent a lifetime building a business and it was ripped away from them, through no fault of their own."

"What happened to the restaurant after you were taken away?" Evelyn asked.

"We entrusted it to a friend," Billy replied. "Letters from him slowed, then eventually stopped. Last we heard, he'd run it into the ground and closed the doors."

"If you never sold it," Nick said, "you should still have claim to it."

"All I know is that when my family came back in 1945, the restaurant was their first stop. It had turned into a diner run by someone we'd never met before. My brother, Hanzo, lost it, started yelling that it was ours and demanding to see their deed. The cops were called and he spent the night in jail."

"There had to be some records," Evelyn insisted.

"And so much red tape," Billy replied. "How could we prove we didn't sell it?"

There was a soft knock on the door and Evelyn looked up to see Julia.

"Sorry for interrupting," she said. "Lewis is gone for the day."

"Please set up a meeting with him in the morning."

Julia nodded, jotting down a note in the small notebook she carried everywhere.

"I can't change what happened to your family," Evelyn said, turning back to Billy. "Nor can I give you back your restaurant. When we started preparing for construction, I didn't know its history. We leveled the entire site."

"My family didn't want me coming here today. They thought it was pointless. At least you listened to me," Billy said as he turned to leave. "That's more than I expected."

"If you didn't think Evelyn could help you, why did you come?" Nick asked.

"I had to say my piece," Billy replied. "I needed you to know what happened."

"And now that we do?" Carl prodded gently.

"I don't feel much better," Billy admitted, turning to Evelyn. "Maybe your family stole the land. Maybe they didn't. Most people aren't evil, but they didn't speak up when it mattered."

Evelyn felt the guilt of his indictment. It was true, she did not protest what happened. She remembered reading in the paper about the mass roundup of Japanese Americans and thinking it was atrocious. It also felt like a foregone conclusion by the federal government. There was nothing she could do to change it, nor did she try. By then, her brother was a POW and her mind had room for little else. Not that it was an excuse.

"I'm sorry," Evelyn said, hoping those words would cover a multitude of sins.

"Thank you," Billy replied. It was not the apology he deserved, but it was all she could offer at that moment.

Chapter 3

Evelyn and Nick's house sat on the edge of the beach. A concrete boardwalk divided the sand from their front lawn. In the distance, they heard the waves crashing and the constant calls of the seagulls. Theirs was a relatively small two-bedroom house that came furnished in various shades of white and beige. In the right light, it mimicked the look of the sand beyond their windows. Evelyn sought to break up the monotony with a rug, pillows, and a throw blanket in a riot of colors. Their other addition to the space were the books that lined the shelves from floor to ceiling. Both she and Nick were avid readers and appreciated distractions when thoughts of the past made it impossible to sleep.

While the crisp, clean ocean air was pleasant in the daytime, night had fallen and it was not quite summer enough to fully invite nature to take up residence. Evelyn closed most of the windows, except in the living room, where Nick lay on the couch reading. Upon seeing her, he set his book aside and opened his arms. She slid into them, resting her head on his chest. The subtle thump of his heartbeat was a metronome quieting her thoughts to a measured pace. Inhaling, she was comforted by his scent. She would know it anywhere, signaling that she was home. He held her close and she slowly felt the tension flow out of her. It was not just Billy's pronouncement and all of the implications it carried, but also the anxiety she had carried while preparing for the groundbreaking ceremony.

"Not exactly the day you were hoping for," Nick said, twirling a lock of her hair around his finger.

"No, not exactly."

Their plan had been to go to dinner and celebrate with their closest friends and family. That promise of that evening had been her bright light amidst all of the late nights and drudgery of finalizing the plans for the expansion. No matter how many times she thought she had signed the last form or approved the newest revision, there was always more. She longed for the time when the construction was complete and they were producing planes on a regular schedule, just like her current factory. Though she was a person constantly drawn to adventure, the stress of this project left her longing for a steady routine.

"Your father would be proud," Nick said. Against his chest, he felt Evelyn's lips curve into a smile.

"Well, he did most of the work."

"That's not true," Nick replied. "Maybe he started the process, but it was your sheer force of will that got the project approved."

"Oh, no," Evelyn corrected. "That was Colette convincing Alan Hunsaker to get the right people to sign off. Did you notice she brought him to the ceremony today?"

"I did, in fact, notice she was not alone," Nick commented. They had both known and liked Colette's late husband, George Palmer. Solving his murder had brought them together again after three long years apart. Nick would never feel pleasure at a good man's death, but he was eternally grateful to reconnect with the woman he now called his wife.

"I wonder what it means," Evelyn said.

"Maybe all city planners are required to attend groundbreaking ceremonies," Nick teased. "Maybe he was there for the free champagne."

"Nothing more?"

"Nothing that's any of my business," Nick replied.

"If you can't indulge in a little innocent speculation—"

"Gossip."

"—With your wife, who can you?" Evelyn said.

"You don't give yourself enough credit," Nick replied, ignoring her question. "You traveled all over the country getting new contracts approved. You made sure there was enough business to justify the new factory. You hired the right engineers and scientists to build jet engines. I know this was your father's dream, but you're making it a reality."

"Thanks," she replied quietly.

"You don't talk about him as much as you used to," Nick observed. "Nor Matthew."

"Since we moved here, I'm not surrounded by reminders of my family in the same way."

The prevailing wisdom was that grief could be conquered with time and space. Evelyn knew the truth. It would forever be her constant companion, making itself known in strange and unexpected moments. After her mother died when Evelyn was eight years old, Logan's sole focus in life, even more than his company, was to ensure his children felt loved. He had succeeded admirably. For years, Evelyn's father was her hero and the first person she turned to for advice. When her brother died, they mourned together. Now, even those memories were clouded with his betrayal.

"You must miss Logan," Nick began. "It's been almost a year and a half since he . . . um."

"Fled. It's okay, you can say it. He fled from justice. And I helped him."

"What he did was wrong, but he was trying to save his son," Nick said. "If we had children, I'd probably make the same decision."

"If we had children . . ." Evelyn repeated quietly.

It was not a topic they discussed often. Nick wanted a family, but Evelyn was not sure she shared the sentiment. She knew herself to be a kind, loving person, but that did not always translate into being a good parent. Mothers, especially, were often expected to give more of themselves than she was willing to sacrifice. She loved her work, she loved Nick, and she loved her current life. Who knows how that would change with the addition of a child? Nick was aware of Evelyn's uncertainty before they married and made the conscious decision to choose her over that dream. Yet, he had not given up hope. He wanted to give his kids all of the love he had never known.

Growing up, Nick thought all disagreements started with raised voices and ended with raised fists. His parents were volatile people whose drinking did not improve their moods. Though they never said it outright, Nick believed he and his siblings were a product of carelessness rather than planning. Nick could not remember a single time his mother gathered him in her arms or his father treated him to a gentle word. From his earliest moments, he was on guard, feeling like home was a place of conditional safety.

When he was twelve, he returned from school to find his parents and siblings had left without him. The next few years, he survived only by the goodness of strangers turned friends. He found backbreaking work, and developed the skills he needed to protect himself. He never sought a fight, but he also learned the hard way that sometimes he had to strike first. After a few instances that made people think he was crazy, they mostly left him alone. He still had scars as rewards for his independence.

The one hope that survived the awful shock of abandonment was that his siblings would return for him. Nick's eldest brother, Brennan, lied about his age and joined the merchant marines when Nick was eleven. However, Nick's middle brother, Cassian, was four years older and had often defied their parents. What was once more, to rescue Nick from the streets? His sister, Paula, was three years older. She had shown him the closest thing he had ever known to a mother's love. There were so many nights when he prayed his siblings would come find him. Perhaps to take him home. Perhaps to start fresh, just the three of them. Whatever passed for a fairy godmother never came. With the distance of time, he could see that this path led him to Evelyn. However, he often wondered if it could have been slightly easier.

Evelyn pushed herself up far enough to kiss Nick. He wrapped his arms more tightly around her as their kiss deepened. Theirs were rarely the sedate kisses of people long married. They always lingered and sometimes, like now, they caught fire. She reached down to the narrow space between their bodies and began unbuttoning his shirt. Her breath caught as his hands trailed along the bare skin of her lower back. He loved her small gasps of pleasure when he touched her. She smiled as he turned her to look into her eyes. Unfortunately, this current couch was not as wide as their previous one. Evelyn rolled a smidge too far and Nick followed. They landed in a heap on the floor.

"This fits in well with the rest of my day," Evelyn said.

"I had a feeling we'd end up here, but I was hoping for a bit more fun beforehand."

They looked at each other again, then started to laugh. The mood was officially ruined. Evelyn sat up, leaning against the couch.

"What did you think of Captain Takemura?" Evelyn asked.

"You're thinking about another man right now?"

Evelyn raised an eyebrow at him.

"Yeah, okay," Nick sighed. "It can't have been easy for members of the 442nd. Fighting for a country that threw them and their families into camps? I don't think I'd be able to do it . . . and yet, they fought like demons."

"Almost like they had something to prove."

"Billy Takemura still does," Nick commented. "You can see it in the way he walks. His expression."

"There's more to it. He needs someone to acknowledge the injustice of it all," Evelyn mused. "I'm curious about his family."

"You want to visit them?"

"Not sure I'd be welcome. They have no reason to trust me," Evelyn said. "Do you currently have a case?"

"Nothing I can't delay."

"Then let me be your client. Help me figure out what happened to their restaurant."

"I have to warn you," Nick began, "I'm very expensive."

"Perhaps we could work out a trade," Evelyn said with a sly smile.

"Very, very expensive," Nick replied. They stared at each other for a moment; then Nick stood, swooped Evelyn up in his arms and carried her upstairs to their bedroom.

Chapter 4

The face that opened the door of the modest brick house in Crenshaw was not friendly. It belonged to a Japanese American man, with rumpled black hair and wary eyes. Evelyn offered a smile, which was dead on arrival.

"What?" the man demanded.

"Is this the Takemura residence?" Nick asked. "We're looking for Billy."

"Why?"

"He came to see us yesterday," Evelyn said. "About your family's former restaurant."

The man's expression hardened. He turned inside and called out in Japanese. Then they heard Billy respond. What started at conversational volume quickly grew in anger and ferocity. Nick and Evelyn were forgotten. The battle occurring in this house was one of raised decibels from different rooms. A soft woman's voice soon joined the chorus in a tone that could only be described as pleading. Finally another woman spoke sternly. She did not have to raise her voice; authority was embodied within it. The man at the door responded once, but she did not tolerate dissent. Her retort was sharp and he deflated slightly before turning back to Evelyn and Nick.

"You might as well come in," he said, opening the door wider.

Evelyn and Nick stepped over the threshold. The man motioned to where a few pairs of shoes were lined up neatly by the door. Evelyn stepped out of her heels and Nick untied his brogues. They were ushered into the living room. It was furnished with pieces that looked like they had come from a local rummage sale. There were a few family photos on a side table and a beautiful silk scroll hanging on one wall. Beyond that, there was little decoration.

Billy hurried into the room, trailed by a young woman in her twenties. She had shoulder-length black hair, pulled back into a low ponytail. Her dress looked to be secondhand, the cuffs and hem worn, with the pattern of the fabric faded slightly. She wore no makeup and looked exhausted. It was not the tired of a few too many late nights, it was slumped shoulders and the haggard appearance of a woman weighed down by something larger than herself. In one of the family pictures, her head was thrown back laughing. Her hair and makeup were perfect. The joy in her expression made her beautiful. It was a sharp contrast between the quiet, solemn woman in front of them. Leaning on her arm was an older woman in her late sixties. The woman shuffled slightly, grimacing in pain, as she was helped into a chair. Her face was pallid and her breath shallow and gasping. Evelyn guessed cancer having seen it firsthand with her mother.

"What are you doing here?" Billy asked Evelyn and Nick.

"I'm trying to learn more about what happened to the restaurant," Evelyn said.

"I don't understand," Billy replied.

"I'm a private investigator," Nick explained. "You say you never sold that land. I believe you. I'm trying to figure out how it came to be part of Bishop Aeronautics."

"I . . . I didn't think I'd ever see you again," Billy said, perplexed.

The other man snapped at Billy in Japanese. Billy responded angrily.

"English," the older woman commanded. "We have guests and this is no way to treat them. Come sit." She gestured Evelyn and Nick to the couch. "Mary, please make some tea."

"Yes, Mama," the young woman answered, and vanished into another room.

Evelyn and Nick took their seats. The older woman nodded to Billy, who sat in a chair beside her. The other man had a restless energy that made it impossible to imagine him still.

"My name is Maiko," the older woman began. "These are my sons. Billy, you seem to have met, and Hanzo, my eldest. My youngest, Mary—"

"Himari," Hanzo muttered under his breath.

"She has chosen to go by the English name Mary and we'll respect her wishes."

"Just because we conform doesn't mean they'll respect us," Hanzo insisted. "Did these past years teach you nothing?"

"Don't speak to our mother like that," Billy admonished.

Hanzo looked to his mother. She held his gaze until he dropped it and muttered, "Sorry, Mama."

"It's not about them respecting us," Maiko said. "It's about us respecting each other."

The brothers looked chastened, but Evelyn doubted the détente would last.

"Can you tell us a bit more about your restaurant?" Nick asked.

Maiko smiled. "It was our dream, Kenji and me. My

husband always said I was a good cook and I love to do it."

"Me too," Nick said.

"We'll have to trade recipes," she promised.

"I'd love that, though I'd be getting the better deal. I have much more to learn from you than I could ever hope to offer," Nick replied.

"Sometimes we surprise ourselves," Maiko said, before continuing her story. "We opened the restaurant back in 1929. Not the best timing, but how could we know? It was a struggle just to get there. I had dreams of serving all of the food I grew up with, but after the crash, we changed toward a more casual setting. It was important to me that everyone could walk in and get a good meal."

"You kept some traditions," Hanzo said. "It was a mix of my mother's Japanese cooking and American diner food. Completely unique."

"We did our best. We survived, which is more than most people could say at the time," Maiko continued. "When Kenji first arrived from Osaka in 1916, he took a job working at a farm. He was a good worker and his boss, Raijin Nagasaki, saw his talent and gave him more responsibilities. Kenji worked for years to save up enough money to buy that plot of land and build the restaurant. He was so proud when we opened our doors. Finally a future that was ours."

"But not officially," Hanzo grumbled.

"My parents were both born in Japan," Billy explained. "After 1919, they were not allowed to become citizens, and only citizens could own businesses or buy land. It was all in Hanzo's name."

"For all of the good it did," Hanzo said. "Dad—"

"Enough," Maiko said sharply, before dissolving into a fit of coughing. Mary entered with the tea tray, set it on the coffee table, and poured a glass for her mother. She carefully held the cup to Maiko's lips, raising it gently to help her drink. It was another minute before Maiko regained her breath. She leaned back in her chair, spent. Mary sat next to her mother and took her hand. Maiko gestured to Mary to continue the story.

"Of course, there was Pearl Harbor," Mary said. "We were sent away."

"Not all of us," Billy retorted.

"Some of us refused to be lambs, willingly led to the slaughter," Hanzo replied tartly.

"Some of us chose to take responsibility for our families," Billy said.

"Until you left."

"You left first," Billy countered, glaring at his brother for a minute before turning back to Evelyn and Nick. "We were rounded up like cattle. We brought only what we could carry: mostly clothing and bedding because the latter would not be provided. There was no room to bring a lifetime's worth of memories. One of our neighbors stored some of our things and we sold my father's car for pennies. Our furniture, appliances, and art were left behind. The vultures circled—white men who showed up at our door offering to 'help' by buying family heirlooms for almost nothing. The Army took us to a racetrack and made us live in stables that had not been cleaned of the soiled hay. Latrines were a single open room, as if we were animals with no more dignity than the horses that previously occupied our new homes.

"Eventually they moved us to Manzanar. The living quarters were smaller than our former dining room and they offered almost no protection from the winter wind or the summer's heat. Our old life was gone."

"And Hanzo?" Nick asked.

Maiko sighed heavily. "When it became clear we would be taken, Hanzo left to avoid being sent to Tule Lake with his father."

"Tule Lake?" Evelyn asked. "I thought they sent people to Manzanar or Poston."

"Or Gila River or Topaz or Jerome," Hanzo drawled. "I could keep going."

"Didn't realize there were so many," Nick said.

"Easy to ignore when you're not in the middle of it," Hanzo replied.

"Tule Lake is where they sent people they thought were suspicious," Mary said.

"As opposed to the ones they randomly locked up," Hanzo added.

"Because of the restaurant, my father imported a variety of food and supplies from Japan," Billy explained. "The FBI accused him of using those shipments to pass secrets or . . . I don't know."

"They picked up a lot of fishermen on the suspicion they were guiding Japanese boats to California," Mary continued. "Of course, none landed here, but people were afraid of their own shadows."

"Hanzo had been arrested a bunch of times . . ." Billy trailed off.

"Most of those were bullshit," Hanzo explained.

"Language," Maiko said.

"Sorry, Mama," Hanzo replied. Then, turning to Nick and Evelyn, he shrugged. "I got into a couple of fights when I was growing up. A lot of people didn't know how to keep their opinions to themselves."

"Hanzo thought he was protecting me," Mary said.

"He had a rotten temper," Billy added.

Ignoring him, Hanzo stated, "I went to Utah, then made my way inland to Chicago. I got a job as an orderly at a hospital, of all things."

"Hanzo is starting his first year of medical school in the fall," Maiko added proudly.

"Never thought I could be a doctor until one of the physicians took me under his wing. I started college at DePaul and made a life," Hanzo explained. "When they finally began releasing people inland, my mother and Mary couldn't return to Los Angeles. I got an apartment for all of us, helped them find jobs, and introduced them to new people. I was there when they needed me. Where were you, my dear brother?"

"You can't keep blaming me for what happened," Billy said.

"Watch me," Hanzo replied.

"There's no point rehashing this," Mary interrupted. "You two are free to hate each other on your own time. Inside this house, you will be civil. If not for me, then for our mother."

Abashed, both brothers apologized. Maiko looked as though she had heard all of this before and did not believe it any more than the last time.

"Can you tell me more about what happened to your restaurant?" Evelyn asked.

"Forget it," Hanzo said. "As everyone keeps reminding us, the past is in the past."

Maiko leaned forward, her voice raspy. "We had a friend—"

"Mama, it doesn't matter," Mary said. "It's gone. We have to make peace with that."

"Less than three months ago, you two were railing about how we had to take action," Billy said. "What changed?"

"The restaurant was bulldozed. We're not going to start over somewhere new," Mary replied. "I wish you could let this go."

"Well, I can't," Billy said. Then he turned to Evelyn and Nick. "The writing was on the wall in February, when

Roosevelt issued Executive Order 9066. I don't think we realized how quickly it would happen. A month later, a new proclamation came out giving us forty-eight hours to leave our homes. We had to figure out what to do with everything, especially the restaurant. Donald Holcomb, who worked with Mama in the kitchen, offered to keep it running. We'd known him for years and we trusted him."

Hanzo snorted.

"That didn't work out?" Evelyn asked.

"At first, he sent us updates and some of the profits," Mary explained. "Then the letters got less frequent and the money disappeared. Eventually we got a letter saying that Donald had to shut the doors."

"The bastard sold the place," Hanzo said angrily. "We never saw a penny."

"You're lucky he didn't press charges," Mary said.

Evelyn looked between them. "What happened?"

"Hanzo ran into Holcomb on the street and couldn't control his temper," Billy explained. "Beat the man bloody and put him in the hospital."

"He deserved it."

"It almost cost you your acceptance to med school," Mary replied fiercely. "You've built a good life. I'm not going to let anything threaten that."

"Know where I can find Mr. Holcomb?" Nick asked.

"There's no point in going over there," Hanzo said. "We talked and got it sorted out."

"So, he shouldn't mind chatting with Nick," Evelyn suggested.

"It's not that we think he'd mind," Mary said quickly. "It's just after everything that happened, we don't want to bother him."

"Bothering people is kind of what I do," Nick replied.

"No kidding," Hanzo said under his breath.

"Holcomb's got a place near Sepulveda and Pico," Billy said. "I went to check on him in the hospital, but they'd already released him. Got his address, but didn't quite feel right about stopping by unannounced. Not after all that happened."

Billy stood up and went to a side table. A pen and a pad of paper filled with messages were beside the phone. He flipped to the first blank page, tore it out, and wrote down the address.

"Here," Billy said, handing it to Nick.

"I know you want to help," Mary said to Evelyn and Nick. "However, this is a family matter. I don't want to waste your time when nothing will change."

"Maybe not," Evelyn replied. "But for my own sake, I need to know what happened."

Chapter 5

Donald Holcomb's house had a dingy, neglected feel. Though the counters were clean and the floor recently mopped, the faded wallpaper still had faint rectangles where pictures used to hang. A door on the cabinets was missing and Nick saw the sparse shelves holding a few glasses and some mismatched plates. The whole place had a feeling of bare minimum. Enough furniture, but nothing comfortable. Enough food, but nothing appetizing. Enough house, but nothing that made it a home. It was impossible to imagine joy here. Nick sipped the coffee in front of him from a chipped mug, surprised at how its quality far exceeded his expectations.

"You make a good cup," Nick said to the man sitting across from him.

Donald Holcomb matched his kitchen. Once upon a time, he might have been considered attractive. He had dishwater-blond hair and blue eyes that had faded into the color of a cloudless sky at high noon. His shoulders slumped and his skin was sallow, with premature wrinkles. Nick knew he was still somewhere south of forty, yet he appeared to have lost all hopes for whatever came next.

"Thanks," Donald said to Nick's compliment. "Maiko taught me. Eggshells in the grounds take away the bitterness."

"Learn something new every day," Nick replied, filing away the information for tomorrow's breakfast. They sat in silence for a moment, appreciating their drinks.

"My wife left me," Donald said, apropos of nothing. "It was after I lost the restaurant. I couldn't forgive myself. I became . . . I don't know."

"Someone else?" Nick offered.

"Before the war, that place was hopping," Donald explained. "Morning, noon, and night, there was a line out the door. Maiko's food . . . you had to try it to believe it. The whole family worked there. Little Mary seating people when they came in. Billy serving food and Hanzo bussing the tables. And, of course, Kenji managing the details."

"How did you come to work for them?" Nick asked.

"I showed up in Los Angeles for the same reason as anyone else. Thought I could be the next Clark Gable," Donald said. "Turns out it's not that easy. Everyone here was the best-looking kid in their hometown. I was heading down to Long Beach after another failed casting call, when I stopped at the diner for a bite. Kenji took pity on me. Saw I was down on my luck and offered me a job waiting tables. He was a fair boss, paid decent, and let me skip work whenever I had an audition. Which, to be honest, wasn't that often. I'd say Hollywood was a dream that died hard, but Maiko made me realize that my move here was less about stardom and more about leaving Idaho for somewhere new. She believed each of us could be whatever we wanted.

"Over the years, I moved up until I was Maiko's sous chef. She taught me everything I know. The Takemuras treated me like family. They invited me for Thanksgiving dinner and catered my wedding all of those years ago. They were the best of people."

"Do the best of people beat you up in the street?" Nick asked.

Donald shrugged.

"You didn't even put up a fight, did you?"

"I deserved it."

"That why you didn't press charges?"

"Can't blame Hanzo. I would've done the same thing."

"What happened after Pearl Harbor?"

"Everyone was on edge. There's always been a lot of anti-Japanese sentiment, but this was more than I could have imagined. Overnight their customers disappeared. Then the government grabbed Kenji. The thought of him being a spy is ridiculous. If you'd known him . . . He loved this country more than anyone I've ever met. He was the living embodiment of the American dream. He came here from somewhere else, worked hard, and had a thriving business. Sure, it wasn't perfect, but he was damned proud of what he and Maiko built. They drafted some paperwork that let me make decisions regarding the restaurant on their behalf. I don't even know if it was legal, but I was supposed to keep running it. Maiko suggested giving it a new name and getting rid of anything that reminded people of them. A complete fresh start. It broke her heart, but she also believed it was the only way for it to survive. I'd been watching the Takemuras for years. I thought it would be easy," Donald confessed ruefully.

"It's never as easy as it looks from the outside," Nick replied.

"I was never as good a cook as Maiko," Donald said. "And I had no idea how Kenji did the ordering. One week I had way too much sirloin, the next I ran out after only a day. Our staff was almost all Japanese, and, of course, they were imprisoned. The new girls I found were unreliable at best. They barely worked and sometimes didn't show up at all. More than a few nights, the till was short. I did my best to send the Takemuras money in the camps. I know it wasn't like what they made previously, but I promise you, I was doing my best."

"I believe you," Nick said. It was his standard encouragement to keep someone talking, but Nick realized it was true. There was something so broken and guileless about Donald Holcomb, it was hard to imagine him intentionally cheating someone.

"I think we would have been okay," Donald said. "Maybe not great, but I think I could have held on. Then these kids started coming around."

"Kids?"

"Hooligans," Donald corrected himself. "They were sixteen, seventeen. They came in and harassed the customers. I tried to drive them out, but they kept coming back. They were loud and disruptive. Order a coffee and stay all morning. They'd sit down at a woman's table and make crude jokes. They'd sit down at a man's and mock his . . . endowments. Our waitresses quit and we lost customers left and right."

"What did you do?"

"I went to the sheriff, who said it was just boys being boys. Nothing he could do," Donald said. "Funny, how he never extended that excuse to Hanzo."

"He was in trouble?" Nick asked.

"All of the time. I was never sure how much of it was him being difficult and how much was the fact that Sheriff Richardson didn't like folks who didn't look like him."

"Don't hold back, tell me how you really feel," Nick said.

"You have no idea the shame Kenji felt every time he had to bail Hanzo out of jail. Maiko worried America was corrupting her children. It became even more challenging when the family was separated. They didn't even have each other. Losing the restaurant was the final straw. I had no idea what it would do to Kenji."

Nick waited a minute for Donald to explain, but when it became clear he would not, Nick prompted, "Which was?"

"He killed himself."

Nick sat back in his chair, the air exiting his lungs. No wonder the Takemura children were so angry at each other. Both Billy and Hanzo thought the other could have saved him, if they made different choices.

"Kenji had just been released from Tule Lake and went to join Maiko and Mary at Manzanar. Billy was in the Army by that point and Hanzo was in Chicago. When Kenji arrived at Manzanar, there were rumors that he had implicated other people in exchange for being reunited with his family. He was ostracized. Not even his oldest friends spoke to him. I think the loss of the restaurant broke him. Mary found him in their quarters, dangling from a length of rope around his neck."

"That poor girl," Nick replied.

"You see why I don't blame Hanzo for his reaction?" Donald asked.

"You clearly care about the Takemuras. Why didn't you send them the money from the sale of the restaurant?" Nick asked.

"I know they gave me those papers saying I could do what I thought was best, but I'd never sell it without Maiko's permission."

"You didn't wonder what happened to it?"

"When it became impossible to keep going, I shuttered the doors and walked away. Few months later, I drove by and it was a diner called Ruby's. I assumed Maiko leased the space to someone else. Until I ran into Hanzo a few months ago, I had no idea they didn't own it."

"So, if you didn't sell it, and they didn't sell it, how did Logan Bishop buy the land?" Nick wondered.

Donald had no answer.

Chapter 6

Evelyn never understood why Lewis Bryson always wanted to conduct meetings in the conference room. It was a plain room, across the lobby from her office, with one long wall covered in photographs of Bishop Aeronautics' planes. The other side had a window overlooking the factory floor. The table was created from the biplane wing of Logan's first creation. It crashed thirty-one seconds into its maiden voyage and Logan kept it to remind himself that everyone is fallible. Whenever Evelyn ran her hands over it, she could feel a part of her father's spirit. Around it, Logan had placed low metal stools. It was his belief that most meetings were a waste of time. The more uncomfortable people were, the quicker they got to the point. Lewis had argued for years to make the room more professional, but Logan refused. Any deal he had ever done came down to the two people who could make decisions finding their way into the same place. They usually sealed the agreement with a handshake and left the lawyers to write up the details.

When Evelyn took over, Lewis brought her plans to make the room into something so formal it belonged in a legal office. She refused, partially because she did not want to be mistaken for an interior designer. Largely, though, if it was not broken, she saw no reason to fix it. Especially seeing Lewis loved the sound of his own voice. He was in his late fifties and kept himself fit with twice-weekly tennis games. While he had to dye his gray hair back to its original brown, his sharp blue eyes were filled with intelligence. He never let anyone forget he graduated from Dartmouth. At times, Evelyn wondered why her father chose Lewis as his right-hand man, but it was a moot point. He had been with the company almost twenty-five years.

Across the table from Lewis, on a stool that was comically small for his large frame, was Ben Strover, the contractor Lewis hired to build the new factory. He wore chinos and a button-down shirt, whose sleeves were rolled up over his tanned, muscular forearms. With wavy light brown hair, he was an undeniably handsome man, who thoroughly appreciated the deference that came with it. At the groundbreaking ceremony, Evelyn remembered meeting a petite blond woman and two adorable children, who called Ben "Daddy". The way he looked at his wife, with admiration and devotion, was a sentiment not seen in all marriages. Evelyn had not spent much time with him, but that moment lingered favorably in her mind.

"Doesn't matter," Lewis huffed. "We have the deed. The plans have been approved by the city. We're not going back now."

"Nor am I asking you to," Evelyn replied. "But if we build on land we don't own, it opens us up to all kinds of lawsuits."

Lewis snorted. "No court in the world would side with them over us."

"Tell that to Fred Oyama," Evelyn said. The two men looked at her blankly. "Supreme Court case. California tried to seize his land and it was ruled unconstitutional."

"We didn't seize anyone's land," Lewis replied. "Moreover, we build planes essential to national defense. They're not going to shut us down."

"The deed must have been submitted with the permit applications," Ben said.

"Sure, but what about the sales documents?" Evelyn asked. "I talked to Ruth, my father's secretary. She's an encyclopedia and she can't find it."

"You're worrying over nothing," Lewis insisted.

"The Takemuras spent years building their restaurant, just like my father spent years building this company."

"We were at war," Lewis said. "Roosevelt made hard decisions to keep us safe."

"Sacrificing a group of people for the supposed safety of others doesn't sit well with me," Evelyn retorted sharply. "Shouldn't sit well with anyone."

"Listen," Ben began. "I'm sympathetic to what happened to the Japanese Americans during the war. It was wrong. Evelyn, I think you're smart to confirm we're doing this by the book. It will save us trouble down the line. Lewis, I also agree with you. This train has left the station and it's going to keep moving."

"What happens if the sale proves illegal? Why are we opening this can of worms? We don't have time to sit around a fire singing songs and holding hands," Lewis snapped at Evelyn. "Business requires decisive action, strong leadership, taking advantage of opportunities, and not seeking out trouble."

For a moment, Evelyn stared at Lewis, fighting her anger at the dressing down. Then she stood, went to the door, and held it open.

"Ben, would you give us a moment, please? Lewis and I have some matters to discuss."

Ben glanced at Lewis, before standing up, gathering his

papers, and heading out to the lobby. Evelyn closed the door quietly behind him, then took a seat next to Lewis.

"You think you'd be better at running this company than me," Evelyn said.

"I have more experience," he replied.

"Well, you're certainly older," Evelyn agreed. "But I grew up with the world's best teacher. Every day, my father talked about his work. He loved it almost as much as he loved us. When was the last time you felt joy here?"

Lewis did not answer.

"My father cared about the bottom line. Of course, he did, but not so he could stash it away in some bank. He reinvested it here in gyroscopic navigation systems and laminar flow wings. Look at Loening. Look at Davis. Look at Grinnell, Bach, or Fowler Aeronautics. We succeeded when so many others failed because my father never stopped innovating. He never rested on his laurels. Every single night, he came home and explained how things could be better. He taught us to look for how we could be better."

"Which is why we're building the new factory," Lewis said. "Logan was also definitive. When he made a decision, that was it. Done. He never looked back and he never second-guessed himself."

"No, but he did incorporate new information as he learned it."

"I worked with your father every single day for almost twenty-five years. We built this company from the ground up. You ask about all of those other companies that failed? It wasn't just Logan. I did the work he could not be bothered with. He was the dreamer, and God knows he was brilliant at it. I made sure we were always standing on a solid foundation."

"I remember when I was little," Evelyn began, her voice

softening. "Sometimes my mom brought Dad lunch. Matthew and I tagged along. We loved coming over to your office because you always had caramels hidden in your desk drawers."

Lewis smiled. "I kept them for the two of you."

"Dad sometimes said that it was his prerogative as a father to always see me as his little girl. I've known you almost my whole life. You watched Matthew and me grow from children to adults. It's hard to revise our first impressions of someone. In my mind, you were always the man hidden behind stacks of papers, barking orders at someone. I don't give you enough credit for all that you have done for my father and for this company."

Lewis did not disagree.

"You're right," Evelyn continued. "Dad never cared about all of the steps it takes to get a government contract. The senators you need to talk with, their aides. Which committees oversee what and who is good at persuading others to support us. When he wanted something done, he expected it would be . . . and he was usually right. He could close a deal, but you set up the meetings and connections. You did the hard work and we have a lot more ahead of us. I know this past year has been challenging, but I believe we can do great things together. We have a whole new world of airplanes to design and build."

"It starts with the new factory."

"I know," Evelyn replied. "But I'm not taking shortcuts. We can be a moral company and a successful company at the same time. Despite his actions during the war, it was one of my father's founding principles."

"There were times your father hated me," Lewis confessed. "It was my job to bring him unpleasant facts."

"It's still your job."

"I don't think you appreciate how much this new factory is costing us."

"Trust me, I do," Evelyn said.

"Every type of expansion is a risk. We've already borrowed a substantial amount to get this project off the ground. While we have a line of credit, any delay is more than we can afford."

"When Dad first came to you with this idea, what did you think?"

"That it was the right one. What you said about the future is true. We have to keep growing."

"This is your baby," Evelyn said.

"In a way," Lewis admitted.

"Then let's figure out a way to earn each other's trust," Evelyn replied. "We stay on schedule for the new factory, but I'm also going to figure out what happened to the Takemuras' land. I don't know that I can make it right, but I can try. I believe it's what my father would have done."

Lewis looked less certain, but nodded and stood up. As he did, his knees creaked.

"When your father built this conference room, he never accounted for us getting older."

Evelyn laughed as she opened the door. "I don't think he ever expected that to happen."

As Evelyn stepped into the lobby of her office, she found Ben sitting on the edge of Julia's desk. Willa, an engineer, had her head thrown back, laughing. Julia wore the trace of a smile as Ben continued his story.

"So, there we were, frantically propping up one thing after the other, the rain is still coming down in sheets, and I realize that we're on a hill. Lost six good bottles of bourbon that day."

"Should have drunk them faster," Willa chided.

Now it was Ben's turn to laugh, putting his hand on her arm. "Where were you when I needed you?"

"Kindergarten, I think," she replied.

"My God! Everyone is so young!" Ben exclaimed.

"You're only what . . . ?" Evelyn began, not willing to hazard a guess.

"Forty," Ben admitted.

"Ancient," Evelyn teased.

"Let me tell you, it was a rough birthday," Ben said. Then he turned to Lewis. "Did you get it all sorted out?"

"Full steam ahead."

"That's what I love to hear," Ben said, jumping to his feet. "In that case, I'm back to work. Ladies."

He bowed to Evelyn, Julia, and Willa, before heading downstairs with Lewis. Evelyn shook her head, then noticed a slight blush on Willa's cheeks.

"He's certainly a charmer," Evelyn said.

"Indeed," Julia agreed dryly.

Evelyn turned her attention to Willa. Tall, lanky, and prone to wearing trousers, she had strawberry-blond hair, cut in a chin-length bob. She had both chemistry and engineering degrees from UCLA. Having gone there herself, Evelyn knew the work and intelligence involved in just one of those tasks, never mind both. It was no surprise Willa was now the new favorite protégé of Hank, the curmudgeonly head of the engineering department.

"What can I do for you?" Evelyn said.

"Is this a bad time?" Willa asked. "I can come back."

"Nonsense. What's going on?"

"Remember how I applied to UCLA to get my PhD?"

"Of course," Evelyn replied.

"And remember how you wrote me that wonderful recommendation?"

"All of it true."

"They must have believed you. I got in!"

Willa's face lit up and Evelyn gave her a huge hug.

"That is the best news!" Evelyn exclaimed. "I knew you could do it! You're going to be brilliant there."

"I can't thank you enough," Willa said. "I wouldn't have applied, except for . . . I mean, that is to say . . . um."

"You want to make sure the company's still going to pay for it."

"Tuition is a bit . . ."

"I made you a promise," Evelyn replied. "Bring the bills to Julia and we'll cover them. Books and other expenses, too. Ten years from now, you'll be designing the next-generation airplane for me."

"You've got a deal," Willa agreed happily.

Chapter 7

The bell above the diner door chimed as Nick walked inside. It was a relatively small restaurant—twelve orange vinyl booths with a chrome-and-polished-wood counter in the middle. The floor, black-and-white–checked tiles, showed both years of shoe prints and diligent daily cleaning. The front wall was plate glass and gave the place enough sun to render the fluorescent lights unnecessary. It was two in the afternoon and the lunch rush had cleared out. In one booth a woman nursed her coffee and read a book. In another, a man in shirtsleeves circled Help Wanted ads in the newspaper, while absently eating French fries. Nick took a seat at the counter and the waitress brought over a pot of coffee.

"Freshly made," she said.

"How can I resist?" Nick asked.

She gave him a smile as she turned over his cup, filled it, then set it back in its saucer. Her moves were efficient and practiced. She looked to be in her late twenties, with red hair piled messily on top of her head. It was not especially stylish, but she made it work. The ill-fitting uniform barely contained her curvy figure and a small dimple in her left cheek made her seem warm and approachable. It had taken a few hours spent at city hall for Nick to look up her full name on the restaurant license for the Takemuras' former place. Then he placed a call to her apartment, where her roommate told Nick where she worked.

"Ruby DuBois?" Nick asked. "Formerly of Ruby's Diner?"

"That all depends," she replied. "You here to offer me money? Or a good time?"

"Wish I could do both."

"That's the dream, isn't it?" she asked. Her tone carried hints of flirtation, but Nick also sensed a keen intelligence. She knew how people, men especially, viewed her, and she would not waste their low expectations until she knew what they wanted. "What can I do for you?"

"I have some questions about your former diner, out by Bishop Aeronautics. I'm trying to figure out what happened."

"Same thing that always happens," she said. "Men are real bastards."

"Aren't you supposed to say, 'Present company excluded'?"

"No," Ruby replied. "At some point, you were probably a bastard to someone."

Nick thought about it for a minute before agreeing, "I was."

"Least you can admit it," she replied. "Pie?"

"Why not?"

"Apple, peach, or blueberry?" she asked as she picked up a white ceramic plate and headed over to a glass display case, where three pies rotated slowly.

"Blueberry," Nick replied.

"Wise man," Ruby said. "It's our best."

She cut out a piece, then slid it in front of Nick. He

picked up a fork and took a bite, his eyes widening in surprise.

"Jesus," he said, taking another bite.

"I do like to believe my pies are a religious experience."

"You made this?"

Ruby nodded.

"You certainly deserved your own diner," Nick said, savoring another bite.

"Being a baker was my dream for years. I know little girls are supposed to want to be wives and mothers . . ."

"Not all of them," Nick commented.

"My mama taught me how to make pies. Best damned baker in the whole world. She worked in a diner like this, after my daddy died. I'd come help her after school."

"Where was this?" Nick asked.

"We bounced around for a while, each place less expensive than the last. Finally ended up near Redding."

"I've never been."

"I've spent enough time there for both of us," Ruby said.

"Let me guess, you came south to be an actress."

"Hell no. And don't be one of those guys who thinks telling a woman she could be an actress is a compliment. It's not. No, I figured everyone's gotta eat. Knew I could always get a job in a restaurant, ideally making desserts. Figured maybe one day I'd impress someone enough for them to take a chance on me opening my own place."

"And you did."

"In a way," Ruby said. "Wasn't my baking, though. Man came in when I was working a counter like this. Struck up a conversation, not too different from this one."

"What happened?"

"He started coming in every day. Just sat at the counter

and watched me work. We chatted sometimes when I had a minute. The way he looked at me made me feel so alive. Like he was the first person who had ever really seen me. When he next suggested going away for a long weekend, I said yes."

"Sounds like a good start . . ." Nick offered.

"It was great. Until I started talking about our future. Turns out, he had a wife. I broke up with him immediately, but he kept coming back and every time, I let him stay a little bit longer. Damned if I wasn't in love with him. He told me twice a week was all I'd ever have. I told myself that would have to be good enough. I tried to make peace with it."

"His wife ever make peace with it?"

"Never asked. He made his limits very clear and set me up with the diner to keep me busy. I loved designing the menus, redoing the décor, hiring the cooks, and making those pies. Even though he was footing the bill, it felt like it was really mine."

"What was his name?" Nick asked.

A fleeting smile crossed Ruby's lips and her eyes softened for just a moment.

"Russell Clements."

"Weren't you worried that the same harassment that happened to the previous owner would happen to you?"

"What? Old Don Holcomb?" Ruby laughed. "No."

"Why not?"

Ruby looked at Nick like he was a child. "Those hooligans didn't randomly decide to show up. Russell sent them. He wanted a diner, so he took it. Holcomb closed up and a month later, Russell surprised me with the keys and the chance to make it mine."

"You ever ask about how he got it? Did he buy the place from the Takemuras? Lease it from them?" Nick asked.

Ruby shrugged. "My mama taught me not to look a gift horse in the mouth."

"So, what happened?" Nick asked. "Why are you here, instead of there?"

Ruby laughed to herself. "Broke the cardinal rule. I cared too much. Throughout our relationship, Russell would disappear for weeks at a time. He always told me it was work and I chose not to ask too many questions. Then one day, I discovered a matchbook in his pocket from a hotel in Palm Springs. He said he'd gone to New York. I could handle sharing him with his wife, but someone else? I demanded he give up the other woman. Made a big stink of it and he said no. Came in to work the next day to find the locks changed, the electricity cut off, and everyone had been fired. The rug was pulled out from under me."

"What'd you do?" Nick asked.

"Felt real sorry for myself. Drank for a solid seventy-two hours. Then got my life together and found this job. At least I still get to make pies."

"Damned good ones, too."

Ruby raised the coffeepot toward Nick, offering a refill. He shook his head and picked up his hat. Reaching into his wallet, he pulled out five dollars to generously cover the coffee, pie, and tip. He set it down in front of Ruby. She nodded her appreciation as she swept the money into her pocket.

"One last thing," Nick said. "You know where I can find your former paramour?"

"Russell was real cagey about where he lived," Ruby said. "But he had a company. Clements and Winston? Wilson? Weston? C and W maybe. They did real estate and development. I always got the sense that it wasn't aboveboard, but I didn't ask too many questions. Sometimes you don't want to know the answers."

"I always want to know," Nick countered with a smile.

"Bet that gets you into trouble."

"More often than I can say."

With that, he picked up his hat and headed out, still savoring the memory of that blueberry pie.

Chapter 8

The afternoon sun streamed in through the large picture window in Nick's office. It was on the second floor, above the Beverly Hills boutique of one of Evelyn's closest friends, Lily Shen. Years ago, when Evelyn was still a private investigator, she helped Lily find the man embezzling her money. In return, Lily rented Evelyn the second floor of the building she owned. Nick had inherited the space, fully furnished. It was decorated with soft blue walls, dove-gray couches, Tiffany lamps, and a Persian rug. He liked the address, too, feeling it gave him an air of respectability. Plus, being in Beverly Hills allowed him to charge enough to make a living.

Nick was going over his notes, trying to discover how Russell Clements ended up with the deed to the restaurant. Something was missing. Sitting back in his chair, Nick stared out the window. A boy, maybe twelve or fourteen, paced outside Lily's store. He looked out of place on Rodeo Drive. It wasn't just his age or the fact that he was alone. It was his poverty. The bottom of his pants were frayed from where someone undid the hem to give him a little more length. Even so, they still displayed three inches of ankle. His white T-shirt showed through the moth holes in his sweater. If he was closer, Nick would probably be able to see the sole peeling away from his shoe.

Nick watched as Lily stepped out from her boutique. She approached the boy slowly, with a soft smile. It was meant to be welcoming, but it reminded Nick how someone might approach a fawn. Nick knew Lily well, and though he was too far away to hear their conversation, he imagined her gentle voice offering help. The boy shook his head and backed away. With a frightened look, he turned and fled down the street. She gazed after him for a moment, then headed back inside. Nick went downstairs to her boutique.

As always, it smelled like lavender. The clothes were lined up on metal bars, exactly two inches apart. Each item was well curated and even Nick could identify the quality from a distance. Lily smiled at him as she leaned against the counter, looking toward the street.

"What's the kid's story?" Nick asked.

"Second day here. Sometimes he's right in front. Sometimes down the street. He might disappear for a few hours, but then he returns."

"Think he's casing the joint?"

"If he is, he's very bad at it. He's barely looked in the shop. He keeps looking up toward your office. You ever seen him before?"

Nick shook his head.

"Wonder if he's in trouble," Lily said.

"You think he needs a private detective?"

"Wouldn't be the first time you worked a case without pay."

It was true. Nick had a soft spot for those who were struggling.

"If he shows up again, will you give me a call?" Nick asked.

"Of course."

Twenty minutes later, Nick was sitting at his desk when his phone rang. It was Lily.

"He's across the street behind the lamppost."

"Thanks," Nick said.

Lily's direct approach had yielded no results, so Nick tried a different tactic. He slipped out the back entrance of their building and darted down the alley. When Nick came out, he glanced down the street to see if the boy was still there. He was. Nick circled the block so he could sneak up from behind. The boy jumped like a startled rabbit and looked around as if to flee.

"I'm not gonna hurt you, kid," Nick said, holding his hands up in a pacifying manner. "You're not in trouble. Though I noticed you seem to have an outsized interest in my window."

"You're Nick Gallagher?" the boy asked.

"Last time I checked."

The boy's eyes widened, looking as though he was gathering his courage. Nick waited. There was absolutely no part of him that missed being the boy's age. So much uncertainty, fear, and posturing came with those first tentative steps into manhood.

"I . . . I . . . um," the boy began. Then he smiled awkwardly and shrugged. "I'm your nephew."

"My what?" Nick asked.

"Nephew. Rory Gallagher. Paula's son."

Nick stared at the boy for a long moment, piecing his features together in a new light.

"I was named after your grandfather," Rory added.

"Christ. You look just like him. Never knew him as a young man, but I see it now," Nick said. "Come upstairs and we can talk."

Rory followed Nick across the street and up to the office. Nick opened the door, but Rory hesitated. Then he carefully stepped out of his shoes and entered the room.

"I don't want to track in dirt," he said. "It's so nice in here."

"Not what you were expecting?"

"I always thought detectives worked in dusty old buildings with broken couches and slanted floors," Rory admitted, "You should have seen me two years ago. I would have fit that description perfectly."

"How'd you end up here?"

A bemused Nick pondered that question. Should he tell Rory about Evelyn? Start with how they met as spies during the war? Or describe the case that brought them back together? Finally he settled on the simplest answer.

"I got lucky," Nick said. Then he motioned to a couch. "Please sit. Can I get you something to drink? Coffee? Tea?"

"Um, uh, maybe water? Is that okay?"

"Of course." Nick filled up a glass from the tap. He set it in front of Rory, who gulped it gratefully. Nick refilled the glass, then sat down across from him. "How's your mom?"

"She's okay. Fine."

"I'm surprised she told you about me," Nick said.

"Oh, yeah. When I was growing up, she talked about you, Brennan and Cassian. Said they used to get into all kinds of trouble and you'd tag along behind, not wanting to be left out."

"Sounds about right."

"Having brothers would be the best. Then you'd never be alone," Rory said.

Nick did not have the heart to disabuse the boy of his fantasy. He had almost always felt alone. Yet, as much as Nick might protest that he had no interest in learning more about his family, when answers were standing in front of him, it was almost impossible not to ask all of the questions at once. What happened to his parents? His brothers? Why did they leave him? Did they ever miss him? Did they ever come looking for him? All of those "whys" were too much of a burden to put on this kid. Especially when Nick knew no answer would satisfy him.

"So, no siblings?" Nick asked. Rory shook his head no. "Do you spend a lot of time by yourself?"

"Mom has to work. She's a cleaner during the day. Waits tables at night."

"Who takes care of you?"

Rory scoffed. "I'm thirteen. Been looking after myself for years."

The thought made Nick incredibly sad. Rory had Paula's last name, which probably meant his father was not in the picture.

"Where do you live?" Nick said, instead.

"Near Barstow."

"How'd Paula get out there?" Nick wondered aloud.

"Followed a guy," Rory said. "Mom had me when she was twenty-four. Her folks—yours, too, I guess—were up in Santa Cruz. Refused to take her in, so we moved around a lot trying to find someplace decent."

"Growing up, I never felt settled, either. It's tough to reckon with," Nick replied.

"Mom does her best."

"I'm sure she does," Nick said. "She come with you?"

Rory shook his head.

"I'm thrilled to meet you, so please don't take this question the wrong way . . ." Nick said. "Why did you come find me?"

"I don't want anything," Rory insisted quickly. "I'm not asking for money or a handout."

"Didn't say you were," Nick replied. "I'm just wondering, why now?"

"I dunno. You had that big, fancy party last year. It was in all of the papers."

"My engagement party," Nick confirmed. "Usually, no one notices me when I am standing next to Evelyn."

"When I saw that picture, I guess I got curious," Rory confessed. "Other than Mom, I don't have any family."

"Not your uncles or your grandparents?" Nick asked.

"I mean, they must exist somewhere, but I've never met them."

"Your mom know you're here?"

"It's summer break. She doesn't much care where I am, as long as I'm not in trouble."

It wasn't quite an answer, but Nick decided not to push it. "Where are you staying? Why don't you come home with me? You can meet Evelyn. Have some dinner . . . I'm a fairly decent cook."

"That's okay. I've got some friends nearby. Should probably get back. It was nice meeting you," Rory said as he stood up. He extended his hand to Nick, who noticed his long, bony arms. It was a very formal gesture and Nick rose to shake his hand with the solemnity it deserved.

"You too."

Nick walked him to the door and watched from the top of the stairs as Rory descended and disappeared down the sidewalk. For a moment, Nick stared into the darkness. He had a nephew.

Chapter 9

Carl was on his second bottle of wine. He was with Evelyn and Nick at their kitchen table for their weekly Friday night dinner. Usually, he drank slowly to appreciate the subtleties of a good pinot noir, but at the moment, he looked like a man trying to escape his life. His eyes were unfocused and he ate without much appetite. At first, neither of them noticed Carl's silence. He was often quiet, preferring to wait until he had something of substance to share. However, at a certain point, they realized his mind had drifted. They stopped speaking and waited. It took Carl a good minute and a half before he looked up, startled out of his reverie.

"Sorry," he said as he reached out an unsteady hand and poured the rest of the wine into his glass.

"What's going on?" Evelyn asked.

"Nothing. It's fine. Everything's fine," he replied.

Nick and Evelyn just looked at him. Carl was quiet for a long moment, as if struggling with himself.

"What do you think of homosexuals?" he asked eventually.

Nick glanced at Evelyn, surprised by the shift in conversation. She shrugged in response.

"I don't, really," Nick said. "Can't see how the personal behavior of two consenting adults is any of my business."

"You don't think it's morally wrong?" Carl asked.

"We've seen a wealth of things that are morally wrong," Evelyn replied. "Everything that happened during the war. Much of what followed after. The Russians raped their way through Eastern Germany. Children were murdered for sport. Whole families were thrown into extermination camps. Those are morally wrong."

"Leviticus 18:22—'You shall not lie with a male as with a woman; it is an abomination,' " Carl quoted.

"The Catholic Church also insists sex should be for procreation," Nick noted dryly.

"If you're going to start living according to the Bible," Evelyn said. "You'll have to give up cheeseburgers."

"And Easter ham," Nick agreed.

"No more cioppino for you."

"What would you do without paella?"

"Bacon!" Evelyn gasped in mock horror.

Carl threw up his hands in defeat, laughing slightly. "All right, all right, I get it."

"Where is all of this coming from?" Evelyn asked gently. She knew Carl was religious and often went to Mass with his father on Sunday mornings.

"Remember how the FBI had me looking for Communists under couch cushions?" Carl began.

"In fairness, you did find one," Evelyn said.

"Only after he tried to kill you. Twice," Carl replied. "Made himself a bit of a target."

Evelyn nodded in agreement.

"Now they have me hunting for homosexual men and women," Carl said. "Apparently, they're a security risk. More likely to be blackmailed . . ."

"Seems to me that if you stopped criminalizing people

living their lives, they wouldn't feel the need to hide them," Evelyn said.

"Besides, the same could be said of someone cheating on their wife," Nick added. "Don't see the FBI cutting people loose for having an affair."

"I guess," Carl said.

"Carl, you know I love you," Evelyn began. "Which is why I'm saying this. You're not happy at the FBI. You could do anything you want. Why this?"

"America took my father in when he left Mexico. It took my mother in from Morocco. Even if it was a bit grudgingly, it gave them a home. Now it's my home. During the war, the job was simple, I understood what we were doing and why. I believed in the mission and I trusted General Gibson when he sent us behind enemy lines. Our work mattered. Now I don't know. I don't like spying on other Americans."

Evelyn wanted to suggest this was a witch hunt perpetrated by a corrupt agency, but she would never say that to him. Both she and Nick knew Carl's patriotism far outstripped their own. They each had reasons for joining the OSS that had little to do with serving their government. Carl joined for God and country.

"If you ever decide enough is enough, you can always come work with me," Nick offered.

Carl laughed. "Already did three years of that during the war. No, thank you."

"I said 'with,' not 'for.' We'd be equal partners. For the first time in my life, I have more cases than I can handle."

"I still have some sense of order in the world," Carl insisted.

Nick pretended to stab himself in the chest while calling out, "Wounded! I am wounded."

"You'll survive," Evelyn said, patting his arm.

"This is the sympathy I get," Nick complained sarcastically.

"We've heard the routine before," Carl replied.

"Gotta hit us with something new," Evelyn agreed.

"How about this? Apparently, I'm an uncle," Nick replied. "Kid showed up at my office today, claiming he was my nephew from Barstow."

"Do you think he is?" Carl asked.

"Says my sister, Paula, is his mother, and he's got the Gallagher nose," Nick replied. "Poor guy."

"How old is he?" Evelyn asked.

"Thirteen."

"And he was alone?" she continued.

"Think so," Nick said. "He's on summer break. Said he was staying with some friends. He skirted around the question and I didn't want to push."

"You didn't want to push?" Evelyn asked incredulously.

"Yeah, why?"

"Which friends? Where do they live? How does a kid like that have contacts in Los Angeles?" Evelyn asked as the realization dawned on Nick's face. "He doesn't know people here. He just doesn't want to be a burden. It's too hard to ask for help and risk being rejected."

"Shit," Nick swore, feeling like an asshole. "I don't even know where to go look."

"Start with anywhere that might be familiar," Evelyn replied as she got up from the table, grabbed Nick's car keys, and shoved them into his chest. "Don't come home until you've found him."

Chagrined, Nick nodded and headed out into the night.

Chapter 10

The empty streets of Beverly Hills reminded Nick of a Hollywood backlot after filming had wrapped for the day. The windows, sidewalks, and roads looked a bit too clean to be real. Concrete colonnades separated the plate glass windows of storefronts. They were emptied of their costly displays each night, giving them a haunted feeling.

Nick looked into doorways, hoping to find Rory. Evelyn was right. If Nick were a kid in a new city, with no money and nowhere to go, he would stay wherever seemed safest, which was usually the most familiar. He walked the length of Rodeo, then cut over to Charleville Boulevard to El Camino, and back up Beverly Drive. There was no sign of Rory. As Nick returned to Rodeo, intending to head west toward Camden, a police officer flipped on his lights and signaled to Nick.

"Help you?" Nick asked.

"Just going to ask you the same question," the cop said. "What's your business here?"

The question was insulting in its implication that Nick had criminal intentions. Then he looked down at his frayed khakis and the shirtsleeves rolled up to cover the hole in the elbow. Though he was loath to admit it, perhaps Evelyn's aunt Taffy was right—his wardrobe could use an upgrade.

"Beautiful night," Nick said. "Thought I'd take a walk."

"Well, I'd suggest you keep walking," the cop said.

"You mean to my office?" Nick asked. "Which you can see from this corner."

"Buddy, I don't give a shit where you go, so long as it's not here."

Nick reached into his pocket and pulled out a business card with his address.

"Lemme see some ID."

For a moment, Nick thought about refusing, just to be ornery, but he didn't fancy a trip down to the station. His driver's license still had the address of the Bishop Estate. The cop clocked that, then looked between Nick and the license a few times.

"If you doubt my right to be here," Nick said, "I can always call Captain Wharton and have him explain it to you. Though, if you know Wharton, you know how much he hates being woken up."

The cop handed Nick back his license and tucked the business card into his shirt pocket.

"I'll be keeping an eye on you," he threatened.

After the cop disappeared around the corner, Nick cursed his own stupidity. Of course, Rory would not be hiding in a doorway. The police would have scared him off long ago. Nick hurried to the alley behind his building. There, in the darkness, Nick found a small bundle of rags that belonged to a thirteen-year-old boy. Upon hearing Nick's footsteps, Rory woke with a start, the panic of discovering himself in an unfamiliar place written large across his face.

"It's okay, it's okay," Nick said, kneeling beside him. "It's just me. Nick."

"Oh, hi . . ." Rory replied uncertainly.

"You should have told me you needed a place to stay."

"Why would you help me? You don't know me. I could be lying about being your nephew."

"Want to know a secret? Even if you were, I'd still help you," Nick said.

"Why?"

"No one should sleep on the streets." Nick stated. "My family left when I was a year younger than you. I spent a couple of days wandering the streets, with no money, not knowing where to go. We'd never had much food, but for the first time, I found myself searching through garbage cans behind restaurants trying to find enough to keep me alive. It was disgusting, but I was hungry. Hungry people will do almost anything."

"I know," Rory replied quietly.

Nick wondered about the boy's life. What drove him to come to Los Angeles seeking a stranger?

"There was one night when it was raining. I was wet and couldn't stop shivering. Didn't know it was possible to feel that miserable. I'd barely fallen asleep—or what counts for sleep when nowhere feels safe—when I heard footsteps and boys' laughter. Before I could stand, they kicked me in my stomach. I was curled in a ball, trying to protect myself. I didn't have anything worth stealing. No money. No food. Just the clothes on my back. Suppose that was good enough for them. When they went for my jacket, a new part of me woke up. I kicked one of them in the shin. Hard. Another I punched in the balls. The third one came for me, but by then, I was on my feet. I knew this was a battle I couldn't win. Yet, after all of the sorrow and frustration and helplessness, I'd lost the instinct for self-preservation. I swung wildly. One of them I bit hard enough to take off some skin. They circled around me and I braced for the inevitable beating. Then a wooden bat smashed the shoulder of their leader. We all turned to see this girl, not much older than us, pulling back to swing again. She hit the next kid in the ribs. If I was wild, she was crazed. Turns out, unpredictability is more frightening than all of the fighting skills in the world. They fled."

"Was that my mom coming back for you?" Rory asked hopefully.

"No," Nick replied. "It was the girl who would become my best friend and savior, Hildy. Well, Helen now. The first words she said to me: 'I guess you're a fighter, after all. Might be worth my time.' I didn't know what to say to that, and to be honest, I could barely speak at all. A few of my ribs were broken and I'd never known such pain. Helen took me under her wing. Gave me the first real food I'd had in days and made me believe I could survive."

"Why are you telling me all of this?" Rory asked.

"A few reasons. One is to say that sleeping on the streets is terrifying, cold, and lonely. The second is that someone once helped me."

"I don't need your pity," Rory said defiantly.

"Then how about my empathy? We've got an extra room, clean sheets, and plenty to eat. Come stay with us."

"Don't need your charity, either," Rory replied.

"Before this afternoon, I didn't know you existed," Nick said. "Now I do and I want the chance to get to know you. Family is family. We take care of our own."

"Yours didn't."

"My wife does," Nick said. "Besides, Evelyn made it clear that I'm not allowed to come home without you."

Nick pressed himself up to standing, then held out his hand to Rory. It was a minute before the boy took it and allowed himself to be helped to his feet. As they walked to the car, Rory turned to Nick.

"I don't know what to call you. 'Uncle Nick' seems too familiar and 'Mr. Gallagher' doesn't feel right, either."

"How about just 'Nick'?"

Rory nodded. "I can do that."

Chapter 11

Evelyn rinsed the sink as Carl finished drying the last dish. He had sobered up a bit as they cleared the table, but neither trusted him with a car.

"Let me give you a ride home," Evelyn offered.

"I can walk."

"It's five miles."

Carl lived in a small bungalow on the west side of Culver City. "I could use the air."

"Call me when you get home, so I know you're safe," Evelyn said.

"Yes, Mom," Carl teased.

Evelyn gave him a hug goodbye, then watched from the doorway as he disappeared around the corner. Once he vanished from sight, Evelyn grabbed her car keys, coat, and a large sack of quarters she kept around to make these particular phone calls. She pulled out of her driveway and headed east towards Twenty-Third Street. Out of an abundance of caution, she rotated locations, rarely going to the same one twice. She found herself standing outside gas stations, inside late-night diners, and on random street corners—wherever she would not be disturbed by someone impatiently waiting to make a call. Tonight it was the far edge of the Santa Monica Airport.

Evelyn stepped into the phone booth, leaving the door open behind her. The cool evening breeze was preferable to the stale air inside. She wrapped her sweater around her more tightly before feeding a stack of quarters into the slot and asking the operator to connect her to a house in Cuba. Her father answered, sounding slightly groggy.

"Did I wake you?" Evelyn asked.

"Yes, but it's worth it. When my phone rings, I always know it's you."

"No one else calls?"

"Like who? The FBI?"

"I was hoping you made some friends," Evelyn said.

The silence on the end of the line was all the answer she needed. Even from this distance, she could feel her father's loneliness. When he fled, he left his entire life behind: his daughter, the home he shared with his late wife and son, and the company he had built from nothing. It was not easy starting over.

"How did the groundbreaking go?" Logan asked before the silence stretched out long enough to feel like pity.

"Interesting," Evelyn replied. "Lots of politicians. Lots of champagne. Lots of speeches."

"Hope you kept yours short."

"I wrote one to rival Tolstoy. Then I realized no one was listening."

"Proof that you've always been the smartest one in the room," Logan said with a laugh. It was good to hear that sound, even if Evelyn could not quite match it. Moments like these reminded her so much of the father she once knew. The warm, caring man who had a moral code that went as deep as the Grand Canyon.

"Dad, did you know the Takemura family?"

"Of course. They owned the restaurant where you're building the new factory."

"How did you get that land?"

"What do you mean?" Logan asked, confused. "I bought it."

"From whom?"

"Hanzo, their eldest son. He'd changed so much I didn't even recognize him, but I suppose being driven out of your home will do that to a person."

"What can you tell me about buying the farm and the restaurant?"

"What's this about, honey? Are there issues with the deeds?" Logan asked.

"Just trying to figure some stuff out," Evelyn replied.

"Initially I tried to buy the farm back in 1939, but Raijin Nagasaki said it wasn't for sale. He'd grown up there with his father working the land. He wanted to keep it for his son."

"What changed after the war?"

"He said Los Angeles would never feel like home again. His neighbors stood by while he and his family were dragged away. They weren't even on the truck before people he once considered friends began stealing the items they were forced to leave behind. No one offered to help. No one offered to keep their belongings safe. No one even said goodbye. He'd never felt so alone. During the war, when people were allowed to move inland, the Nagasakis made their way to Madison, Wisconsin. Raijin found a job with a farmer, who appreciated Raijin's expertise. They became good friends, and eventually Raijin used the money from selling his farm here to buy one there."

"Did he personally sell you the land?"

"Raijin called me first to work out his details. Then he sent his son, Daniel, to sign the papers. They offered me what I felt was a fair price and I took it. Probably could have gotten them to go a bit lower, but it didn't feel right to bargain."

"What about the Takemuras' property?"

"To be honest, I didn't even need that part. You know the plans. It's in the corner of the parking lot. We could have easily worked around them."

"So, why buy it?"

"They offered. Better to have the whole parcel than deal with whoever else might move in there. Hanzo told me his father had passed and it broke his mother. The lease from the previous tenant was not renewed, the family had no interest in starting over, and besides, they needed the money. I was surprised he came with a real estate broker. Hanzo never struck me as a person who would pay for something he could do himself."

"So, you met with Hanzo personally?" Evelyn asked.

"Of course," Logan said. "Why?"

Evelyn filled Logan in on Billy showing up at the groundbreaking and Hanzo's assault on Donald Holcomb.

"That's so strange," Logan replied. "I wrote a check specifically to Hanzo Takemura. It was cashed a few days later at Farmers and Merchants Bank. The returned check should bc with the other documents regarding the sale."

"Speaking of . . . We can't find them anywhere."

"They're probably in the dungeon," Logan replied.

Evelyn shuddered. The dungeon was a space below the factory floor. When exploring as children, she and Matthew found every nook and cranny, but they only went there once. Cold and damp, even in the height of summer, there were cobwebs and the constant sounds of small feet scurrying across the floor.

"I'm building a new records room," Evelyn decided. "Calling the architect in the morning. In the meantime, I'll see what I can find."

"You know I'd never take advantage of a situation like the internment camps," Logan said.

Evelyn wanted to answer, "of course", but she struggled with the words that once came so easily. The long silence was finally broken by the sound of the operator asking for more money.

"I love you, honey," Logan offered.

"I love you, too, Daddy."

It was both true and not enough. Evelyn hung up the receiver, then turned to leave the booth. Carl was standing on the sidewalk, his face a mask of barely concealed rage. She stepped out to face him.

"What are you doing here?" Evelyn asked, before realizing one of the paths back to his house crossed Twenty-Third Street.

"Was that Logan?" Carl asked.

Evelyn nodded. Carl punched the phone booth in anger. The glass cracked, sending fine spiderwebs down the length of it.

"I can't believe you're still talking to him," Carl said.

"Your hand," Evelyn said, reaching for it. He pulled away, blood budding on his knuckles.

"How could you do this?" Carl asked. "After all the pain he's caused."

"He's my father," Evelyn replied quietly.

"He's a traitor!" Carl exclaimed.

"You think I don't know that? You think this is easy? When I was growing up, he was my hero . . . and now?"

"Now you're still willing to betray your country for him."

"It's not like that."

"You Bishops have been known to bend the rules when it comes to family. Not just your father. How many times did we almost get caught because you needed to stop and look for your brother? It wasn't only the night he was killed. It was every time you went off mission."

Evelyn stared at him. She had no idea he was carrying this resentment.

"There's no chance in hell Nick would have left you behind. If you'd been caught, he would have moved heaven and earth to get you back, putting all of us at risk. You were reckless and so was he. Most times, we escaped unharmed, but not always."

His words knocked the air from her lungs.

"You're putting Theo's death on me?" Evelyn asked, astounded. "That had nothing to do with Matthew. Our contact was picked up by the SS."

"You joined the OSS with an ulterior motive," Carl retorted.

"We all did. No one becomes a spy out of the goodness of their hearts. We're all a bit broken; otherwise, we couldn't do what we did."

"I thought I could trust you."

"You think I can't tell the difference between gossip and national security? I'm not giving my father specs on the new planes or where the military is sending them. I'm not telling him about government orders or how they're going to be used. I'm asking him for information about a land purchase from years ago."

"The last thing I need is more secrets," Carl snapped. "I put my career, hell, even my freedom, at risk by letting your father escape. We could've been court martialed for abetting a traitor. Your father deserved to be punished for what he did and I still don't know if I made the right decision. I can't believe you've forgiven him."

"I haven't, but he's my father."

"So what?" Carl demanded.

"You still have both your parents. You could hop in your car and twenty minutes later they're giving you a hug. Do you have any idea what I would give to see my mother again? To have one more conversation with her?

To feel her arms around me and tell me it's going to be all right? To have her see the person I've become? If you haven't been through it, you can't begin to imagine the hole it leaves in your heart." Evelyn stopped to wipe away her tears. "My father's alive. Maybe he's not here, and he's certainly not perfect, but I can call him on the phone. That won't always be the case and I'd hate myself if I gave him up sooner than I have to. I know it's complicated, but I still love him. Surely, you can understand that."

"Then you love a monster."

"Carl—"

"Don't talk to me. Don't come find me. Don't send Nick. I no longer know you. Nor do I want to."

Carl turned away and resumed his long walk home. Evelyn stood next to the cracked phone booth, pained by the justice of his accusations.

Chapter 12

Nick parked on the street behind his house. As Rory stepped out, he looked around, confused.

"What's wrong?" Nick asked.

"I thought you lived in a mansion."

"That was Evelyn's, not mine. We moved here when someone burned it down."

"Someone burned down your house?"

"Evelyn's house."

"They set it on fire?"

"It was more like a bomb."

"Someone bombed your old house?"

"They were trying to kill us."

"They *what*?"

"Professional hazard," Nick replied nonchalantly. "We've been known to make a few enemies here and there. Don't worry, as far as we know, things are all quiet on that front."

Nick led Rory to the back door and opened it to reveal Evelyn at the table. A book sat in front of her, but she was staring off into space. Startled out of her reverie, she stood up with a warm smile. Like most men upon whom Evelyn turned her full charm, Rory found himself without words.

"Welcome!" Evelyn said. "It's so good to meet you."

Rory stared at her, wide-eyed for a minute. Then he finally stuttered, "You're . . . you're so pretty."

"That's very kind," Evelyn said. "You're quite a fine-looking young man, yourself."

Rory, self-conscious, smoothed down a cowlick toward the back of his head. Evelyn placed her hand on Rory's shoulder, ushering him to the table.

"I know it's still late, but I kept some dinner warm for you. Are you hungry?"

"Um . . . I guess."

Evelyn pulled the pan of leftover pasta from the oven, spooned some of it onto a plate, then brought it to the table. Rory glanced at Nick questioningly.

"Made it myself," Nick said.

"That's good news," Evelyn added.

Given permission, Rory picked up his fork. He tasted a small bite, then quickly devoured the rest of the plate.

"Thank you, ma'am."

"Ooof. 'Ma'am' seems way too formal," Evelyn said. "Call me Evelyn."

"Evelyn." Rory rolled her name around in his mouth for a moment, before nodding.

Evelyn picked up Rory's plate, filled it with the remainder of the pasta, then set it in front of him.

"Oh, no. It's okay. I'm good," he said quickly.

"If you don't eat it," Evelyn threatened, "it's going to go to waste."

"Please, finish it," Nick seconded.

Rory picked up his fork and began to eat again. When he finished, he carefully carried his plate to the sink.

"Are you still hungry?" Evelyn asked. "Feel free to help yourself to whatever we have. It might not be much, but it's yours."

"Oh, no. That's okay," Rory replied.

Evelyn's heart went out to him. He seemed so overwhelmed and uncertain. Almost like he was trying to take up as little space as possible.

"When I was your age," Nick said, "I wanted to eat everything. I kept growing and my stomach kept rumbling."

"Matthew had a hollow leg, too," Evelyn agreed. Then, for Rory's sake, she clarified, "He was my brother."

"Was?" Rory said.

"The war."

"I . . . I'm sorry. I shouldn't have asked."

"It's okay. I like talking about him. Helps me remember the good times," Evelyn replied. "Nick said your mother didn't come with you. Do you want to use the phone to let her know you're safe?"

Rory shrugged. "She doesn't care."

"I'm sure she does," Evelyn said.

"We don't have a phone at home."

"Then we'll try her tomorrow at work," Nick offered.

"Really, it's fine."

Evelyn caught Nick's eyes. He shook his head, warning her not to push the issue. Silence filled the space until it felt awkward.

"You know," Evelyn began, "Nick has told me very little about your family. What's your mom like? What about your grandparents?"

Rory shrugged again.

"How about school? What grade are you in?"

"I just finished seventh."

"Do you have a favorite subject?" Evelyn asked.

"I like to read."

"Nick's a huge reader," Evelyn said, motioning to their walls. "As you can see from our shelves."

"If you have a book with you, you're never bored," Nick replied. "Do you have a favorite author?"

"Not really."

Nick went into the other room and returned a minute later with Raymond Chandler's *The Big Sleep* and showed it to Rory.

"Read that last year," Rory said.

"How about Hammett's *The Maltese Falcon*?"

Rory nodded.

"Agatha Christie, *The Murder of Roger Ackroyd*?"

"I liked that one, especially the twist at the end," Rory said with a slight smile.

"Who would have guessed the narrator did it?"

"I started wondering about him on page seventy-six," Rory replied.

"Sounds like you read a lot of mysteries," Evelyn said.

"And other books. I recently finished *For Whom the Bell Tolls*. I picked it up because I really loved *The Sun Also Rises*, but I struggled a bit with this one."

"Hemingway can be a pretentious ass," Evelyn agreed.

"I've got it!" Nick exclaimed as he rushed into the living room. Returning a moment later, he handed *The Count of Monte Cristo* to Rory. "You'll love it. Has twists and revenge. Good versus evil. Even a prison break."

Rory opened the book and began flipping through the pages. Evelyn could tell he wanted to be alone to disappear into the world of Dumas.

"Why don't I get you settled?" Evelyn offered.

Rory stood to follow her. Then he stopped and looked at Nick.

"Thanks for finding me," he said quietly.

"You're welcome," Nick replied.

Evelyn led Rory upstairs. Their guest bedroom contained simple, but elegant, white oak furniture. On the floor was a braided rug with all of the colors of the rainbow. The double bed was covered in white sheets, a yellow blanket, and a blue down comforter.

"Sometimes it can get cold at night," she explained.

Rory moved toward the window and stared out into the darkness. He opened it to hear the waves.

"Is that the ocean?" he asked. "I've never seen it before."

"Tomorrow morning we'll put our feet in."

Evelyn opened the bottom of the dresser, which held several fluffy white towels.

"The bathroom is through that door. There should be soap, shampoo, anything you need. I think there's a toothbrush in the vanity—" Then she stopped abruptly, realizing Rory had not brought any bags with him. "Let me get you some pajamas."

Evelyn disappeared into her room, where she grabbed a pair of Nick's pajamas.

"They're probably a bit big, but it's just for tonight," she said as she returned. "We'll get you a few more essentials tomorrow."

"No, that's okay," Rory replied quickly. "You've been so nice already."

"When I first met Nick, he couldn't ask for, or accept, help to save his life. Literally," Evelyn said. "It's a kindness to let people take care of you in whatever small ways they can."

Then Evelyn turned down the bed, brushing the sheets straight.

"Our room is down the hall." Evelyn pointed through the open door. "If you need anything, let us know."

Rory nodded. Evelyn wanted to give him a hug, but knew it was too soon.

"I'm really glad you're here," she said.

"Me too."

Those two words felt like a triumph. Evelyn gave him a smile, then left the room, closing the door quietly behind her. Downstairs she found Nick drying the pasta pan.

"You get any more from him?" Nick asked.

"Gonna take some time," Evenly said. "Was that what you were like at his age?"

"Worse."

Evelyn did not know how to respond. Instead, she reached out a hand to him. "Let's go to sleep."

"My second favorite thing to do upstairs," Nick replied.

Fondly, she shook her head at the innuendo, kissing him before they turned out the lights.

Chapter 13

Before breakfast, Nick, Evelyn, and Rory ran down to the beach, still in their pajamas, to wade into the ocean. The water was icy, but with Evelyn's encouragement, Rory rolled up the bottom of his pants and made it to his knees. Evelyn followed to her ankles before complaining she could not feel her toes. Nick took this as a personal challenge. He pulled off his top and dove under the surface, popping up a few yards out. Rory's eyes were wide, but Evelyn just laughed.

"Your uncle's an idiot," Evelyn said with deep affection in her voice.

Nick fought against the undertow to make his way back to them.

"You're an idiot," Evelyn repeated.

"Am I?" Nick asked, a mischievous look in his eyes. Then he charged at Evelyn, scooping her up in a huge hug and carrying her deeper.

"Not fair!" Evelyn yelled, still laughing. "Put me down."

Nick did and she sank to her thighs, yelling at the shock of the water. It took her a moment to recover, but when she did, she gave Nick a huge push, sending him tumbling back into the waves as she darted towards shore. She grabbed Rory's hand.

"Run!"

With their head start, they made it back to the cottage before Nick could catch them. He came in dripping wet and looked to Evelyn. She smiled sweetly. "Love you!"

Nick shook his head, grinning; then he glanced toward Rory. It was the first real smile he had seen on the boy's face. He did not want to ruin the moment by commenting on it.

"All right!" Nick called out. "Everyone get changed. Breakfast will be on the table in fifteen minutes."

Evelyn and Nick headed toward the stairs, but Rory hung back.

"Clothes," Evelyn mouthed to Nick.

"Yes, yes!" Nick said. "Let's see what I have that might fit you."

Nick went upstairs, with Rory trailing behind him. Nick found some khakis and a blue plaid button-down shirt. The clothes were large, but not as much as Nick expected. Rory folded back the sleeves and rolled up the pants. For a moment, Nick saw himself. He had always bought clothes that were too big, so he would not outgrow them as quickly.

"You look great," Nick said. Then he changed into a similar outfit.

By the time Evelyn came downstairs, having showered and pulled her hair into a low bun, the coffee was made and breakfast was almost on the table. Rory leaned against the counter, watching Nick cook. As always, Nick's movements were sure and steady. He sautéed vegetables, while keeping an eye on the eggs, waiting for the perfect moment to fold everything into an omelet. There was toast in the oven and bacon on the skillet. Evelyn snuck behind Nick to pour some coffee. Then she held up the pot to Rory, who shook his head.

"Don't give him ideas," Nick said. "Just because it's your particular addiction does not mean it's for everyone. It will stunt his growth."

Properly chastised, Evelyn went to the kitchen table and sat down, motioning for Rory to take a seat beside her. Nick set breakfast down.

"Help yourself."

Rory began to eat and his food was gone before Nick had a chance to pick up his fork. Nick piled more bacon and toast onto Rory's plate, along with the fruit. He ate it quickly, looking embarrassed afterward.

"Guess I was hungry."

"Don't apologize," Nick said. "I can make more."

"No, really. Thank you for this."

"Are you still intending to go to the JACL meeting this afternoon?" Evelyn asked.

"I was, but Rory came all of this way. We should take him to see the sights."

"JACL?" Rory asked.

"Japanese American Citizens League," Nick explained.

"Can I come?" Rory wanted to know.

"Isn't there something else you'd rather do?" Nick asked.

"I came here to meet you."

Nick did not know what to do with that honest admission. It felt too intimate.

"Before we go, I need to find some paperwork," Evelyn said. "You don't happen to like dark, creepy spaces, do you?"

During work hours, Bishop Aeronautics felt like a living, breathing animal. Even after everyone had gone home, it still thrummed with an undercurrent of energy. Evelyn dug her keys out of her purse and unlocked the front door. Throwing it open, she led Rory into the factory. All of the planes stood in various stages of completion. Some were recognizable as vehicles to take people cross-country, others were skeletons of what they would become. They cast long shadows and Evelyn loved each one fiercely. To her, the quiet was not oppressive; it was the silent sigh of watching a loved one sleep.

"Wow!" Rory said as he walked onto the factory floor. "This is . . . incredible."

"Thanks," Evelyn replied, feeling like a proud parent. Nick smiled at her expression. Her love for this place rivaled her love for him.

"You want a tour?" Evelyn asked.

Rory nodded. She took him around the whole factory, showing him various parts and how they would go together. There was one finished plane that would fly out later that week. Rory stepped in it reverentially.

"I've never been inside one before."

"Remind me," Evelyn said. "I'll take you flying."

Rory nodded, though he clearly did not believe her. Nick remembered a time when promises felt as insubstantial as dreams.

"Take us to the dungeon!" Nick commanded with a flourish.

Evelyn found three flashlights. They headed toward a hidden set of stairs, but stopped when they reached engineering. Seeing movement through the glass door of the main drafting room, Evelyn opened it and stepped inside. Willa was sitting on a high stool, studying plans for the Bishop 523. It was their most popular commercial plane. Nearby were rows and rows of photographs displaying the engine mountings for both the propeller and the jet planes.

"What are you doing here on a Saturday?" Evelyn asked.

Willa jumped up, startled. "Oh, hi! I'm just looking into something."

"Hank shouldn't ask you to come in on your day off," Evelyn admonished.

"He doesn't know I'm here," Willa replied. "I like coming in on the weekends. It's quiet, which is a rare commodity in my life. I've got three roommates."

"What are you concerned about?"

"Nothing," Willa said a bit too quickly. "It's all fine."

"When you say it like that, I definitely believe you," Evelyn replied.

"If it's of concern, I promise to tell you."

Evelyn wanted to remind her that everything inside these walls was her concern, but she trusted Willa's judgment.

"I'm always here if you want to talk it through," Evelyn said.

Willa nodded. Leaving her to her work, Evelyn, Nick, and Rory continued to the basement. There was an unmarked door at the end of a long hallway. It took a minute for Evelyn to force it open. She wondered when someone had last been down here. Evelyn turned on her flashlight and walked carefully down the aluminum steps, dreading each one that drew her farther into the dark. When her feet finally hit solid ground, Evelyn felt along the damp wall until her fingers found a switch. She turned it on, but it was not especially helpful. The dim bulbs were few and far between. Rory and Nick followed her and shuddered at the view. The floors were rough concrete. Cobwebs hung from the light fixtures, and rat droppings littered the floor. The temperature was ten degrees lower than upstairs and the air reeked of mildew. Stacks of Bankers Boxes stood in haphazard rows, labeled by month and year.

"We're looking for 1945. Sometime after June, I'm guessing."

They spread out, quickly realizing there was no filing system. Boxes from 1925 stood next to those from 1947. Even the more recent ones carried a thick layer of dust. Half-filled boxes were crushed under the weight of fully packed ones. The writing on some of the older ones was faded to illegibility. They streamlined the chaos down to those that looked relatively new, but it was still a huge number.

Rory was the first to find records from 1945; Evelyn began paging through unmarked manila folders to find the sales documents. When Logan first filed the plans to expand the factory, he had to include the deed with their submission. However, Evelyn wanted to see every transaction leading up to transfer of ownership. It took two hours of eye-straining effort before they found the right box. Evelyn found the original letter from Raijin Nagasaki offering Logan the land, as well as subsequent correspondence arranging for his son, Daniel, to come out to finish the paperwork. Afterward, there was a kind letter from Raijin to Logan telling him how much the farm had meant to his family and that he was certain Logan would be a good steward. Evelyn also found a carbon copy of Logan's response thanking the Nagasakis for the opportunity.

They discovered the documents for the sale of the Takemuras' land in a different box. There were no friendly missives, but she did find Hanzo's signature across the transfer of ownership, as well as the cashed check that was written in his name. She held it up for Nick and Rory to see.

"Hanzo sold the land out from under his family."

"The JACL meeting is about to get a lot more interesting," Nick said as he brushed the dirt and cobwebs from his clothes.

Chapter 14

It was not hard to find the Japanese American Citizens League meeting. Loud voices provided all the direction Evelyn, Nick, and Rory needed. It was held in a community center in Boyle Heights. They walked down the generic halls decorated in colorful announcements advertising camp for grade school kids and a baseball league for dads looking to get out of the house on a Thursday night. People were gathered in a large room that functioned as both a theater, as evidenced by the stage at one end, and a basketball court, whose markings covered the floor. Wood folding chairs formed a haphazard circle around a man standing in the middle. He was young, though he carried an air of exhausted authority. All three Takemura children were in attendance. Mary stood in a corner near the back. Hanzo was right up front, with Billy in the middle, watching everyone warily.

Nick leaned over and whispered to Rory, "Keep your eyes open for anything that seems unusual or out of place."

"Even if you don't know why," Evelyn added. "Trust your gut."

Rory nodded eagerly. They fanned out through the room.

"Please, please!" the man in the center called, raising his hands. He was a slender Japanese American man in his late twenties, with rumpled hair and thick glasses. "This isn't helping. Could you please yell at me, one at a time?"

"What's happening with the reparations, Joe?" a man wearing faded dungarees asked. "I submitted all of my paperwork months ago and I haven't seen a thing."

"I know, Kaito. I reached out to the attorney general's office on Thursday. They're singing the same old song. A lot of claims. It's going to take time."

Another man jumped into the mix. "I heard Bruce Abe's claims were denied and the Yamamotos only got a fraction of what they requested."

"That's all true. I wish I had better news for you, but even if they threw thousands of dollars at you, it still wouldn't make this right. Most of us lost our homes and the heirlooms from our grandparents. Many of us are still missing people we loved."

Joe shot a quick glance at Mary, who was standing toward the back. She gave him a sad smile.

"Tell me, Tony, if the government gave you back your farm, would it be the same? You'd have to start tilling the ground from scratch, not knowing what kind of condition they left the fields. You'd have to hire new workers and train them. All of that is possible, but you'd never get back those years of seeing your daughters pick strawberries for breakfast."

A man in his forties nodded his head in agreement.

"Mr. Inoue, you were a fisherman who dreamed of passing the business down to your son. Where is Richard, now?"

"In college in New Jersey," a middle-aged man said.

"Do you think he'll ever come home?" Joe asked.

The man shook his head angrily.

"How many people in our community are gone, never

to return? Our friends. Our family. The government stole three and a half years of our lives," Joe said. "Nothing will ever make this right, so it's time to stop looking to them for a way to move forward. It's up to us to build a future."

A few people grumbled a slight agreement. A young woman rose, wiping her eyes, and left. Nick saw Rory follow her outside. From the second row, Hanzo stood up.

"How do we do that when they don't see us as equal citizens? Many of our parents still can't legally own their own businesses."

Joe began to answer, but another man interrupted.

"Don't tell us that the JACL is working on a new legislation. It didn't matter whether we were citizens when they put us in those camps. It didn't matter that we were loyal. It didn't matter that we served our country!"

The crowd cheered the new speaker and others started shouting their opinions. Joe crossed from frustrated to resigned. He let the yelling continue until it was clear that it was growing, rather than abating. Joe stepped out from the center of the group and headed toward Mary.

"That went well," Mary joked quietly.

"They have a right to be angry," Joe replied.

"Not at you. You're trying to help."

He reached out and took Mary's hand. "I miss you."

"I miss you, too."

They stared into each other's eyes for a long minute, before tears formed in Mary's eyes, and she took her hand back to wipe them away.

"Please, Mary, why won't you let me—"

His plea was cut off by Billy's angry approach.

"What the hell do you think you're doing?" Billy demanded.

"He's not doing anything," Mary said.

"You broke her heart and now you're . . . ? I trusted you. I thought you were our friend."

Joe looked to Mary with a sad smile. "I should go."

Mary watched him walk out the door.

"I can't believe that guy," Billy said.

"Stay the hell out of my business," Mary retorted. "You have no idea what's going on."

She turned on her heel and stormed out of the room. For a moment, Billy looked helpless, overwhelmed. Then he saw Nick standing nearby.

"Guess you caught all of that?" Billy asked.

Nick nodded. "What happened there?"

Billy waved his hand, as if seeking to brush off the confrontation. In the center of the room, the meeting began to dissolve. People broke into small groups, venting their anger to each other. Evelyn approached Hanzo, waiting on the periphery until the last person had moved on to a different conversation.

"You," Hanzo said without the slightest hint of friendliness.

"Me," Evelyn agreed. "Tell me about your land."

"What do you want to know? Why it's important to us, or why it hurts so much that it's gone?"

"You signed papers selling it to my father," Evelyn said, withdrawing the documents from her handbag and handing them to Hanzo.

"What the hell are these?"

"My father's records," Evelyn said. "It's the bill of sale, signed by you, and the canceled check . . . cashed by you."

"I've never seen that before in my life," Hanzo insisted. "And I certainly never got any money."

"My father said that you came to him shortly after the war, offering to sell your family's restaurant."

"I wouldn't do that," Hanzo replied coldly.

"Far as I can tell, these documents are legal. There's no way my father would have opened up his company to lawsuits that could potentially bankrupt the company," Evelyn said.

"You come in where you're not wanted, accusing me of betraying my family, and for what? So you can parade around, pretending you care? That, somehow, you're innocent in all of this?" Hanzo said. "You're just like every other person who profited when we were thrown into camps."

"What's he talking about?" Billy asked from behind Evelyn.

Hanzo grabbed the papers from Evelyn and thrust them at Billy. "There's some fake documents saying I signed over the restaurant. This wouldn't be happening if you didn't bring outsiders into our business."

Billy looked over the papers, stopping at Hanzo's signature. "Did you sign these?"

"Go to hell," Hanzo snapped.

Billy swung his fist, connecting with the side of Hanzo's cheek. For a moment, Hanzo stood there, without words. Then he hit Billy back. In a matter of moments, they were grappling with one another, knocking over chairs and trading wild punches. Billy was the better fighter, but Hanzo had more anger. Finally a commanding voice rang out.

"Stop!"

The brothers released each other, then turned to face an older man.

"This is not how the grown sons of Kenji Takemura behave."

Both Billy and Hanzo mumbled an apology.

"Go home. Take care of your mother and don't let word of this reach her. It's the last thing she needs," the man said. "In the future, when you think of misbehaving, remember your father is watching over you. Stop making a spectacle of yourself. Especially in front of outsiders." The older man turned to Nick and Evelyn. "You should leave. You're not welcome here."

Evelyn picked up her documents, which were lost in the scuffle. Together she and Nick exited the now-silent room, with everyone's eyes upon them.

Chapter 15

"You want to avoid the root for as long as possible," Nick said to Rory, who stood beside him in the kitchen. "Try making a crosshatch structure at the top before slicing down."

Rory picked up the knife and followed Nick's directions. In a minute, he had a large pile of chopped onions.

"You've done this before?" Nick asked.

"Not fancy, like onions or peppers. When Mom comes home from work, she's usually tired, so I make something simple. Scrambled eggs or a sandwich."

"Being able to feed yourself is no small skill," Evelyn said. "And despite what Nick would have you believe, I can manage at least that."

"Wine is not dinner," Nick said.

"It is when you pair it with cheese," Evelyn replied with a smile. Then she looked to Rory. "What did you think of the meeting today?"

"Seems like a lot of people are angry."

"They have a right to be," Nick said.

"Did you notice anything particular?" Evelyn wondered.

"Was I supposed to?" Rory asked.

"Nick and I can go to the same place and have the same experience and remember it very differently. Each of us is coming at it from our own perspectives," Evelyn said. "I'm curious about yours."

"The man who was speaking when we came in seemed really young, but also really smart. Some people wanted to listen to him. Others almost seemed mad at him."

Evelyn nodded in agreement. "He was telling some hard truths."

"When he started talking about people who would not come back, one girl started crying and left."

"Good job spotting that," Nick said.

"I followed her," Rory added, looking afraid they might be angry at him.

"Even better!" Evelyn exclaimed. "Did you learn anything interesting?"

"At first, she didn't want to talk to me, but then I gave her my handkerchief. Well, actually, Nick, it was your handkerchief. I found it in your pants pocket. You're probably not getting it back."

"That's fine," Nick said reassuringly.

"She cried for a little longer and I felt awkward. Sometimes, though, when I'm sad, it helps to have people there. Even if I don't really know them."

Evelyn nodded her encouragement.

"When she stopped crying, I asked her if she was okay. Turns out Suzy Nagasaki was her best friend from high school. They were in Manzanar together, and then their families moved to Madison, Wisconsin, together. When the war was over, Suzy's older brother, Daniel, sold their land, while her family returned here."

"Nice work!" Evelyn exclaimed.

"I even got you their phone number," Rory said, handing Evelyn a slip of paper.

"She just gave that to you?" Nick asked.

"I might have fibbed a little," Rory admitted. "I told her that you were the one who bought their land, and since you were building on it, you wanted to make sure they got their tax refund. I don't know if that's a thing, but I figured if you had good news, she'd be more likely to give me their information."

"God, you're a natural," Nick said.

Rory blushed slightly.

"Thank you for this," Evelyn said. "Seriously, thank you."

She looked to Nick, who already anticipated her next words. "Go, make the call. I've got dinner under control."

Evelyn kissed him lightly, then disappeared into a small den she used as her home office. Nick turned to Rory and handed him several potatoes.

"Peel these before we boil them," Nick instructed.

Rory picked up the small paring knife and got to work.

"How did you become a detective?" Rory asked.

"I was a spy during the war. OSS," Nick began. "A lot of those skills are helpful as a private eye. When I came home after V-E Day, I was pretty useless. My friend Carl got me a job with the LAPD, but I couldn't hold on to it. I was drinking too much and angry at the world. Working for myself let me off the hook. I made my own hours and no one cared if I was sober."

"What changed?" Rory asked.

"Evelyn," Nick said. "During the war, I was at my best when I was with her. Afterward, we both made mistakes, and went our separate ways. Mine was the bottom of a whisky bottle. When I saw her again, three years later, I knew I had to pull myself together and become a man worthy of her."

"You really love her," Rory said.

"More than anything in the world," Nick answered. He scooped up the peeled potatoes and began to chop them before putting them into the water to boil. The doorbell rang and Rory looked up, startled. "That's Evelyn's aunt Taffy. Would you let her in?"

Rory made his way to the door and opened it to find a regal woman with blond-tinted hair, wearing a cashmere sweater, and neatly creased pants over leather loafers. Despite being the weekend, she still wore a thick gold necklace and a diamond ring that could be seen from space. With an unreadable expression, she looked Rory up and down.

"Well, you're too young to be their new architect and not fluffy enough to be a new puppy . . ." Taffy said.

Rory gulped awkwardly. "I'm Nick's nephew."

"Nephew?" Taffy asked. "I didn't know Nick had a nephew. Or any family. Come to think of it, what I don't know about Nick Gallagher could fill a library."

"Oh, I'm not that interesting," Nick said as he came from the kitchen to rescue Rory. He gave Taffy a kiss on the cheek and ushered her inside.

"Tell me, young man, do you have a name?" Taffy asked.

"I . . . um . . . It's Rory, ma'am."

"Rory what?" Taffy asked.

"Gallagher," Rory stammered.

"Well, Rory Gallagher, I am Mrs. William Winslow Foster III, née Tabitha Gardner. However, seeing you are family, you may call me Taffy."

"Yes, ma'am," Rory said.

Nick wondered if Rory would ever feel comfortable enough to use Taffy's first name. He barely managed it himself.

An hour and a half later, everyone was finishing the shepherd's pie Nick made for dinner. Rory was on his third helping and Nick realized he might have to start doubling his recipes. They had spent most of the meal discussing the construction of Evelyn's factory expansion.

"Remind me again," Taffy said. "How did you get your contractor?"

"Lewis found him. I think they belong to the same club," Evelyn said.

"Old boys network," Taffy said. "Alive and well."

"As long as he finishes on time and on budget, I don't really care if Lewis pulled him straight out of the ocean."

"Hmph," Taffy snorted before turning her attention to Rory. "So, young man, I'm assuming you're in town to see Nick. Where are you from?"

Her imperious tone made Rory sit up a little straighter in his chair.

"I live in Barstow, but we've been all over."

"All over is not a destination. Can you be more specific?" Taffy asked.

"When I was young, we were in Barstow with a guy named Dean."

"Dean Haynes?" Nick asked, an edge to his voice.

"Yeah. You know him?" Rory asked.

"When I was growing up, he was . . . around. I remember Paula had feelings for him."

"Still does," Rory said. "He lives with us."

"You like him?" Nick asked.

Rory paused long enough to make them realize this was a sensitive subject.

"How long were you in Barstow?" Taffy asked.

"Until I was about five," Rory replied, happy to be on another topic. "We moved to Sacramento, I don't remember how long we were there. Then we went down to San Luis Obispo for a year or two. After that, it was San Diego, then Temecula for about six months. Next, Palm Desert,

Ojai, Santa Cruz, Oakland, back to Palm Desert, then Oxnard. That lasted barely five weeks. Does it count? Went to Reno for almost eight months, then finally got back to Barstow. We've been there a year and a half."

"Why did you move so often?" Evelyn asked.

"My mom met different guys. Each one seemed like he was going to be the one. She almost married Richard—or Robert?—in Reno, but it fell apart a few days before the wedding."

"How did you go to school?" Evelyn asked. "How did you make friends?"

"My math could probably use some work, but I got the essentials," Rory said. "As for everything else, I'll find an interesting subject and read whatever I can about it."

"I was like that, too," Nick said. "You don't need a fancy school to get a good education, you just have to be curious. And have access to books."

"The local library is pretty small, but Mr. Prichard at the bus station lets me go through the lost and found," Rory explained. "Moving wasn't so bad. I liked the times it was only me and Mom. We didn't always have a place to stay, so we'd sleep outside and tell ourselves we were camping in the Grand Canyon. Other times, we'd find shelter in a train station or an abandoned building and we'd pretend we were knights out on an important quest. King Arthur was waiting for us at the end with a reward for our service. It was us against the world."

"Paula could always tell a good story," Nick remembered with a smile. "When my parents fought, we'd pretend we were foxes, hiding in our den, while angry bears marauded outside. We had to be very quiet so they didn't find us. Sometimes she played a game talking about all of the places we'd visit when we grew up. I'd research the different cities and plan our itineraries."

"Mom could make the boring stuff feel special. It wasn't that we were cleaning other people's homes, we were searching for treasure," Rory remembered.

"Do you have any siblings?" Taffy asked.

"I was Mom's big mistake," Rory said. "After that, I guess, she found places to take care of things."

"She said you were a 'big mistake'?" Evelyn asked, trying to keep her tone neutral.

"Mom says I should be grateful. We almost always have food and a place to live, even if it is with some guy or another. And I got to see a lot of places. Sometimes, though, I just . . ."

"Just, what?" Nick asked gently.

"Want to be a normal kid," Rory confessed in a rush.

"When I was your age," Nick said, "that's all I wanted, too."

Rory gave him a small, grateful smile. There was a moment of silence, when no one seemed to know what to say.

Finally Evelyn spoke. "Nick rarely talks about his childhood. Thank you for getting him to share a little bit more."

"What are your plans while you're here?" Taffy asked. "Obviously, you'll want to see the sights. Santa Monica Pier, Grauman's Chinese Theatre, the Hollywoodland Sign?"

Rory's eyes lit up briefly, but he said, "No, that's okay. I can't really afford . . ."

"Well, I can," Taffy insisted. "And we're going shopping. Nick's clothes don't fit properly, and I've never liked his taste, to begin with."

"How kind," Nick intoned dryly.

"I don't want to take advantage," Rory replied.

"Nonsense. It's been ages since I've played tourist. You'd be doing me a favor."

As far as Evelyn knew, Taffy had never been a tourist in Los Angeles, but there was a first for everything.

"Besides, these two will be working all day," Taffy said.

Rory glanced between Evelyn and Nick, trying to gauge if it would be all right to say yes.

"It's best not to resist," Nick agreed. "It won't do you any good."

"Taffy always gets her way," Evelyn added.

"It's not that I always get my way," Taffy said. "It's just that I always have the best plan."

She looked around the table, but no one could deny the truth. In another minute, they had Monday's agenda sorted.

Chapter 16

Joe Aoki's office was a small, crowded room above a bakery. The pleasant smell of flour and yeast rose up, perfuming the air.

"How are you not three hundred pounds?" Nick asked Joe.

"I'm going to have to pick up a few pastries before we leave," Evelyn agreed.

"You should," Joe replied with a laugh. "I encourage everyone to support them because they keep me fed. I get so busy I forget to eat."

Evelyn and Nick were sitting in two client chairs across a desk from Joe. He wore a white dress shirt, with the sleeves rolled up. A tie and a suit jacket hung on a hook by the door. Though it was only nine in the morning, his hands were already stained with ink. Evelyn wondered if he had slept there.

"Yesterday's meeting was rough," Nick said.

"If someone took everything you owned, everything you spent your life building, shut you away for three years, then set you free with nothing, I'd bet you'd be angry, too," Joe replied. His tone was matter-of-fact, but it did not hide his underlying frustration.

"I don't know if there are enough synonyms for 'wildly unfair,' " Evelyn said.

"How about 'criminal'?" Joe asked. " 'Fascist'? 'Racist'?"

"Yep, those would work," Nick agreed.

Evelyn looked around. The two filing cabinets in the corners were pushed past their capacity. Thick manila folders formed precarious stacks against the walls. Someone else might wonder how Joe found anything, but Evelyn—were she left to her own devices—would have organized her office in the exact same way. She was one of those people who could recall exactly where a specific document was, based more on its location in space than in any rational system.

"My clients are mostly people who were incarcerated by the U.S. government. Trying to get any kind of compensation for them is a fool's errand, but I do what I can," Joe said. "Sometimes that means filing for reparations, which almost never get paid. Sometimes it means suing the government or individuals. Sometimes I'm just the person they come to when they realize their old life is never going to return."

"It must be difficult," Evelyn said.

"I was too angry to volunteer for the 442nd, so I went to law school. I don't ever expect to see justice, but that doesn't mean it's not a worthy fight."

"I'm trying to find out more about the Takemura family and the land they sold to my father," Evelyn said. "I spoke with the Nagasaki family and they confirmed the sale of the farm. Billy, however, is convinced the restaurant was stolen from them. Hanzo seems to want the whole thing to go away."

"They've been at odds since childhood," Joe began. "Billy was the good kid. Always getting great grades, destined for college, meant to fit squarely into the middle class. Hanzo struggled more. Kenji and Maiko could not own property, so they put the restaurant in Hanzo's name when he was only eleven years old. That responsibility was difficult, but he wanted to make his parents proud."

"Did he?" Nick asked.

Joe thought about it for a long moment. "Maiko appreciated Hanzo's spirit. He was a fighter, for better or worse. A few years before the war, there was a man who didn't like people of Japanese heritage. He made a fuss, saying that the restaurant was dirty, that he got food poisoning, that they were spies."

"Charming," Evelyn replied.

"Hanzo followed him home one night. I don't think anyone knows exactly what he said to the man, but they never saw or heard from him again."

"Hanzo threatened people?" Nick asked. "He ever follow through on those threats?"

"Childhood legal records are sealed," Joe replied. "But the sheriff picked him up on a regular basis."

"He didn't go to Manzanar," Evelyn said.

"Maiko insisted," Joe explained. "She's a wise woman who sees her children clearly. It's a rare gift. She knew that Billy was a rule-follower and would make the best of a situation. Mary was strong enough to survive almost anything. But Hanzo . . . ? His instinct was always to fight. At best, he would end up in Tulle Lake with his father. At worst, he'd get shot by some trigger-happy guard. When they came for Kenji, Maiko realized it wouldn't be long before they came for Hanzo. Maiko heard of a group fleeing east. She packed him a bag and made sure he left with the others."

"Does Billy know that?" Evelyn asked.

"Maiko told him. At first, he didn't believe her; then he figured Hanzo should have stayed with the family, regardless. He owed it to them."

"Instead, he got settled in Chicago and made sure Mary and Maiko had a place to go" Evelyn said.

"Doesn't matter. The two brothers are like oil and water."

"So, what happened with you and Billy?" Nick asked.

"Mary and I were engaged. We met in Manzanar. They randomly assigned my family rooms next to the Takemuras'. Billy and I became friends. Through him, I got to know Mary. You can't imagine what those first days were like. We had nothing. No beds, no blankets, no food other than what they gave us. It was humiliating to be treated like prisoners, though we had broken no law. I felt powerless for the first time in my life. My emotions ran from rage to hopelessness, to frustration and fear. Yet, whenever I was with Mary, I felt a little better. She was kind and funny, and five years younger than me. I thought of her as a little sister.

"1942, I was in my senior year of college. Some of my professors helped me graduate via correspondence courses. Those same professors helped me apply to law school. It took another year, but when they finally opened the camps and allowed us to move inland, I had a place at the University of Chicago. Billy had already left for the Army, and unfortunately, Kenji was gone. I encouraged Mary and Maiko to come to Chicago. I always took Mary's presence for granted. Then, one weekend, she had a date. Hanzo and I went along as chaperones, but I kept glaring at the guy, hating every time he made her laugh or reached for her hand. I was cranky for the next few weeks, snapping at Hanzo and avoiding Mary. Finally Maiko pulled me aside and said that Mary was old enough to hear all of the things that I did not yet realize I needed to say. I'm ashamed to say it took me another two months to finally figure out what she meant. When I did, I showed up on the

Takemuras' front doorstep at five in the morning and told Mary I was in love with her. She'd figured that out months ago, but wondered if I would ever catch up. Then she told me to court her properly. So I did. Showed up with flowers, took her to the theater, went with them to church, and stayed for dinner. Her family began to feel like my own.

"After the war, I spent another year in Chicago, finishing up my law degree before moving back to California to take the bar. When I got here, Hanzo, Mary, and Maiko were set up in their house. Mary got a job working at the Central Library, and Hanzo was an orderly at St. Vincent's. Hanzo was lax in his chaperoning of Mary and my dates. He knew I was a good guy with good intentions. I would never dishonor her. Billy returned from the war early in 1947, and took his duties very, very seriously. He was on our heels whenever we took a walk. Sat between us at the movies. Never gave us a moment alone. It was long overdue, but finally I proposed. Billy eased up once our engagement was public. We planned a small wedding at the church down the street. There was a courtyard where we could have the reception. Initially Maiko insisted on making all of the food, but obviously . . ." Joe trailed off.

"So, what happened?" Evelyn asked.

"I don't know," Joe admitted. "Mary came to me about two months ago, incredibly upset. Usually, Hanzo or Billy came with her into my apartment, but Hanzo simply dropped her off, then drove away. She wouldn't tell me what was wrong; instead, we . . ." For a moment, Joe looked embarrassed. "When she left, Mary handed me her engagement ring. She told me that she loved me, but she couldn't marry me."

"She ever say why?" Evelyn asked.

"No," Joe replied. "I kept trying to talk to her about it. First to get her to change her mind. Then just to understand. The person you see today is not the woman I know. She always used to pride herself on doing her hair. She sewed her own dresses. There was this lipstick, Tangee Red Majesty. Mary wore it every day. It was her favorite. Now? I can't remember the last time I saw it. She's beautiful, regardless—it's not about that. It's that she lost that spark that makes her Mary. I wanted to help her, whatever is going on, but finally Hanzo asked me to respect her decision and stop coming around. He was not unkind, but it broke my heart. Whenever I run into Mary, like Saturday, it's so hard. I know she still loves me, and I still love her."

"So, why is Billy upset with you?" Nick asked.

"He thinks I disgraced his sister. We both told him that she was the one to end our engagement, but he insists I must have done something wrong. Billy cares a lot about what people think. He works so hard to look perfect on the outside. It must be exhausting. I think he's hoping that Mary will forget me and find someone else. Or that she'll come back to me."

"Is that what you hope?" Evelyn asked gently.

"Yes. No. I just want her to be happy."

"Sounds like you and Hanzo became very close," Evelyn said.

"We did. I hesitate to say that he feels like a brother, considering all that's between him and Billy, but he's definitely a good friend."

"What about you and Billy?" Nick asked.

"I respect him and I'm grateful for all he did in Manzanar, but we're very different people. Billy is tightly wound, like if he lets go for an instant, the world will fall apart. I've never known him to date or let himself get close to anyone. Maybe he's lonely."

"Hanzo was furious Billy came to see me about their land," Evelyn said.

"If one says 'black,' the other's going to say 'white,'" Joe sighed.

"What if it was more?" Evelyn began. She reached into her bag and pulled out the sales documents she found in the dungeon. "My father said Hanzo came to him personally, looking to sell the land."

Joe looked at the paper briefly, before setting it on his desk. He stood and went to a corner of the room. He moved one pile of folders out of the way, before reaching a file buried in another. He opened it to confirm its contents, then carried it back to his desk.

"Hanzo didn't sign that," Joe said. Then he laid out several other documents, all recording the sale of land. "These are all supposedly signed by the Nisei sons of Japanese parents. This one is dated when the man was still in Europe. This one here was signed by a man who is buried in Northern France. These others came home to find their land occupied by strangers. For the past two years, we've been trying to prove these were forged. Look at the signatures. The writing is the same. The contracts have the same wording. And they were all handled by the same company—C and W Developers."

"Wait, did you say C and W?" Nick asked.

Joe nodded.

"Why?" Evelyn asked.

"Russell Clements, the C in C and W, told Ruby DuBois that he bought the restaurant for her."

"But my father bought it from Hanzo."

"Or someone pretending to be Hanzo," Joe clarified.

"According to my father, they knew a lot of personal information: Kenji's death, the functioning of the restaurant before the war, details about the Takemura family," Evelyn replied.

"So it could be someone from our community," Joe suggested. "If we found them, we could prove the sales were illegal. Might be able to reverse the transaction."

"Or at least get money from Russell Clements," Nick agreed.

"Let me look into it," Joe said, a hint of excitement creeping into his voice.

"While you do that," Nick replied, "I'm going to have a chat with Mr. Clements."

Chapter 17

The office of C&W Developers left a lot to be desired. It was a two-story beige cinder block building, facing La Cienega. It was bordered by a parking lot on one side and a dive bar on the other. The front door had a metal gate, which did not exactly scream welcome. Upon entering, Nick found a receptionist sitting at the far end of a gray room. A few mass-produced art prints hung on the wall and vinyl couches lined both sides. The receptionist's greeting was perfunctory, as if surprised to see someone come through the door. When Nick had asked to see Russell Clements, she simply responded, "Not here."

The receptionist turned back to *Look* magazine. Nick waited a moment to see if she would add onto that statement. She did not.

"Do you know where I can find him?" Nick asked.

The woman shrugged.

"Who's the *W* in C and W?" Nick asked.

"Patrick Wilson."

"Is he here?"

She heaved a huge sigh. Then she picked up the phone and spoke into it. A minute later, she turned back to Nick.

"You can go up."

The receptionist motioned to a door behind her. Opening it, Nick found a stairway leading to the second floor. Upstairs, there were two offices, facing each other across a small foyer. In the middle stood a large drafting table, with shelves underneath that held rolls and rolls of blueprints. Waiting next to it was a man in his early forties. He looked to be a person who was athletic in high school and struggled to maintain his physique. His hair was still thick and black and his skin carried both the tan and the wrinkles of too much time spent outside.

"Patrick Wilson," the man introduced himself.

"Nick Gallagher."

"We don't have an appointment, do we?" Wilson asked. "Wouldn't be the first time Kitty let something fall through the cracks."

"She seems eager," Nick replied sarcastically of the receptionist.

"My sister's kid. What can you do?" Wilson said, before leading Nick into his office. The furnishings inside were the standard executive model, with a large wood desk and a leather chair behind it. Wilson took his seat and motioned Nick to one of his guest chairs.

"I appreciate you taking the time to see me," Nick began. "I'm curious about the type of development your company specializes in. Specifically, how you choose your locations."

"And I'm curious why you want to know," Wilson said, his voice guarded.

"I can't tell you the name of my client," Nick said, "but it rhymes with Bishop Aeronautics."

"They're building that huge expansion," Wilson said, his eyes widening. "We had a small part in the project. I saw a deal come across for a plot of land."

"Might be more to come. All of those new workers need a place to live. I really can't say more," Nick continued.

"We're jacks-of-all-trades when it comes to real estate," Wilson informed Nick proudly. "If you can buy it, sell it, or build it, we're your people."

"How long have you been in business?" Nick asked.

"My father started it before the turn of the century, but I took it over in the early thirties. Not the easiest time. Very few people were looking to buy a house, even fewer looking to build one. Not ashamed to admit that I often took side jobs to make ends meet."

"What kind of side jobs?" Nick asked.

"Dad wanted me to know what goes into making a quality house. I grew up learning plumbing, woodworking, electrical work. People got to know me as honest and fair. Eventually I got licensed by the city to do inspections. Made enough to stay afloat."

"When did Russell Clements join the firm?" Nick asked.

"In 1939. Things were starting to pick up. What can I say? War's good business. People were pouring in for factory jobs. All of them needed a place to live. Look what William Levitt is doing out in the East. Mass-produced single-family homes. Quality that will last for generations at a price people can afford."

"These housing developments," Nick said. "Were they your idea or your partner's?"

"Wish I could take credit for it," Wilson said. "But Russell's always been the idea guy. He's found ways to streamline the process and make it more affordable. Of course, we pass those savings on to our customers."

"Of course," Nick echoed. "I'd love to hear more about it from him. He's not in today, is he?"

"Nah," Wilson replied. "I haven't seen him in a while."

"How long?" Nick asked.

"I can tell you that should your client, no names mentioned, wish to begin exploring a real estate purchase or further construction, I am more than capable of handling it myself. After all, this is my company."

"Even though the *C* comes first?" Nick asked. Sometimes he liked to provoke people who seemed a little too polished. "How did that happen?"

Wilson tried to cover his annoyance with a slight smile. It did not work.

"Russell can be . . . persuasive when he wants."

"Care to explain?" Nick asked.

"No."

"You don't like him, do you?"

Wilson sighed. "This won't go into your report, will it? I mean, it has nothing to do with business."

"Then I can't imagine how it would be relevant," Nick replied.

"Russell is a man who does not appreciate what he has at home. He's got a wandering eye. When he meets a new girl, he'll disappear for a while. Sometimes just a few days, at most a couple of weeks. This is the longest time he's been gone."

"How long?"

"About two months."

"Has he checked in?" Nick asked.

Wilson shook his head no. "Russell's a great salesman. There are people you think will never, ever sell their land. He gets them to sign on the dotted line. He has a way with zoning commissioners and knows how to motivate contractors. If he wants to disappear for a while, I guess I can't complain. He'll show up when he's ready."

"Can you show me the plans for your housing developments?"

Wilson stood up from his desk and led Nick to the drafting table. He checked the tags on some rolls, then pulled out a few blueprints. They displayed neat little communities, patterned around the swirling veins and arteries of the streets. There were a few hundred houses, with a school and a church located at the center.

"Everything you could need right here. Imagine your children being able to ride their bikes to school or run over to play at their friends' houses, all with the reassurance that they're safe and will be home for dinner. We're not just selling a place to live, we're selling security and community. The opportunities of a big city, with the friendliness of a small town."

"Seems like you have it all figured out," Nick said. "Where are they located?"

Wilson pulled out a larger map of Los Angeles and highlighted the sprawling developments.

"These are huge tracts of land. Was there any difficulty in obtaining them?" Nick asked.

"Not at all. Most of it was farmland."

"Largely cultivated by Japanese farmers who were shipped off to internment camps."

"I didn't create the situation," Wilson replied. "The government did what they thought was best and we made it through the war without an enemy ship running up on our shores. Staying safe is worth any sacrifice."

"Easier to say when you're not the one making it."

"We helped people! They took that money and started over somewhere else. Or maybe they came back here and found a new job. It's not my problem. Russell handled that side of it. Did we profit? Sure, but if it wasn't us, it would be someone else."

"I'm not so sure about that," Nick said, pulling out mimeograph copies of the sales documents Joe Aoki had shown him and Evelyn. "Here's the paperwork for Bishop Aeronautics' purchase of the Takemuras' land. Look at the signature. Now here is the paperwork for the Watanabe's' land. And the deed to the Yamamotos' farm. And this one—"

"What's your point?" Wilson snapped.

"All of these deals were made by Russell Clements, via C and W Developers. All of them have the same handwriting. All of their owners deny selling their land. Do you understand why I'd like a word with him?" Nick asked.

"I didn't have anything to do with that!" Wilson said.

"As you said, it's still your company."

"Now, listen, buddy. I'm tired of your innuendo and your snotty little asides. I don't owe you an explanation."

"No, but you might owe one to the courts. If these land sales are fraudulent, you'll be looking at some impressive lawsuits."

"You son of a bitch. Coming in here and threatening me?"

"Not threatening. Just pointing out the reality of a situation."

"Leave or I'm calling the police."

Those were words Nick had heard more often that he liked to admit. Then, as now, he took it as a sign the conversation was over.

Chapter 18

Evelyn finished briefing Lewis and Ben about her meeting with Joe Aoki. Ben relaxed in a chair in her office, while Lewis paced the small space between her desk and the couch upon which she sat. Unlike the conference room, where he could really get into stride, he was hampered by the lack of square footage. Instead of seeming powerful, it reminded Evelyn more of a child stomping through a tantrum. She wanted to tell him to sit down, but would not give him the satisfaction of seeing her annoyance.

"We have paperwork transferring ownership of the land. We have proof of payment and we have the deed," Lewis insisted. "Why are we still discussing this?"

"Morality?" Evelyn suggested.

"We're a business," Lewis retorted.

Evelyn wondered if he could squeeze any more condescension into those three words.

"The difference between my family and the Takemuras is the random chance of where we were born. I know I can't fix this, but I still want to help them."

"You're opening up a Pandora's box," Lewis snapped.

There was a soft knock on the door and Evelyn looked up to see Julia.

"Hank and Willa are here. Is it a good time?"

Hank, a stocky, medium-height man, with glasses perched atop his salt-and-pepper hair, pushed past Julia. "I don't give a damn if it's a good time."

"Tell them to come in," Evelyn replied wryly. Julia ushered Willa in, then went to close the door. "You should probably stay, too, Julia. Hank's only this rude when something is wrong."

"Willa found a problem," Hank said.

"That's what had you here on a Saturday?" Evelyn asked.

"Hank told me to stay quiet until I was certain," Willa replied. "As you know, we're developing prototypes for our new jet engines. There's a small bracket on the engine mount that broke in extreme heat."

"So, design a new one," Lewis instructed.

"Happy to," Hank said. "That's not the problem."

"We use the same bracket in our current planes," Evelyn guessed.

Willa nodded grimly.

"What happens if it fails?" Lewis asked.

"Short version? The plane would fall out of the sky," Hank said.

"Our current engines are under less heat and stress than the new jets," Willa began. "My best estimate is that it might happen in one in every 2,536 flights."

"Don't hesitate to be specific," Evelyn said.

"Of those, assuming the pilot is competent, and depending on when it happened, the plane would land intact about ninety-eight percent of the time," Willa finished.

"That doesn't seem so bad," Lewis said.

Evelyn did a quick calculation in her head, then looked up at Hank, horrified. "How did we not know this?"

"Luck," Hank replied.

"What's the big deal?" Lewis asked.

"There are approximately 3.1 million flights per year.

Let's say a quarter of those are our planes. That's about 766,000 flights. One in every 2,536 is approximately 302 flights. Assuming a ninety-eight percent ability to land, that still leaves up to six crashes per year," Willa replied.

"We haven't had a crash in three years," Lewis stated.

"You said the timing of the breakage would matter," Evelyn said.

"The beginning or the end of the flight would be the worst," Willa explained. "There's less time for the pilot to adjust or find a glide into a safe airstrip."

"Ascent and descent is where we put the most stress on our planes," Evelyn noted.

"Now you see the problem," Hank replied.

Evelyn sat back in her seat, suddenly wishing this meeting had taken place in the conference room so she could be the one pacing. Finally she raised the question whose answer she dreaded.

"How much?"

"Assuming a total grounding of the fleet? Sending trained mechanics to every airport we serve? Plus, the lost revenue for the airlines?" Hank asked.

Evelyn nodded. Hank handed her a sheet of paper with his calculations. Evelyn glanced at the number, blanched, then handed it to Lewis.

"Forty-five million dollars?" he asked incredulously.

"You couldn't have come at a worse time," Evelyn said.

"I know," Hank replied. "This is the last thing you need."

"I . . . I'm sorry," Willa offered.

"Don't ever apologize for doing your job well," Evelyn replied.

"You're not considering a recall?" Lewis gasped, horrified. Then he looked at Evelyn's expression and saw the truth. "No. Absolutely not. I forbid it!"

"You forbid it?" Hank asked. "Last I checked, you didn't have the right to forbid serving tuna casserole in the cafeteria. Which, by the way, should really be off the menu."

Evelyn smiled slightly, like Hank knew she would.

"Julia," Evelyn began. "please make a note to remove tuna casserole from the lunch rotation."

"Mrs. Hanihan will not be pleased," Julia warned. "It's one of her favorites."

"Perhaps we can let her have kidney pie," Evelyn countered, before diving back into the topic at hand. "What happens if we do this quietly and wait until the plane's next service?"

"Our planes are usually inspected every two hundred hours of flight time. Which is a little more than once every three months. Their major service isn't until every thousand hours. Basically, once a year. We could be fine," Willa said. "It's a slow rotation, but our luck might hold."

"Would you fly on one of our planes?" Evelyn asked.

"No," came Willa's immediate answer.

"We don't have to alert the airlines," Lewis suggested. "Just send our people out for a surprise inspection."

"You don't think they're going to get suspicious?" Hank asked.

"If we tell them something is wrong, they're going to lose all faith in us," Lewis said.

"We're not telling them something is wrong," Evelyn clarified. "We're telling them we have a concern and we're preemptively fixing it."

"It's the same thing," Lewis snapped.

"No one would ever trust us again if a plane crashed and they discovered we knew about the issue," Evelyn said. "Besides, the quickest way to double or triple the cost would be the fines from the CAA and the CAB for trying to cover this up."

"How would they find that out?" Lewis asked.

"Proof might be somewhere in the burning wreckage," Hank said.

"We're talking about 390 potential deaths," Lewis began. "Even if their families sued us, it's still less than the cost of the recall."

Evelyn and Hank stared at Lewis incredulously.

"What exactly is a life worth? A hundred dollars? A thousand? Six months' pay?" Evelyn demanded, bitterly quoting the Army's payment for a soldier lost in active duty. "Does it matter whether it's a man because he might be supporting a family? How about a mother taken from her child? If they're older, is it okay because they have less life ahead of them? Explain the math to me."

"It might never happen," Lewis argued.

"Are you going to comfort a grieving family?" Hank asked.

"At least it's better than Logan. He never went to see any of those boys' families, did he?" Lewis said. "Yet he was perfectly happy to trade them for Matthew."

For a moment, Evelyn felt time stop. There was a numbness that came with hearing the unmentionable. Even worse was the fact that he was right. Willa and Ben looked uncertain, not knowing what they were referencing. Julia's expression told Evelyn she had learned exactly how Evelyn came to be running the company. Hank watched Evelyn as if she were a grenade without a pin. Even Lewis saw he had gone too far.

"I didn't mean it like that," he backtracked.

"Yes, you did," Evelyn replied.

"You know we've all been under a lot of stress and it just came out," Lewis explained. "I meant that—"

"Get out," Evelyn said. She did not raise her voice, but it was a command nonetheless. Everyone left.

Chapter 19

Nick walked up the driveway to a large house in the flats of Beverly Hills. It was flanked by marble statues stretching ten feet into the air. They were classically posed, and Nick thought he recognized Aphrodite, Hermes, and perhaps Dionysus. Their clothes were made of gold, highlighting the pale white of their skin. Though Nick knew the original figures of the Parthenon were brightly painted, his modern eye found it jarring. The lawn was neatly maintained and a Cadillac, freshly washed and polished to a high shine, was parked in front of the garage. Nick wasn't sure Russell Clements had style, but he certainly had money.

Reaching the front door, Nick rang the bell. It was loud and deep, echoing through the whole house. Nick waited a minute or two, then rang again. Finally he heard high heels clicking toward him. The door opened, revealing a woman in her mid-forties whose short stature was offset by her three-inch heels. Her blond hair was freshly dyed and set, her nails cherry red, and her makeup immaculate. Nick might have expected this kind of effort from someone on her way out or just returning home, but her shirtwaist blouse and Capri pants made Nick think this was her perpetual status, even when alone. Diamonds glittered on her left wrist while a gold-and-ruby bracelet with a lion clasp encircled her right. The only thing on her fingers, though, was a simple gold band.

"Yes?" she asked. Her voice was not curious, warm, or cold. It was the neutral resignation of a person who has been interrupted while doing a not particularly interesting task.

"Are you Mrs. Cheryl Clements? The wife of Russell Clements?"

She nodded briefly. Nick introduced himself, then told her he was looking for her husband.

"He's not home," Cheryl replied.

"I spoke with his business partner, Patrick Wilson, who said he had not seen Russell in at least two months."

"You spoke with Patrick?" she asked, her interest slightly piqued.

Nick nodded. "May I come in?"

"Do you have a card?"

Nick pulled one out of his wallet and handed it to her. She studied it for a moment, decided he was legitimate, then stepped back to let him enter.

"We can sit on the lanai," Cheryl said.

Nick stepped inside. Not only were the floors marble, but the whole two-story atrium was lined with it. There was a circular staircase, leading the eye up to a crystal chandelier, which could have come from the Paris Opera House. Cheryl led Nick past a formal living room, with its white rug, white furniture, and even a white piano. Across from it was a dining room that could easily seat twenty-four people.

"You must like entertaining," Nick said.

"Not particularly," Cheryl replied.

They continued through to the back of the house, where

a wall of windows displayed outdoor seating and an azure-blue pool in the distance. Cheryl headed outside and gestured to a patio chair. Without asking, she poured gin into a shaker, added a hint of vermouth, threw in some ice, and shook it to within an inch of its life.

"Olive or a twist?" she asked.

"Olive," he replied.

She skewered a few on a stick, dropped them into his glass, peeled a small curl of lemon into hers, then poured the drinks. Handing Nick his, she toasted before sitting in the chair beside him.

"So, you want to know about my husband," Cheryl said, taking a small sip of her drink, before setting it on a low table between them.

"Any idea where I can find him?"

"Nope."

"When was the last time you saw him?"

"Probably the same day as Patrick. April fourteenth. I made him breakfast, he packed up his briefcase, then never came home," she explained.

"Isn't that unusual?" Nick asked.

"For most men?" she replied, laughing bitterly to herself. "Sure. For my husband? No."

"So, the fact that he's been gone two months . . . ?"

Cheryl took another tiny sip of her drink. She motioned for Nick to do the same. He did.

"Do you know where he went?" Nick asked.

"Nope."

"Have you heard from him since?"

"Nope."

"Do you . . . um . . . know who he might be with?"

"I appreciate that you're doing your very best not to imply he's shacked up with some floozy, but let's not kid ourselves."

"He's done this before?" Nick asked.

"First time was about three years into our marriage. He went on a 'research trip.' Supposed to come home on a Tuesday. I didn't see him until Sunday. I was worried sick for five days. Then he wandered in as if nothing had happened and got angry with me when I demanded he explain himself. We had a roaring fight, slept in separate rooms. The next day, he came home from work with this."

Cheryl held up her wrist encircled by a diamond bracelet. For a moment, she admired the way it reflected light. Then she turned back to Nick.

"I was given a choice. Accept his occasional absences, while keeping my current life, or get a divorce." Cheryl was silent for a minute before looking to Nick. "I know how it looks. This place is . . . But it's not the house or the cars or the jewelry. Russell and I met when we were in grade school. He was the rich boy across the tracks. I was the daughter of the local handyman. Somehow, we became friends. It wasn't one of those situations where he pulled my pigtails. Instead, he beat up the kid who pulled my pigtails. Maybe I've always seen him as the larger-than-life hero who rescued me from a Podunk existence.

"We began dating in high school. He was the varsity quarterback and I was the valedictorian. I had a full scholarship to Bryn Mawr and I gave it up to stay close to him. My father never forgave me, but I thought that was love. Russell had so many small hints and instructions. I learned how to do my hair, my makeup, my clothes, so that I wouldn't lose him to a college girl. Ironic, right? We married the summer after he graduated and the rest is history."

"Sometimes it doesn't feel like a choice until long after we've made our decisions," Nick replied.

"The first time he cheated on me, it felt like I would break in two. I thought about leaving, but I had no idea how to support myself and no faith there was anyone better out there. The next time, it hurt a little less. Time after that . . . ? The worst was when he set that woman up in a restaurant. It wasn't just a few weeks. He cared about her enough to go through the effort of making her happy. I went to see her once. Had lunch at the diner. She could make a great pie, I'll give her that, but otherwise, I didn't see the appeal."

"Does it still hurt?"

"Always. I want to hate him, but I can't. For the longest time, he was the only man I ever loved."

"And now?" Nick asked gently.

Cheryl flushed, realizing she had inadvertently confessed to adultery. Then she squared her shoulders and put on a bravado that did not seem to come naturally.

"I was lonely," she said. "Maybe it would be different if we had children. I tried. Went to every doctor you can imagine, but I never got lucky. Russell refused to get tested, but there haven't been any random kids showing up on our doorstep. Makes me think I was not the problem."

"It does take two," Nick agreed.

"I don't even know why I'm telling you all of this."

Cheryl reached out and took another sip of her drink. It was still two-thirds full.

"Because I'm a stranger," Nick offered.

"You must think I'm pathetic," Cheryl said. "Spilling my guts like this."

"You're not pathetic," Nick replied. "Though you do seem sad."

Cheryl reached for her drink, but stopped herself midway. Her hands shook and it took Nick a minute to realize she was sobbing. It was noiseless, with tears streaking down her cheeks, her shoulders shuddering as she curled into herself.

How long does it take a person to train herself to cry in silence? Nick wondered.

Cheryl stood up and fled inside. It was twenty minutes before she returned, her makeup redone, her shirt changed.

"I'm sorry," she said, her reserve back in place.

"Don't apologize," Nick said.

Cheryl seated herself again, picked up her drink, and tasted it. Then she tossed the liquid to the side.

"Warm," she explained. "Care for a refill?"

Nick's drink sat untouched on the small table.

"No, thanks," he said.

She sat back in her chair, twirling the stem of the empty glass between her fingers.

"What can you tell me about your husband?" Nick asked. "Patrick Wilson gave the impression that Russell was a big personality. Something of a bulldozer."

"I never saw it when I was younger, but he's the most selfish man I've ever known. Thinks of himself first. And second. And third. Maybe, at some point, I make the list of priorities. Maybe not. He knows looking respectable is important, so he takes me to business dinners or company parties. I read quite a lot and can hold my own in a conversation. It looks good for him to have an intelligent wife. Sometimes I still see flashes of the man I married, but those are rare."

"What about his business?"

"He keeps that part of his life very separate from me. I stopped trying to understand it a long time ago."

"Can I ask you one more question?" Nick began.

"Why not?" Cheryl said. "We're on a roll."

"What would you have studied at Bryn Mawr?"

A quiet smile crossed her face. "Economics. And before you give me some patronizing bullshit about how I can still do it, I'm going to stop you. It is too late to start over. At least for me."

"Fair enough."

"Got anything else?"

"You say you became this person to make your husband happy. The hair, the makeup. It's beautiful, but it's also a lot of work."

"Not many men realize that," Cheryl said, reassessing Nick.

"Why bother when he's gone?"

"For the time when he comes home," she replied quietly.

"You still love him," Nick said.

"I honestly don't know any longer. Maybe all of this is just reflex."

Cheryl stood and Nick took it as his cue. She walked him to the door. On the threshold, he stopped.

"You have my card. Will you give me a call when your husband returns?"

Cheryl thought about it for a minute. "No. Probably not."

With that, she closed the door, leaving Nick outside with the marble statues.

Chapter 20

Nick found a pay phone after his conversation with Cheryl and gave Evelyn the update. She was at her desk, with the phone clasped between her shoulders and her ear while she reviewed the potential schedule for the recalls. She liked to believe she could do many tasks at once, but now, like always, she had to set one aside to focus on the other.

"You think it was C and W that stole the land," Evelyn said.

"I'm not certain, but yes. The only question is whether it was done legally."

"I don't understand."

"Unscrupulous bankers could have called in the loan, then sold the land for nonpayment," Nick began. "Insurance companies could have canceled their policies, which would cause a bank to revoke the mortgage. Tax statements might have been intercepted or never forwarded to the camps. When they went unpaid, the land could be sold at auction. All of those maneuvers are technically within the confines of the law, despite people not being here to receive notice. Take it to any court in California and they'll find for the new owners."

"Why bother with a fake owner?" Evelyn asked.

"Two reasons," Nick suggested. "The first is that the Takemuras might have done everything right. There might not have been a mortgage to default on, or they were able to keep up with their taxes. Donald Holcomb struck me as a decent sort, who would have done his best to stay on top of that."

"And the second?"

"Do you think your father would have bought the land if he thought someone was cheated out of it?"

"No," Evelyn answered.

"They bring in someone they said was the original owner."

"And have him convince people that his family endorsed the sale."

There was a knock and Hank opened the door to her office. She gestured him inside. He walked to where she kept the whisky, uncorked the bottle, and poured himself a glass.

"It's a plausible scenario," Nick said. "A lot of people did not return after the war."

"I'd love to ask Clements about this land I may or may not own," Evelyn said.

"If I can find some of the women he had affairs with, I might be able to find one of his romantic hideouts," Nick mused.

"You really think Mrs. Clements is going to offer up names?"

"No, but Ruby might," Nick replied. "She could still be angry enough to share them."

"I've always loved diner food," Evelyn said.

"Hash browns, here we come," Nick joked before saying goodbye.

Evelyn hung up the phone and walked past Hank to Julia's desk.

"Do you have it?"

Julia handed Evelyn a draft of the notice to alert their customers of the voluntary recall. It strongly emphasized the point that no one was forcing Bishop Aeronautics to take this step. They chose to do it out of an abundance of caution, before there were any incidents. Included was a timeline of when they could expect the issue to be resolved. When Evelyn finished reading, she handed back the paper to Julia.

"Looks good. Telegraph the people who need to know tonight and we'll put copies in the mail tomorrow morning. I'd suggest setting up calls with our major customers, but I have a feeling they'll be on the phone first thing in the morning. Tomorrow's gonna be a rough day."

"We've had them before," Julia said. "We'll have them again."

Evelyn nodded, before heading back into her office, and closing the door behind her. Hank sat on her couch, halfway through his first drink. She sat beside him. He pushed a second glass of whisky toward her and she took a long swig.

"We're doing the recall," Evelyn said.

"It's the right decision," Hank replied.

"It's going to cost us every penny we have in reserve, and a lot more. Finances were already tight with the new construction. Now? I have no idea how we're going to make it work."

"You didn't see us at the beginning," Hank laughed. "Back then, I built airplanes because I thought it was fun. Never really considered making a business out of it, until your father came along. We worked out of a barn and kept crashing planes into the ground. Logan also made several that flew better than anything I'd ever seen. Those early days were grueling—sixteen, eighteen-hours. I think your father kept us afloat from sheer force of will. Money was going out faster than it was going in, yet Logan could always sweet-talk a banker into lending us a little more. This was his passion and everyone wanted to be part of it.

"It was easier for me. I wasn't married. If it all fell apart, I'd pick up the pieces and start over. Logan had Anna, then Matthew and you. He needed it to work, not only to support his family, but to prove to your mother she was right to take a chance on him. It was pure chaos, and I wouldn't have traded it for the world."

Evelyn always enjoyed the stories of her father, back when he seemed a larger-than-life figure.

"Lewis wasn't there," Hank continued. "He had no idea what it was like to survive on canned tuna and peanut butter sandwiches."

"I'm guessing he would not have fared particularly well," Evelyn replied sardonically.

"Probably not, but he had the right connections. Knew how to use them to our advantage. I don't always understand exactly what he does, but he brought in new customers when we desperately needed them. Between him and your father, we managed to weather the Depression, and, of course, the war put us on top. It wasn't the way Logan wanted to get there, but we took what we could get. The money coming in from the Navy and the Army Air Corp allowed us to take more risks and innovate faster. I like to believe the technology we created helped those planes stay up just a little longer. Keep those crews just a little safer."

"I flew on our planes more than once," Evelyn confessed.

"It's a good thing you never told your father what you were doing. He would have flown over to London and throttled you himself."

"He would have had to find me first," Evelyn replied. "I didn't spend too much time in one place."

"The OSS gave you a lot of skills most young women never learn," Hank said. "You're smart, tougher than nails and can read people better than almost anyone I've ever met. Maybe you wouldn't have been fit for this job before the war, but you certainly are now."

"Try telling that to Lewis," Evelyn replied.

"It's hard for him," Hank admitted. "He always wanted the top job. Or at least to be equal partners with Logan. He was out of line today."

"But was he wrong?"

"What your father did? It shocked the hell out of both of us. We'd known Logan all of these years. The betrayal felt personal. He wasn't just giving away his work, he was giving away ours. Something I created might have caused American deaths. I don't think I'll ever get over that. Yet, if I had a son in a POW camp, I probably would have made the same choice."

"Can you forgive him?" Evelyn asked.

"I don't know," Hank answered honestly. "I do know that I'm grateful for the life I have now. Logan was never going to make anyone a partner, but he always treated me well. I was more than fairly compensated. He never hesitated to give me credit and he was incredibly supportive when I took all of that time off for Jenny's illness."

Hank's wife had died of cancer a few years back and he had yet to recover from that loss.

"One day, Logan's name will probably be in the history books, while mine won't even be a footnote. The top job came with stress, struggle, and hard choices. I got to spend my time focusing on the work I love. How can I complain about that?"

Evelyn smiled, but it didn't reach her eyes.

"Airlines and government are going to give you hell," Hank said. "But they're also gonna realize they can trust you."

"I needed to hear that," Evelyn said quietly.

"Come on," Hank said as he stood and pulled her to her feet. "You're too much in your head. Let's take a walk and see that new factory of yours."

"They're still digging the foundation. All we're going to see are piles of dirt," Evelyn replied.

"Ah, yes. But it's dirt with potential."

Evelyn laughed and allowed Hank to lead her outside. They took a winding path toward the construction site, idly discussing new projects. It was close to quitting time, but the sun was still high in the sky when they arrived. A few diggers moved earth, slowly winding down for the day, while others filled dump trucks with soil to be hauled away. Hank was right. She found a sense of peace outside and seeing the project gave her hope.

That is, until she heard the screaming.

They ran out into the field to find a mangled body caught in the teeth of an excavator. Evelyn couldn't tell what damage was from the machine and what was natural decomposition. The corpse had been in the ground for a while.

Evelyn suspected they had found Russell Clements.

Chapter 21

Nick was making dinner for Evelyn and Rory while she told them about finding Russell Clements. The state police took a surprisingly long time to arrive and she did not get the sense that they had a lot of experience. A bunch of people tromped across the field and she had to suggest that they take photographs before moving the body.

Nick raised his eyebrows at that. It was basic police work.

“Did the sheriff come?” he asked.

“I wish he hadn’t,” Evelyn replied. “He was the last to arrive and blustered around giving contradictory orders, before closing off the entire construction site, with no clue as to when we’ll be able to reopen.”

“I suppose when you don’t know how to collect evidence, you want the option to go back,” Nick said.

“When I told Lewis, he started yelling numbers at me,” Evelyn said. “I’ve been making Rory answer our phone all night.”

“I’m getting good at saying no—‘No, she’s not home.’ ‘No, I don’t know where she is.’ ‘No, I don’t know when she’ll be back.’ ”

"Saying no is a useful skill," Evelyn replied. "One day, you'll thank me."

Rory grinned. The few days he stayed with them were enough to help him relax.

"Clements was not beloved by his business partner. I'd like to get into their office and see their records," Nick said.

"Especially before that sheriff gets his hands on the evidence," Evelyn agreed. "Would it be wrong to take a quick look around?"

"It's not as if we're stealing anything," Nick offered.

"We're gonna break in!" Rory exclaimed.

"There is no 'we' in this scenario," Nick replied.

"I could be the lookout. I'm really useful," Rory said.

Nick looked to Evelyn. "He's your nephew."

Rory looked between the two of them before reading the answer on Nick's face. An excited smile lit up the boy's face.

"You're staying in the car," Nick insisted.

Evelyn, Nick, and Rory parked two blocks away and walked up to the offices of Clements and Wilson. The building was shut tight. While Evelyn could easily pick the locks on the metal gate and front door, the bar next door was so crowded, people spilled out into the street. Their goal was to be in and out unnoticed. They circled the entire building, but only found the one entrance. All of the windows were barred, except for a small one at the back of the building. It was about six feet off the ground.

"No way I can fit through there," Evelyn said.

"Obviously," Rory said.

"Excuse me?" Evelyn asked.

"No, no. Sorry. I'm not implying you're fat! Oh, God. I just meant that you're old," Rory explained quickly, before realizing that was not a better answer. "No! Not old, just . . . I just meant that I'm . . ."

"A kid?" Nick offered.

"No, a"—Rory seemed desperate to avoid mentioning his age, for fear that they would not allow him inside—"less fully developed, though still an incredibly capable, human."

Remembering what it was like to be thirteen and desperate for Matthew to let her join his adventures, Evelyn struggled to suppress a smile.

"What happens if the police show up?" Nick asked. "It would be bad enough for Evelyn and me to get caught. But you? You have the rest of your life ahead of you."

"Exactly," Rory said. "A decent lawyer could get my record expunged when I turn eighteen."

Evelyn couldn't help it. She began to laugh.

"What's so funny?" Nick asked in exasperation.

"It's like watching you argue with a younger version of yourself," Evelyn replied.

Rory looked to Nick expectantly.

"Fine!" Nick said. "But don't touch anything."

"Scout's honor," Rory said, holding up three fingers in a Boy Scout salute.

"Were you ever in the Boy Scouts?" Evelyn asked.

"I know how to set a fire, if that's what you're asking."

"No!" Nick said emphatically. "That is definitely *not* what we're asking."

Then Nick glanced at Rory, saw his grin, and sighed. The kid had teed up his reaction as surely as a professional golfer at St. Andrews.

"I'll give you a boost," he said finally.

Nick brought his hands together in a makeshift step, then lifted Rory up so he could reach the window. After a moment's fiddling, Rory pushed the glass open. Nick raised him higher as Rory wriggled his shoulders through the narrow opening and inched farther inward. Then, with a sudden yell, the boy disappeared, followed by the sound of a crash.

"Rory!" Evelyn cried. "Are you okay?"

There was a muffled response. If he had hurt himself, they would have to break in through the front door—bystanders be damned.

"Give me a boost," Evelyn said.

"You're not going in there! "Nick exclaimed.

"Rory made it perfectly clear I won't fit," Evelyn said. "I want to see if he's okay."

Nick formed another step with his hands and boosted Evelyn up. She pulled open the window and looked inside. Rory was on the floor, near a cascade of boxes.

"I made a mess," Rory said sheepishly.

"Are you hurt?" Evelyn asked.

Rory shook his head.

"Then go open the front door. Nick and I will help you clean this up."

Rory nodded. When Nick and Evelyn arrived at the front of the building, a drunk couple was madly groping each other. They probably would not have noticed if a wrecking ball took down the building. Evelyn was loath to disrupt them, except they were leaning against the front gate. Rory opened the inside door, but there was no way of pushing two people off the metal bars. Evelyn glanced to Nick.

"Fine," he said, correctly reading her look. He stepped up to the couple and politely tapped the man on the shoulder. At first, he didn't notice, but when Nick did it three more times, he finally turned around angrily.

"What!"

"Would you kindly move about four feet to the side?"

Nick asked. The couple glanced at the building, to see Rory smiling from behind them. Grudgingly, they moved the required distance, before recommitting to each other. Rory opened the gate. Nick and Evelyn stepped inside.

"Now we have witnesses," Evelyn sighed.

"They'll never remember us," Nick promised.

Nick, Evelyn, and Rory made quick work of putting the storeroom back into reasonable shape before heading upstairs to the offices. Both Clements and Wilson had several file cabinets. There was not too much of interest in Wilson's office, though Nick did find a jeweler's receipt for a wildly expensive gold-and-ruby bracelet with a lion clasp. Now Nick understood why Clements's disappearance did not especially bother his partner. He wondered whether Wilson's animosity toward Clements was just business or if it had more to do with the fact that he was sleeping with Cheryl Clements.

Rory searched the secretary's desk downstairs, with no luck. Evelyn's search of Clements's office was a bit more fruitful. The top drawer held a pack of Lucky Strikes and matchbooks from nearly every club in town.

"He got around," Evelyn noted.

"Wish we could find his flavor of the week," Nick replied.

"I didn't see his calendar in the secretary's desk," Rory said. "Maybe it was on him. Could have her name in it."

"It's a good thought," Nick said.

Evelyn flipped through Clements's address book. There were a few familiar names, like those she had gotten to know at the city planning office. There were some local politicians and the direct numbers for a variety of police officers. Evelyn stopped when she found the contact information for Ben Strover. It was not unusual for a builder to have the name of a contractor, yet she was not a fan of coincidence . . . especially since Clements's body was found where Ben worked. She showed it to Nick, who raised an eyebrow in surprise.

In the bottom drawer of Clements's desk were letters tied in different-sized bundles. Evelyn opened some from a man named Pete Oster. The letters started off discussing Clements's potential purchase of his land. At first, it was largely business, but quickly devolved into threats of violence. Evelyn looked through the other stacks. Some were anonymous, suggesting Clements watch his back. They knew where he lived. Others gave him an ultimatum of paying back what he owed or face the business end of a baseball bat. Several were demand letters from lawyers representing homeowners, contractors, and fellow builders. There were also a few from Hanzo.

Evelyn opened them.

"Hanzo didn't even give Clements the benefit of the doubt," she said. "They started off angry, then got worse."

"Death threats?" Nick asked.

"Yep. But that's not the problematic part," Evelyn replied. "The letters stopped right around the time Clements disappeared."

"I don't understand," Rory said.

"Why send letters to someone you know is dead," Nick explained.

"I understand that he's angry," Evelyn said. "But I got the impression that it was mostly bluster—a desire to protect his family. Do you think he really could have killed someone?"

"Anyone can do anything if they're pushed far enough," Rory answered matter-of-factly.

Both Evelyn and Nick looked at him. It was not that they disagreed, they just remembered the horrors it took for them to gain that knowledge.

"Might be time for another chat with Hanzo," Evelyn said.

"The grieving widow, too," Nick added. "It's not the fact she was having an affair. It's who she was having an affair with. Patrick Wilson had a lot of reasons to want Clements out of the picture."

"Even more so if these lawsuits keep growing," Evelyn agreed.

Chapter 22

When Evelyn drove past her construction site the next morning, she was greeted by a large stretch of police tape and absolutely no police. No construction vehicles, either. Until the crime scene was released, there would be no progress on the new factory. She could not bring herself to tally up the cost of this delay.

Rather than turn toward her office, she kept driving to the sheriff's station. It was a low gray building that looked as though it was designed by a two-year-old playing with blocks—a rectangle with a flat roof and a door facing the parking lot. The interior matched the creativity of the outside, with a few vinyl chairs along the wall and a four-foot-high partition dividing the waiting room from the bullpen. Six desks were lined up in neat rows, leading to the sheriff's private office. Evelyn saw Sheriff Richardson with his feet up, leaning back in his chair, a cup of coffee balanced nearby. When a deputy told him Evelyn wanted a word, the request was greeted with laughter and the pronouncement "uppity broad."

"Sorry," the deputy said with a blush, knowing full well she heard the interaction.

"Do you know whether the sheriff will be at the crime scene today?" Evelyn asked.

"At some point," the deputy replied. Then lowered his voice. "Perhaps someone else might have more luck with these questions."

"Someone not in a skirt?"

He nodded. It was not the first time she had heard this suggestion.

"Thank you, Deputy . . . ?" Evelyn said.

"Polansky," he provided.

Evelyn committed the name to memory.

Three hours later, Teddy, the security guard who kept watch of the construction site, called Evelyn's office to let her know the sheriff had finally arrived. She murmured a couple of choice words about the time, then went to find Ben. Though his workers were off for the day, Lewis wanted him here, if for no other reason than to witness his frustration. Julia directed Evelyn to engineering.

"He's been spending a lot of time there," she offered. There was a note in her voice that caught Evelyn's attention, but Julia did not elaborate.

Evelyn headed down to the drafting room, where she found Willa standing with Ben. They were chatting amiably, but Evelyn sensed an undercurrent of something more. They stood closer than most colleagues. Upon seeing her, Ben quickly stepped away.

"Willa pointed out that engines will probably get heavier as time goes on," Ben said. "We should reinforce the support beams in the new factory, rather than having to retrofit them later."

"Willa is brilliant," Evelyn replied.

"I'm just finding this out," Ben agreed with a warm smile.

Evelyn wasn't certain, but she detected a small blush on Willa's cheeks.

"I hate to interrupt," Evelyn began, "but I need your help, Ben."

"I'm at your service," he replied gallantly with a slight bow.

As they walked toward the construction site, Evelyn filled Ben in on the frustrations of the morning.

"We could always keep working," Ben joked. "Maybe sweep the crime scene into a dump truck and drop it at his door."

"Tempting," Evelyn replied. "Though it might get us arrested for tampering with evidence."

"But other than that . . ."

"Other than that," Evelyn agreed. "How do you know Russell Clements?"

"I don't," Ben replied a bit too quickly.

"Your name is in his address book."

"How do you know that?"

"How does anyone know anything?" she replied, studying him. His was a strange response to a simple question.

"We knew each other professionally," Ben admitted finally. "He came to me a while ago about working on one of his projects."

"Seems like a substantial paycheck."

"We disagreed on methods. I like my buildings to remain standing in a strong wind," Ben replied.

"And I, for one, am happy to hear that," Evelyn seconded.

"Clements cut corners every chance he got. Used subpar material and shoddy methods. He was so cheap, he even regulated how many nails could be used in the floorboards and walls."

"Seems like it wouldn't cost that much more to build a quality home."

"It's not. His way is less expensive up front, but much more costly down the road."

"After he's already sold the properties," Evelyn noted. "Reputation like that, a lot of people might want him dead."

Ben stopped and looked at Evelyn.

"Listen, I didn't like the guy. Am I bragging about our association to the sheriff? No. That said, I wouldn't kill Clements or anyone else. We decided not to work together. Went our separate ways. That was that." Ben's voice had become aggressive in its defensiveness. The new tone surprised Evelyn.

"I've gotta ask. Where were you around April fourteenth?"

"You think I'm a suspect?" Ben said in disbelief. "What are you? Some lady detective?"

"I can show you my private investigator's license if you want," Evelyn offered.

"Wait, really?" Ben asked. "Like some grown-up Nancy Drew?"

Evelyn could not be bothered filling him in on her history at this particular moment.

"April fourteenth," she reminded him.

"I can't believe you're actually asking me this," Ben said.

Evelyn waited.

"Jesus. I don't know. I'd have to look at my calendar."

Before Evelyn could suggest he get back to her, they had arrived at the crime scene. Seeing them on the sideline, Deputy Polansky came over with the sheriff.

"Do you have any idea how long this will take?" Ben asked.

"You got a problem with the way I work?" Sheriff Richardson barked.

"Of course not," Ben replied. "We would never want a killer to go free. Especially one who went after a respected member of our community. I know you excel at your job and value keeping the streets safe. Thing is, I've had to send my workers home and I'd love to tell them when they can return."

"They can return whenever the hell I say so," Richardson barked. Ben's attempts at flattery had gone approximately nowhere.

"Between us," Ben continued, "this delay is costing quite a lot of money."

"How's that my problem?" Richardson asked.

"I'm just thinking that perhaps there might be a way to speed up the process," Ben suggested. He glanced at Evelyn, who sighed, then nodded. "For instance, I know overtime costs quite a bit. I could give you the extra money to pay your officers."

"Are you offering me a bribe?" The sheriff's voice sounded more intrigued than insulted.

"Certainly not!" Ben exclaimed. "I'm trying to come to a solution that works for everyone. The sheriff's office is wildly underfunded for the important work you do."

"I'll get back to you," Richardson said, then walked to where the body was found. Deputy Polansky looked slightly disgusted with the whole affair, but followed his boss.

"I would've thought he'd take the money," Evelyn mused.

"He'll come back with a higher number, but not yet. He wants us desperate so we'll accept anything," Ben replied.

"Gotta love a dedicated officer," Evelyn replied sarcastically.

"Not much else you can do," Ben said.

"Sheriff's not the only person on the case."

Chapter 23

Nick entered the sheriff's station a few hours later to find several police officers milling about. For a place ostensibly dedicated to keeping people safe, there was a definite lack of urgency. The phones rang. Sometimes they were answered, sometimes they were not. There was nothing to give a person confidence their issues would be handled efficiently, or even at all. Nick approached the clerk sitting on a stool behind the front desk.

"I'm here to see Sheriff Richardson," Nick said.

"Why?" the clerk replied.

"It's about the body discovered at Bishop Aeronautics."

"What's it to you?" the clerk asked.

"I think Sheriff Richardson is just dreamy. I've been writing his name in my notebook with little hearts around it all week!" Nick replied with a girlish squeal.

"That's not getting you anywhere, wise guy," the clerk retorted.

"How about this?" Nick pulled out his old LAPD badge. He was supposed to turn it in when he was fired, but he conveniently forgot. Though it was illegal to impersonate the police, Nick liked to think of it as exploring the road untaken.

"How about a little thing called jurisdiction?" the clerk replied. "You don't got it."

Nick had to admit, he was not expecting the clerk to know this fact. Usually, the badge was magic.

"What about professional courtesy?" Nick replied.

The clerk was unmoved. "Sheriff's not here."

"Is there anyone I can speak with?" Nick asked.

Deputy Polansky had been watching this exchange from his desk and came over to introduce himself.

"Come on back. We can talk in the interrogation room."

Polansky led Nick to a small, dark room. He flipped a switch and the fluorescent lights took a moment of flickering before the gas fully ignited. There were four chairs, two on each side of a plain wood table. A thin layer of dust coated every surface.

"Looks like this place doesn't get much use," Nick said.

"We mostly get drunks and petty crime," Polansky admitted as he gestured for Nick to take a seat. "Sorry for the clerk. He's . . ."

"Spent too much time around your boss?" Nick asked.

The deputy gave a wan smile and took another chair for himself. "Let me guess. You're here to ask when we'll release the crime scene."

Nick nodded.

"Mrs. Bishop was down here this morning about the same issue. Got her contractor to repeat the question a few hours later."

"So I heard," Nick replied. "She also mentioned the sheriff was not especially helpful."

"He's been here a long time. Has his way of doing things," Polansky replied, but Nick heard the annoyance in his voice.

"Is it the same as your way of doing things?"

"Here's what I can tell you," Polansky offered. "Help

me solve this case and we won't need the crime scene anymore."

"I'm no longer a detective with the LAPD."

"You don't say," Polansky replied dryly.

Nick was a little hurt. Between the front-desk clerk and Polansky, he was losing his touch.

"I'm a private investigator looking into land that was stolen from Japanese Americans during the war. The victim's name came up a few times in my case."

"Not exactly a stand-up guy?"

Nick sketched the outline of the evidence he had found, conveniently leaving out their visit to the C&W offices the night before. Impersonating an officer might get a blind eye, but breaking and entering would not.

"You said the Takemura family?" Polansky asked.

Nick nodded.

"Sheriff's not exactly a fan of Hanzo Takemura. I knew him when he was a teenager."

"Hanzo ever get into major trouble?" Nick asked. "The kind that requires more than a night in lockup?"

"Not that I know of. He and some other boys could rough it up. Hanzo was usually the only one arrested, but the other kids never sat for statements."

"Street code," Nick said. "Might hate each other, but you settled it your own way."

"The working theory on Clements's death is a robbery gone wrong. Sheriff thinks some guy tried to steal his car when he was in it. Clements fought back and the rest is history. Killer found an empty field and dumped him there."

"What do you think?" Nick asked.

"It's possible. Last day anyone saw him was April 14th. Fits with the decomposition. Clements died from a blow to the back of the head. Skull is crushed."

"You find a murder weapon?" Nick asked.

"Nope. From the wound, it's probably something flat and heavy. Impact from a pipe or a baseball bat would be more centralized."

"One blow or more?"

"Coroner says it was one," Deputy Polansky said. "Who knows? Maybe he fell backward and cracked his head on a rock."

"You think that's likely?"

"Clements was there two months, so a lot of the evidence was washed away or has sunk deep into the mud. No footprints or drag marks. No tire tracks. No clue one way or another. Only thing we do know is someone dug him a shallow grave. He wasn't alone when he died."

"Heard a rumor that Clements hired local hooligans to drive people out when he wanted their property."

"Can't say anything about that," the deputy replied.

"Can't, or won't?"

Polansky thought for a moment. "As long as you're in town, Henderson's Tavern makes an awful martini. Might stop by there if you're in the mood for a liquid lunch."

Nick nodded his thanks.

Chapter 24

"Lewis!" Evelyn snapped from behind her desk at Bishop Aeronautics. "We've been over this. I don't know what else to do."

"We need to find a shortcut," he replied, sitting in a chair across from her.

"Yes," Evelyn said. "Those are always the most reassuring words when it comes to safety."

Lewis glared at her. "I'm just trying to help. We have orders two, three, five years in advance. Orders we planned to fulfill using the new plant. These were tight deadlines, to begin with, and we cannot default."

"Yes, the government does get a little cranky when you run behind schedule," Evelyn agreed. "General Clay and I have a good relationship. If this is still an issue in a month—"

"A month!" Lewis exclaimed.

"I will fly to DC and have a chat with him. Right now, we've only been shut down for a few days. I don't understand why you're panicking about this."

"Because what if it's not a few days. What if it's weeks. Or months?"

"Then we'll handle it," Evelyn replied. "Let's not borrow trouble."

"Oh, no. Willa found more than enough already."

"This recall isn't anyone's fault. The piece was properly tested. We only discovered the issue because we're putting it under more stress. There's no blame here. We should be grateful Willa found it before anyone was killed."

"From what I hear, the Air Force is taking a second look at our contract," Lewis warned.

"We sell more to the Navy anyway," Evelyn said with a nonchalance she did not feel.

"It's not a joke," Lewis insisted. "Look what they're doing to Convair. They tried to pull the funding for the B-36."

"Which the Army saved," Evelyn replied. "Though I can't imagine why. That thing's a mess."

"We lost an ally when the secretary of the Navy resigned," Lewis said. "John Sullivan is a good man. He always had our back. No one knows what's going on with Russia. Now isn't a good time to be cavalier about our relationships with the military."

"Maybe not, but if I have to, I will fly to DC and gently remind people that the newspapers won't be kind if they learn the government got fussy over a recall that would save soldiers' lives." Lewis looked like he wanted to interrupt, but Evelyn held up her hand. "I am aware of our current financial situation and the probability we'll have to use our line of credit from Security First National Bank."

"Have you spoken to them recently?" Lewis asked.

"Have you?"

"They're concerned about our current situation and—"

"How do they know about our current situation?" Evelyn asked.

"This is a small community. People talk," Lewis replied.

"They haven't called in our loans, but they're unwilling to give us any more."

Evelyn shook her head in frustration. "I know my father skated close to the line, it never felt this tight before."

"Your father was a realist. He wouldn't have authorized the recall."

"We disagree, but the point is moot," Evelyn said. "We're not going to go bankrupt from this recall or anything else."

"Now you're tempting fate," Lewis grumbled.

"And you could use a little more faith," Evelyn replied tartly. "You are right, though. We need to stay up-to-date with our current orders while managing the recall. The only fix I can think of is to hire more people."

"Which requires money," Lewis reminded her.

"There must be outstanding invoices. Call them in."

"That brings ill will," Lewis warned.

"Heaven forbid we ask people to pay us what they owe," Evelyn retorted.

Before she could continue, however, she heard Julia's voice rise.

"No, you can't go in," Julia said. The answer was too quiet to hear. "Yes, I'll tell her. Please have a seat."

There was another response, slightly louder this time.

"Well, I want a pony, but we all have to learn to live with disappointment," Julia replied tartly.

Evelyn opened the door to find Ben in front of Julia's desk, annoyed.

"Your secretary wouldn't let me in to see you," he groused.

"That's her job," Evelyn informed him.

Ben looked between Evelyn and Julia for a moment, his face inscrutable. Then he said, "I was told to come, so I'm here."

Lewis ushered Ben into Evelyn's office. "Yes! I'm glad you could make it."

"You okay?" Evelyn asked Julia quietly.

Julia nodded. Evelyn went back into her office to find Lewis sitting in the chair across from Ben.

"In the future, Lewis, please tell Julia when you plan to include others in our meetings," Evelyn instructed, before resuming her seat behind the desk.

"We were just discussing how to make construction as cost effective as possible," Lewis explained to Ben. "Is there any way we can put the workers on leave while the site is closed?"

"They are on leave," Ben replied.

"No, I meant"—Lewis fished around for a delicate way to say it—"unpaid leave."

"You can't punish them for something they have no control over," Evelyn said.

"Well, they're not working," Lewis grumbled.

"They're also not free to take other jobs," Ben countered. "Unless you fire them. Then we'll have to find a whole new crew, which could take weeks."

"I didn't mean it like that!" Lewis exclaimed. "Just don't pay them until we restart."

"How do you expect them to eat?" Evelyn asked. "Or pay their mortgage? Not everyone has savings."

"Even if they do, I doubt this is what they'd choose to spend it on," Ben added. "If you won't pay them, then you shouldn't pay me. We'll move on to the next job."

"We can't afford to find a new contractor," Lewis said. "Especially on such short notice."

"I know you're trying to save money, Lewis, but you can't do it by taking it out of other people's pockets," Evelyn stated.

"Fine," Lewis muttered.

"Anything else?" Evelyn asked, looking between the two men. There was no response. "Then I think this meeting is over."

She walked Lewis and Ben to the door. Neither looked at Julia as they made their way downstairs. Evelyn caught her expression. It was hard and wary.

"You don't like him, do you?" Evelyn asked.

"I don't trust him."

Julia often understood people even better than they knew themselves. Evelyn had never known her to be wrong. It was only later that Evelyn realized Julia did not specify which man she meant.

Chapter 25

Nick wandered into Henderson's Tavern. Dust swirled in the shafts of light peeking through the gaps in the window shade. A pool table stood to the right of the entrance, and a bar with a dozen stools to the left. A variety of bottles, ranging from drinkable all the way down to something better used for cleaning brass, lined the wall behind it. Looking at the worn handles on the taps, Nick thought better of ordering a draft. Having spent too much time in the back of a bar, he knew how quickly mold formed in the beer lines and he had little desire to test the strength of his constitution.

There were five men in their mid-twenties dispersed through the room. Two were shooting pool, while the other three sat on stools, talking too loudly for the relative emptiness of the space. They were long past the age of being hooligans, but Nick could see the echoes of their boyhood-little love and no tenderness. They tried so hard to be men and saw violence as the only initiation. Nick understood how they would be intimidating, especially in large numbers, yet he had dealt with men like this his entire life. Bravado often crumbled when confronted. Nick grabbed a stool and the bartender ambled over, asking what he wanted.

"Bottle of Schlitz seems safe."

The bartender grabbed a beer from the refrigerator and popped the top. Nick took a pull, then set it aside. Almost everything had an expiration date, and this was long past it. Nick set down a quarter in payment, which the bartender scooped up, before returning to his book. Most of the men pretended to ignore Nick, but one summoned his courage.

"Don't know if you noticed, old man, but this is locals only."

"Seems my money's as good here as anywhere else," Nick replied. The bartender glanced up briefly and Nick knew better than to look to him for help.

"I say it's not," the man said.

"And you're the owner?" Nick guessed. "The manager? The patron saint of all things alcohol."

"I'm the patron saint of screw you."

"Creative," Nick replied.

The other men gave up the pretense of being otherwise occupied and stared at Nick. Reluctantly, he got to his feet. The other man immediately charged at him. Sidestepping gracefully, Nick directed the man's head into the wood railing of the bar. He shook his head, took two steps, and then collapsed. Before anyone else could move, Nick held up his hands in a pacifying gesture.

"You can come at me with whatever you've got. I'll put you down as easily as I did your friend."

"Not all five of us!" one of the men near the pool table shouted.

"Four now," Nick corrected. "It would be a bit messy and I'm willing to bet the bartender would ask you to find a new place to enjoy your afternoon libations."

"Our *what*?" the man near the pool table asked. "I'm not doing that with you, pervert."

"It means 'drinks,' not 'sex,'" said the man on the stool closest to Nick. He was slightly older than the rest, looking bored by it all. Among these men, his authority was unquestioned.

"How about I buy you all a drink?" Nick offered. "You answer some questions and we go our own way, no worse for wear."

The man lying at Nick's feet groaned slightly and the leader nodded to two others to pick him up. They dragged him to a bench near the pool table and propped him in the corner.

"I'm Colin," the leader said to Nick. Then nodded to the man on his other side. "This is Drew."

"Nick. What are you drinking?"

Colin looked to the bartender. "Double whisky all around."

The bartender looked to Nick, who nodded. Pouring six glasses, he handed them out, one by one. Colin raised his glass to Nick, not quite toasting him, then tossed the liquor back. Nick took a sip. As expected, it was cheap and watered down to a barely recognizable ratio.

"What do you want to know?" Colin said.

"You remember the Takemura family?" Nick asked.

Colin laughed without humor. "Had a couple of scrapes with Hanzo. Asshole broke my arm once."

"Payback feel good? You were the ones who destroyed his family's restaurant, right?"

"They were gone," Colin said. "The U.S. government took care of any and all revenge I might want or need. Closing down Holcomb was just business."

"Who paid you?" Nick asked.

"That question's going to cost you," Colin replied. "And more than those watered-down drinks."

Nick pulled out his wallet and slid a few bills across the bar. Colin tapped them, wanting more. Nick doubled the fee. Colin waited again, but Nick put his wallet away.

"We could take the rest from him," Drew said.

"You could try," Nick said calmly. The threat needed no emphasis.

Colin folded the money and put it in his pocket. "A guy named Russell Clements."

"What did he offer you?"

"Gave us a lump sum. We were supposed to drive the current owner out."

"Any particular rules of the assignment?" Nick asked.

"Told not to damage the building."

"You didn't worry about the police?"

Colin laughed. "They were on this guy's payroll, too. Holcomb called them every time we showed up. Somehow, patrol cars never arrived. Gotta give him credit, though. Man hung on longer than I expected. Made his life a misery, but he still opened up every morning for months. He even offered us money to leave him alone. It was a useful bargaining chip to take back to Clements."

"Gotta appreciate loyalty," Nick drawled.

Colin shrugged, but Drew missed the sarcasm. "Guy gave us a ton of other jobs, too."

"Drew!" Colin snapped. "Go take a walk."

Grumbling, Drew got up and headed to the pool table.

"Good help is hard to find," Nick commented.

"You have no idea."

"Care to tell me the other jobs Clements hired you to do?"

"Nope," Colin replied.

"Sorry. I phrased that wrong," Nick said as he pulled out a small notebook and pen. "Write down the other names that Clements gave you to harass. We've already established that the local sheriff is useless. And I'm not a cop . . .

anymore. Gives me a certain latitude when I question people."

Colin took a moment to see if Nick's threat of violence was a bluff. Then he grabbed the paper and began to write. When he was finished, there were more than twenty names, some of whom Nick recognized from the threatening letters in Clements's office.

"I'd better not see you again," Colin said, trying to get in the last word.

"For your own good, I certainly hope that's true," Nick answered as he stood up and walked out into the bright sunshine.

Chapter 26

It had been a frustrating day and Evelyn decided to head home early. Entering the kitchen, she discovered a large stack of books on the table. Rory's head was bent over one of them. Taffy sat next to him, browsing through another. She looked up and smiled at her niece.

"What's all of this?" Evelyn asked.

"We spent the day sightseeing. Or at least we were supposed to," Taffy said, gently teasing Rory. "We ate downtown at Clifton's Cafeteria and—"

"Wait," Evelyn stopped her. "You ate at a cafeteria?"

"The inside is incredible," Rory said. "It's decorated with all kinds of wild animals and the walls are painted with different scenes from across America."

"The food was halfway decent," Taffy admitted.

Evelyn shook her head, amused. She had officially seen everything.

"Then we were going to see *Home of the Brave*," Taffy continued. "But there was a bookstore . . ."

"It's called the Pickwick Book Shop. Like *The Pickwick Papers*," Rory enthused. "How great is that?"

"Somehow, we lost our afternoon there," Taffy finished with a smile.

Evelyn looked to the books and picked up the top one, flipping through it.

"'All animals are equal, but some animals are more equal than others,'" Evelyn quoted.

"You've read *Animal Farm*?" Rory asked.

Evelyn nodded.

"Rory insisted I get it," Taffy said. "He has good taste."

"If you liked that one," Rory continued, "you'll have to try *Homage to Catalonia*. Even though it talks about the war, I still want to go to Barcelona."

"It's beautiful. They're rebuilding it slowly, but one day it will be better than before," Evelyn said.

"You've been?" Rory exclaimed. "Where else have you gone?"

"Growing up, I was fortunate to travel a lot. Both my father and Taffy took me to Europe and parts of Africa. Then, during the war, I saw it again, but differently," Evelyn replied.

"You were over there?" Rory asked. "During the fighting?"

"It's how I met your uncle."

"Wow," Rory said, eyes wide. "I didn't know. Though I did wonder how you two met. I mean . . ."

"They don't travel in the same circles?" Taffy offered.

Rory nodded.

"The world is a wide and wonderful place," Evelyn said.

"Maybe," Rory replied.

"You don't think so?" Taffy asked.

"Sometimes it feels like the future was written before I was born."

"You can change it," Evelyn offered. "I grew up thinking I'd be exactly like my mother. Then the war happened and my life took a left turn."

Taffy slid her hand over Evelyn's and gave it a small squeeze of support.

"Tell me about your books," Evelyn prompted.

There were twelve in all and Rory went through each one, describing what had drawn him to this story or the review that one had received in the *Los Angeles Times*.

"You're going to need a larger suitcase to take all of these home," Taffy teased him gently.

Rory's face fell slightly.

"Or you can read as many as possible during this trip. We'll keep the rest safe until you return," Evelyn said.

"Really?" Rory asked. "I can come back?"

"Always," Evelyn replied, glancing down at her watch. "Let me get changed and we'll figure out dinner."

Rory smiled, then turned back to his books. Evelyn headed upstairs, with Taffy following her to the second-floor landing.

"Rory is a great kid," Taffy began, her voice barely above a whisper. Evelyn tensed, certain she did not want to hear what came next. "But I saw him coming out of your and Nick's bedroom earlier today."

"That doesn't mean anything."

"No, of course not," Taffy agreed. "It was just the expression on his face. It looked . . . I don't know. Almost guilty."

"What are you accusing him of?"

"This boy shows up out of nowhere. How well do you really know him?"

Evelyn sighed deeply. While she loved her aunt dearly, sometimes she also thought her a terrible snob. Taffy would probably agree, though she would reframe it as having standards.

"Did he say anything that makes you think there's an ulterior motive?" Evelyn asked.

"No. He's a polite, kind young man," Taffy replied. "I

don't think he has ill intentions, but perhaps there are things he's not telling us."

"What he's not telling us could fill an ocean. I think some are too painful and others too personal. I don't want to push him. He'll open up when he's ready," Evelyn said. "Nick gave up on the idea of his family. Now that door is creaking open again. It's a fresh start that could be good for both of them."

Taffy nodded. She paused for a moment, as if wanting to add something more, then decided against it and headed back downstairs. Evelyn went into her room and closed the door behind her. She changed into comfortable pants and a sweater. Her jewelry box was sitting on top of her dresser, as always. The angels of her better nature told her to ignore Taffy's allegations. Instead, she opened the lid. Her mother's pearls were missing.

Evelyn swore softly. She wanted, so badly, to believe in Rory. His attitude led her to believe he desired only to be a part of Nick's life. The pain she felt at this betrayal was miniscule compared to Nick's anguish upon learning of this theft. His history was so fraught, she worried he might turn his back on Rory, with little hope of second chances—even if there were extenuating circumstances. She did not know what to do. Before she could come up with a plan, the phone rang.

Evelyn picked it up with a brusque "Hello?" She listened for a moment. "No, he's not home. What's going on?" Then, "I'll be right there."

Chapter 27

Wendy, a thirty-five-year-old woman wearing a starched shirtwaist dress, flawless makeup and patent leather heels, led Nick up her driveway, past her neat two-story house in Long Beach, towards a small garage that had been converted into a studio apartment. It was painted gray with blue trim and its garden held chrysanthemums, zinnias, and marigolds. After three quick knocks, the door opened, revealing Pete Oster, an older man wearing a worn button-down shirt, faded khakis, and work boots. A smile cracked his face, upon seeing his daughter.

"Wendy! You look nice, honey. Going out?"

"Yes, Dad," she replied, her voice carrying a hint of annoyance. "I told you. I have a PTA luncheon to discuss the fall fundraiser."

"Right, right, I forgot," he said. "I can pick up the kids from school."

Wendy hesitated long enough to feel awkward, then nodded. "Thank you. That would be helpful." She turned to Nick. "This gentleman is looking for you. Has some questions about Russell Clements."

Pete's face darkened. "What does that son of a bitch want now?"

"He's dead," Nick replied.

"How?" Pete asked.

"Someone hit him over the head with something heavy."

Pete began to laugh. It was a sound hovering between happiness and hysteria.

"It's not kind to celebrate a man's death," Wendy admonished sternly, before relenting. "Though maybe there are exceptions to be made."

Pete picked up his daughter and swung her around. She smiled briefly, then gently freed herself. "I have to go."

With a nod toward Nick, she walked back into the main house.

"Come in, come in!" Pete enthused. "Tell me all the details."

The apartment was small, with a sink, hot plate, and a small refrigerator against one wall. A double bed was tucked into the corner of the other. Pete led Nick to a round table in the middle of the room and gestured to a coffee mug drying on the dish rack.

"Can I get you a drink? I'd offer something that more properly suits the occasion, but I gave all of that up to live here."

"No, thanks," Nick said, as Pete joined him at the table. "Nice of your daughter to take you in."

"At first, she didn't want to. Not that I can blame her. I was a mess for a while," Pete said. "I hope Clements is being raked over a fiery pit of coals by the devil himself."

"What happened?" Nick asked.

"I was a farmer my whole life. Grew up on the land, planted the fields with my father and granddaddy. Counted the seasons by which crop was ready to go to market at any given time. Planned to pass it all down to my sons, but then they went to war. Son-in-law has no interest in getting his hands dirty. Still, it was mine. It was home. Figured I'd die at some point and let Wendy sell it for whatever she could get."

"When did Clements come into the picture?" Nick asked.

"Couple of years ago. Everywhere around me, these new communities were forming. All of the houses looked the same. All of the streets. Even the people looked alike. Those straight-backed soldiers and their pretty wives. Don't blame them. Everyone deserves a nice place to live."

"Clements offer to buy your place?" Nick asked.

Pete nodded. "How do you leave the only home you've ever known? Said 'no, thank you' and ushered him out the door."

"Guessing that wasn't the last you saw of him."

"He came back a couple of times, but I wasn't interested. One morning, I came out to find some kids had salted my fields overnight. Bastards didn't even bother to hide. They were walking up and down the rows with bags over their shoulders, destroying the soil. Entire life's work was gone. Once the salt is in the ground, nothing's going to grow there for years."

"Jesus," Nick said quietly under his breath.

"Rather the opposite," Pete replied. "Though it did make me question his existence. How could someone be so evil?"

"You must have felt powerless."

"Cops did nothing. I tried to take Clements to court, but there was no way to prove he was behind it. Plus, lawyers cost money."

"Sounds like he left you without many options."

"At first, I'd sell to anyone other than him, but he'd told people we had a deal in place. Made it so messy that no one else wanted to touch it. If I could have burned the place to the ground for insurance money, I would've done it. Perhaps with me inside," Pete confessed.

Nick put a reassuring hand on the older man's shoulder.

"Appreciate your kindness," Pete said. "And listening to me ramble. Sometimes you just gotta get it out of your system."

"Know the feeling," Nick replied.

"Anyway, it was coming up on tax season. I had no crops to sell, nor did I have much left in savings. Despite my best efforts, the place was going to go to Clements or the bank. He gave me a fraction of what it was worth. Much less than his first offer, but he said there had been 'administrative fees' since then. He made me pay for the men he hired to ruin my fields."

"You didn't happen to write him any letters, did you?"

Pete laughed. "So many. I admit, it wasn't my finest hour. Several were threatening. A lot were a product of too much whisky. In one or two, I'm pretty sure I promised to kill him."

"Would you have done it?" Nick asked.

Pete thought for a minute; then a slow smile came on his face. "If I knew I could get away with it, yeah, probably."

"I gotta ask," Nick said. "Where were you on April fourteenth?"

Pete went to the calendar on the wall and flipped back two pages. "That's right. Kitty, Wendy's eldest, was playing Ado Annie in *Oklahoma!*. I helped build sets that week. That when Clements was killed?"

Nick nodded. "You have any idea who did it?"

"Nope, but you find the person, let me know. I want to buy him a drink."

Pete Oster's smile was not an expression Nick would soon forget. He hoped no one felt such joy upon his demise. As Nick walked to his car, he spotted a pay phone on the corner and called home to speak with Evelyn. Instead, Rory answered, informing him that Evelyn was at the police station. They arrested Hanzo for Russell Clements's murder.

Chapter 28

Nick arrived to find Evelyn tapping her foot impatiently while she leaned against the front partition of the sheriff's office. The clerk was glaring at her, but if she sensed his annoyance, she was not bothered by it. Billy and Carl sat against the wall. Evelyn was surprised to see them together, but when she tried to say hello, Billy was too anxious to give anything more than a perfunctory nod and Carl refused to acknowledge her.

"Tell me what happened," Nick said when he arrived.

"They picked up Hanzo this afternoon," Carl replied.

"On what evidence?" Evelyn asked.

Carl glared at Evelyn, not answering. Nick looked between them, curious about the tension.

"On what evidence?" Nick repeated.

"The letters at Russell Clements's office included death threats from Hanzo," Carl said.

"That's it?" Evelyn replied. "There were death threats from dozens of people."

Billy and Carl looked up sharply.

"Or I'm assuming," she amended quickly.

"We definitely—*definitely*—did not break into his office," Nick seconded.

"Why go after Hanzo, particularly?" Evelyn wondered.

"Sheriff Richardson always had a thing against him," Billy said. "Ever since we were kids. If he saw Hanzo with a pack of chewing gum, he'd arrest him for shoplifting until the store owner confirmed he paid for it."

"He do that with everyone?" Nick asked.

"Everyone who looked like us. Richardson liked people being afraid of him. Hanzo wasn't. He had as much right to be on that street as anyone else and he wasn't going to let some bigoted cop scare him off."

"Heard Hanzo got into some scrapes," Nick said.

"I'm sure this will come as a huge shock, but some of the guys around here liked to bully us," Billy replied. "Hanzo never sought out trouble, but he'd stand up for himself . . . and for us. Said if he refused to fight back on the small stuff, the abuse would escalate. Don't know that he was wrong. Hanzo got arrested more times than we could count. They never made the charges stick, but it still broke Mom and Dad's hearts."

"You were the good kid," Carl guessed.

"Always. I had to be perfect so my parents wouldn't worry about me. Then again, it was probably hard on Hanzo fighting all of the battles so Mary and I could walk down the street with our lunch money in our pockets."

"I hate to ask this," Nick said. "Do you think there's any chance Hanzo could have killed Russell Clements?"

From the open doorway, a voice called out, "No!"

They looked up to see Mary enter the building.

"No," she repeated. "There is no way my brother killed anyone. Tell them, Billy."

Billy did not answer.

"Hanzo could get angry, sure. Sometimes he even lost control, but he was getting better," Mary insisted. "More mature. Instead of going after that horrible man, he was working with Joe to get our land back."

"Wait, what?" Billy asked. "Why didn't you tell me?"

"Because Hanzo was handling it," Mary said. "Then you had to go shoot off your big mouth at that groundbreaking ceremony. We don't need outsiders in our affairs."

They both looked at Nick and Evelyn, whose discomfort ratcheted up to eleven.

"You should have included me!" Billy replied.

"Why?" Mary asked. "So you could try to take over and make it worse?"

"That's unfair."

"It's accurate," she snapped. "You made it very clear our family was never your priority."

"What are you talking about? I wasn't the one who ran," Billy said.

"Weren't you?" Mary asked. "You signed up to go fight for a country that locked us away like criminals. Shipped out to basic training and never looked back. Do you have any idea what it was like after Dad got out of Tule Lake? It was hell for him there and it wasn't any better at Manzanar. Everyone in camp assumed he was released because he ratted out others to get a better deal for himself."

"Did he?" Billy asked.

"Go to hell," Mary said.

Billy looked shocked at her profanity.

"There you were, serving this great and glorious country that stole everything from us and threw us in prison. It just proved that we were a family who couldn't be trusted. We were ostracized, with only Joe and a few others speaking up for us."

"I didn't know," Billy said quietly.

"Mom wouldn't let me tell you," Mary said. "She didn't want you distracted when you were at the front. Then you returned, and there didn't seem a point. Hanzo got us out of Manzanar. He set up a place for us in Chicago, found us jobs, made sure we had a roof over our heads and food to eat. You never had to see our mother on her hands and knees scrubbing someone else's floor. You never had to ask for charity or spend hours in line to get your paperwork sorted to prove a loyalty that should never have been questioned. By the time you returned, we were back in Los Angeles. You were the hero, swanning around in your captain's uniform, but you never asked what we endured. You never cared."

"I . . . I'm sorry," Billy said, shamefaced.

Mary turned to Evelyn and Nick, eyes blazing. "Hanzo did not kill Russell Clements."

There was an authenticity in her voice that brooked no argument. Across the room, the door to the interrogation room opened. Sheriff Richardson stepped out first, followed by Hanzo, his shoulders hunched and his hands in cuffs. Joe trailed behind, his hair rumpled, his expression frustrated. Mary rushed to the counter dividing the station.

"Hanzo!" she yelled.

He looked up and shook his head.

"Remember your promise," Hanzo said.

"But . . ." Mary began.

"You promised," he repeated; then the sheriff dragged him away.

Joe offered her a wan smile before heading toward the holding cells in back.

"Hanzo!" Mary yelled again.

A clerk came around the desk.

"All right, everyone out. I can't have you in here causing a ruckus," he said, arms wide, driving them toward the door.

Mary stormed out, followed by Evelyn and Nick. Carl was last, his hand on Billy's shoulder, comforting him.

Chapter 29

After what seemed like forever, but was closer to twenty minutes, Joe Aoki stepped out of the police station to find Mary, Billy, Carl, Nick, and Evelyn.

"What did they say?" Evelyn asked.

"Not much," Joe replied. "They didn't offer any evidence to justify his arrest; though, at this point, it's not required."

"How long is he going to be in there?" Mary demanded.

"They have forty-eight hours before they have to release him or charge him," Joe said. "If they charge him, we'll get a better idea of what they know."

"This is harassment!" Billy exclaimed.

"Yes, but it's also legal," Joe retorted. "They're going to see if they can get him to confess."

"How?" Mary asked.

"There won't be any fingernails yanked out, but they can 'accidentally' leave the lights on or 'forget' to turn off loud music so he doesn't sleep at night. They're required to feed him, but it's possible what they bring might not be edible."

"My God," Mary breathed quietly.

"He's strong," Joe assured her. "It's going to be a rough

two days, but he knows the drill and his Fifth Amendment rights."

Mary looked as though she wanted to say something more; instead, she went to Joe, wrapped her arms around him, and began to sob. He held her, quietly rubbing her back. They clearly still loved each other and Evelyn wondered again what drove them apart.

Billy turned to Evelyn and Nick. "Thanks for taking me seriously, but Mary's right. This is a family matter. We'll handle it on our own."

"I appreciate that," Nick replied. "Unfortunately, there's a dead man and it wasn't only your family he screwed over."

"I'd rather you drop it," Billy said.

"I'll leave you out of it as much as possible," Nick offered.

"I said no!"

"It's not your case anymore," Nick said. "The man who pays the piper, picks the tune. Evelyn needs this murder solved so she can continue building her factory. I need to know what happened because I'm a stubborn ass. And who knows? I might prove Hanzo's innocence."

"Or his guilt," Billy replied. "Who's to say you're not another person trying to lock us away?"

"Billy—" Carl started.

"You don't understand," Billy retorted. "You could never understand."

Billy stormed to his car, got in, slammed the door, and peeled out onto the road.

"He doesn't speak for all of us," Joe said, still holding Mary. "I'll take anything you find. Good or bad. If it exonerates Hanzo, so much the better. If not, I don't want to be surprised at trial."

"You really think it will go that far?" Mary asked.

"Yes," Joe replied.

Nick offered to stop by his office the next morning to go over what he knew. Joe nodded his gratitude, then helped Mary into his car. They drove away, leaving Carl, Evelyn, and Nick standing together. The silence was strangely awkward and Nick did not understand it. Before he could question them, Deputy Polansky waved him over to the back of the building, where they could talk without being seen.

"Tell me what's changed?" Nick asked. "Why Hanzo? Why now?"

"We found Clements's car near the pier in Hermosa," Polansky said. "Someone tried to drive it into the ocean."

"No luck?"

"It's not as easy as you'd think," Polansky replied. "The sand's a pain and most people don't have the stomach to keep going when the water rises."

"There goes the robbery theory."

"Especially seeing his watch and wallet were tossed in the back seat," Polansky added.

"Got anything else?" Nick asked.

"Not much, but we found his datebook. He recorded all of his appointments with initials. The day he disappeared, there was a *DI*, a *BS*, a *PW*, and an *HT*."

"You think it's Hanzo Takemura?"

"That's what Sheriff Richardson is running with," Polansky replied. "You got any other theories?"

"*BS* could be Ben Strover. He's the contractor working on the new Bishop Factory."

"Maybe he put the body there, intending to hide it when the field was dug up?" Polansky asked.

"It's not a bad theory," Nick said. "Man knows how to operate the machines, but he doesn't really have any motive. Just a minor business falling-out. I think the stronger suspect is *PW* for Patrick Wilson, Clements's business partner. He happens to be sleeping with Mrs. Clements."

Polansky raised his eyebrows. "Should I ask how you know that?"

"Nope," Nick replied.

"The car's ashtray held the remains of some Lucky Strikes and a French brand, *G*-something."

"Gauloises?"

"That's it," Polansky said. "I ran across them during the war."

"They were expensive, but you could find them on the black market."

"The theory is that the Luckys were probably Clements's, the other his killer's."

"Besides death threats, what else did you find when you searched Clements's office?"

"How do you know there were death threats?" Polansky started before shaking his head. "Never mind."

"Why are you helping me?"

"I want to be a good cop and there aren't that many opportunities. I don't know who killed Russell Clements, but it seems like we should look at more than a few initials and a person's appearance to make our case."

Nick extended his hand to Polansky. "Well, I appreciate it."

Polansky nodded and headed back inside. Nick turned back to see Evelyn and Carl in the parking lot. Even from this distance, he could see the frustration on Evelyn's face and the anger on Carl's.

"Stop trying to justify it," Carl demanded.

"I'm not justifying it, I'm trying to explain," Evelyn replied.

"It's the same thing. How can I trust you?"

"Because you know, deep down, that I would never betray you."

"It's about more than me!" Carl roared.

"Maybe once, but those days are long gone. He can't hurt anyone anymore."

Nick approached and looked between the two of them. "Enough of this. What is it between you two?"

Evelyn looked at Carl, willing him to respond, but he refused.

"All right, don't talk to me," Evelyn said. "But you need to talk to someone. You look like hell. Whatever's going on, you can't carry it alone."

"Come on," Nick insisted. "I'm taking you out to dinner."

"I'm fine," Carl said.

"No. You're not," Nick replied. "Besides, I give you full permission to complain about my wife."

Carl did not even offer a quirk of a smile. That alarmed Nick.

"Remember during the war, I'd tell you to do something and you'd argue with me? Nine times out of ten, what happened?" Nick asked.

"I'd do it anyway," Carl grunted.

"Get in the car," Nick ordered. "Besides, you have no other way of getting home."

Carl glanced around the parking lot as if realizing this for the first time. He grudgingly got in the passenger side. Nick gave Evelyn a quick kiss.

"See you at home," he said.

Evelyn nodded, her eyes on Carl. "I'm worried about him," she whispered.

"Me too," Nick replied.

Chapter 30

Evelyn entered her kitchen, her arms laden with bags of food. Seeing her, Rory set aside the book he was reading and stood to help.

"I got dinner from the cantina down the road," Evelyn said. "I didn't know what you like, so I ordered a little bit of everything. Tacos, burritos, fajitas, tostadas . . . Is Taffy still here?"

"She left a few hours ago. Said if Nick wasn't cooking, there was no point in staying."

"What am I? Chopped liver!" Evelyn exclaimed.

"She also said you'd be offended, but should take it as a compliment to Nick."

Evelyn laughed. "Fair."

They unpacked the bags and set the feast on the kitchen table. Rory looked at all the food laid out in front of him, but he did not reach for it.

"Please," Evelyn said.

"Oh, no," Rory replied. "You start. I'll take whatever you don't like."

"I like it all," Evelyn said, setting a carne asada burrito on his plate.

As Rory ate, he stopped a few times to mumble through mouthfuls, "This is so good."

Evelyn took a few tacos for herself. "We didn't eat out a lot when I was a kid."

"Was your Mom a good cook?" Rory asked.

"According to my dad, she couldn't boil water. Unfortunately, I don't really remember. She died when I was eight."

Rory stopped eating. "I'm sorry."

"Cancer. It was unbelievably awful."

"What was her name?"

"Anna," Evelyn replied with a smile. "She was the kindest person you'd ever meet. And funny. She could make the whole table laugh. Every night, my brother and I would jostle for who got to go first telling her about our day. She had this way of listening that made you feel like you were the only person in the whole world. Even though we were kids, she took our questions seriously—like we were intelligent and valuable. Being around her felt like being encased in sunlight."

"That sounds really nice," Rory said.

"Dad tried, but when it was just him, Matthew, and me, it wasn't the same. He loved us, but I think Mom's ghost haunted every meal."

"Did you eat together every night?" Rory asked. When Evelyn nodded, he sighed longingly.

"You don't get to do that?"

"Mom works a lot and Dean's around," Rory said. "When it's the two of us, she'll bring home leftovers of whatever people didn't finish from the restaurant. Occasionally I even get steak!"

"One of Nick's favorite memories was a steak dinner with his friend Helen."

"Mom sometimes tells me stories. There was one day

Nick found a dollar on the street. They went to the pier and pretended they were tourists—the kind of kids whose parents took them to see somewhere new and bought them a treat just because they could. They got ice cream and popcorn. Nick even won Mom a small stuffed animal at the shooting gallery."

"Sounds like fun!"

"It was . . . until they went home. When Grandma found out, she was furious with Nick for wasting money."

"How'd she find out?" Evelyn asked.

"Mom told her."

"Why?"

Rory shrugged. Evelyn could imagine what happened next. There was a reason Nick never spoke about that day.

"My brother and I liked ice cream, too," she said. "Matthew ate it so fast; sometimes I wondered whether he even tasted it. I tried to make it last. Good in theory, but I always ended up a sticky, melted mess. There was one time my brother called me hopeless and threw me, fully dressed, into the ocean. It drove him bonkers having to wait for me."

"Were you hurt?" Rory asked, alarmed.

"No, of course not. We made each other crazy, but he was also my best friend. We looked out for each other."

"How did he die?"

Evelyn nodded. "A POW camp. He's the reason I joined the OSS. Without him, I never would have met your uncle."

"Almost like a trade?" Rory asked.

"Oh, no," Evelyn replied. "There was no purpose to Matthew's death and Nick isn't a consolation prize. It's hard to imagine an alternate timeline where I didn't go to war. All of the pain, the fear, the struggle, made me who I am today. There's no point in torturing myself with what might have been. I love my life. I appreciate what I have now. Maybe that's the best any of us can hope for."

"Maybe," Rory said doubtfully.

"Thirteen is a miserable age. One of the worst years of my life."

"Thanks," Rory drolled. "Real encouraging."

"It does get better, though. Look at Nick. It wasn't easy, but he built a family of people he loves and trusts. And now he has you. I know it hasn't been long, but you have no idea what you mean to him."

"Really?" Rory asked with a slight blush.

"When his family abandoned him, it broke Nick. He's been carrying that pain around for so many years. Unfortunately, it makes opening up to new people more difficult. Part of him always worries they're going to betray him. A small mistake takes on grand proportions because his instinct is to protect himself. Once his trust is lost, it's nearly impossible to get it back."

Evelyn pulled a large brooch out of her pocket and set it on the table between them. A massive ruby made up the body of a bird, while diamonds, sapphires, and emeralds constructed the head and the wings. Rory's eyes widened.

"Sometimes it's hard to know what has value," Evelyn continued. "The president of a steel company gave me this for my wedding. I'm sure he thought jewelry so extravagant would buy him good will. You could use it as a paperweight, for all I care. Other pieces, like my mother's pearls, aren't worth much money, but they mean the world to me. When I'm wearing them, it feels like I'm holding a piece of her close to me. Does that make sense?"

Rory nodded.

"Love is one of those things you can't always see. Sometimes you just have to have faith that it exists," Evelyn said. "I know we've been talking a lot about your uncle, but you're my family now, too. That means I trust you. I believe in you and I'm so glad you're here."

Rory didn't know how to respond. Evelyn looked around the table and realized they had finished the food.

"Are you still hungry?" Evelyn asked. "I can rummage up some cheese and crackers."

"No," Rory said. "I'm pretty full. It was great."

"Next time, we'll go to the restaurant. It's even better there," Evelyn replied, as she picked up the dishes and headed toward the sink.

"It's okay," Rory offered, jumping up. "I'll do those."

"Thanks," Evelyn said. "It's been a long day. You need anything before I go to bed?"

Rory shook his head, then glanced at the table where the jewel-encrusted bird sat.

"Don't forget your brooch!" Rory called.

"I'll get it in the morning. Have a good night."

She was almost out of the room when she turned back.

"If you ever need help, money, whatever, we'll give it to you. No questions asked."

He held her eye, then nodded once. Evelyn turned and went upstairs.

Chapter 31

Carl and Nick sat at the horseshoe-shaped bar in Tom Bergin's Tavern. It had recently moved to a new location, but it still had its homey charm. Wood arches at the top of the room gave it a majestic, yet accessible feeling. Almost like sitting in a sixteenth-century English hunting lodge, complete with leaded-glass windows. The bar had a copper top covering up the dark-paneled wood and was flanked by stools to match. There was a dining room with a fireplace at one end, but in all of his years of going to the old place, Nick had never once sat at a table. Didn't make sense to start now. Irish whisky drew him here and the menu was secondary.

Carl was on his fourth Bushmills, while Nick nursed his first. It was unusual for Carl to drink to excess, yet this was the second time in two weeks Nick had seen him drunk. As Carl raised his arm to signal to the bartender for another, Nick put his hand on Carl's shoulder.

"You're really going to criticize me?" Carl asked. "You? Of all people?"

"Not criticism," Nick said. "Concern."

"How much did you appreciate my 'concern' for you? Still have a scar from when you threw a bottle at me."

Carl held up his hand, where a faint scar traced the back. Nick looked at it with regret.

"I was an asshole," Nick said. "I was also in pain. Not an excuse. Just saying you were right to worry."

Carl drained the remainder of his drink and reached for the new one, before setting it back on the bar untasted. After all Nick and Carl had been through, they developed the rarest of things—a friendship where they could be themselves. They had already seen the worst in each other.

"We all have so many secrets and sometimes it feels like it's killing me," Carl confessed. "I know we did it during the war, but then I understood the purpose. Now? I don't know."

Nick waited patiently. They sat in silence for a couple of minutes, each sipping their drinks.

"I was assigned to spy on an officer I knew during the war. Find out if he's a homosexual."

"Are you close?"

"We lodged in the same boardinghouse in London. We'd chat over breakfast or when we passed in the hall. Never spent time together socially, but he's a good man."

"Why's he in California?" Nick asked. "The CIA's mandate is foreign countries."

"His father is sick. He's on leave to take care of him."

"Did you find any evidence?" Nick asked.

"Like I said, I knew him during the war. Everyone was desperate to have one last fling before heading to Normandy and they were not as careful as they might have been. This guy's smart enough not to frequent the bars and clubs where he might get picked up in a raid, but there are still certain upscale places unknown to the cops. Both homosexual men and lesbians visit them; so if anyone shows up looking for trouble, it just seems like a regular heterosexual club."

"How do you know that?"

"It's my job to know," Carl replied.

"Any chance he wandered in there by accident?" Nick asked.

"He went home with another man and stayed there until breakfast. Got pictures of them. It's enough to end his career and maybe force him to inform on other people. Hell, they could put him in prison."

"Any chance those photos got lost and the negatives accidentally caught fire?" Nick suggested.

Carl offered a wan smile. "I haven't turned them over yet. Asked for more time to do further investigating."

"If you report back that you found no evidence?"

"Then I'm technically committing treason."

"So what?" Nick said.

Carl looked at him sideways.

"I mean it," Nick continued. "This is some weird J. Edgar Hoover vendetta against the CIA. It's not about national security."

"I have orders."

"You have morals," Nick countered. "If the war taught us anything, orders cannot be a replacement for your own judgment."

"If it's not me, it's going to be someone else who turns him in."

"So let them. Don't have this on your conscience," Nick said. "Maybe there's a way to warn him he's under surveillance."

Carl laughed humorlessly. "And who's to say I'm not being watched, too?"

"You think Hoover sees the irony in having loyalty tests, like Stalin?"

"Not sure the man knows the meaning of the word 'irony,'" Carl retorted. "Hoover claims this is a necessary part of rooting out Soviet spies, yet this guy had family who were Volga Germans in Russia during the Great Purge of

1937. He's as anti-Communist as they come—exactly the person who should be working for the CIA right now."

"It shouldn't be this hard to serve your country," Nick said.

"No, it shouldn't," Carl sighed. "How do you deal with secrets?"

"I try not to think about them. When I learn one, I usually file it away under 'things that are not my business' and move on with life."

"Wish I could do that," Carl said. "I don't know why it bothers me so much that Evelyn still talks to her father, but it does. Almost like she's betraying me, personally, rather than just her country. Not that she's even doing that. Her father is in the middle of God only knows where. It's not like he's still sharing information . . . or even has any to share."

"What do you mean?"

"Maybe it feels so close to home. Logan was a traitor. Anyone else, I would have turned him in to the FBI and never looked back. Part of me still feels guilty he was never punished."

"Evelyn still talks to her father?" Nick asked slowly.

"You didn't know?"

Nick shook his head. Carl let out a long, low whistle of surprise. Suddenly Nick wondered what else she was keeping from him.

Chapter 32

When Nick got home, all of the lights were out. He and Carl did not shut the bar down, but they came close. Nick found Evelyn asleep in their bed, curled up, with the covers pulled tightly over her shoulders. After debating with himself for a moment, he nudged her awake. She sat up with a jolt, instantly alert. When she saw it was only Nick, she settled back down and frowned at him.

"What time is it?" she asked groggily.

"Almost two in the morning."

"What's going on? Everything okay?"

"You still talk to your father."

"Carl told you."

"Why didn't you?" Nick demanded.

"Why would I? Not like I go around yelling, 'Hey! That fugitive you're looking for? Let me give you his phone number,'" Evelyn replied.

"I'm not some random person. I'm your husband."

"And I don't need your opinion or permission to deal with my family."

"If someone discovers you know where he is . . . ?"

"How would they find out?" Evelyn asked, her voice edged in ice. "The only two people who know about our conversations are the two people I trust most in the world."

"No, no. Don't turn this around on me!" Nick snapped, his voice rising. "We're supposed to be partners. In life . . . in everything. Two people who truly understand each other. Now I find out there's this huge secret between us."

"It's only between us if you put it there. Otherwise, it's just a part of my life that never came up in conversation."

"What else are you keeping from me?" Nick asked.

"It's terribly scandalous. I'm not reporting daily production numbers or the nuances of freight cost."

"You know what I mean."

"I really don't," Evelyn stated. "Do you think I'm cheating on you?"

"No."

"Do you think I'm plotting against you?"

"No."

"Then where the hell is this coming from? When have I ever given you a reason to be suspicious?"

Nick didn't answer.

"I can't believe you woke me up for this," Evelyn said. "Do you have any idea how it feels to have you come in here accusing me of I don't even know what—"

"Keeping secrets."

"We both had lives before our marriage. We both have lives outside our marriage. Why is that so wrong?" Evelyn asked.

"Because we're family. We're supposed to share everything."

"Yeah. You're an open book."

"When have I ever kept something from you?"

Evelyn laughed humorlessly. "Every single day. Our past makes us who we are, but you're hiding yours from me. Do you think I'm going to love you any less?"

"It's not the same!" Nick yelled.

The door creaked open and they turned to see Rory.

"Rory?" Evelyn said as she got out of bed.

"Are . . . are you okay?" His voice was quiet. His eyes darted towards Nick, then quickly looked away.

"Of course, I am," Evelyn replied. "Sorry we woke you up."

"It's fine. It's your house and I . . ."

Evelyn glanced at Nick, uncertainly, but Nick understood all too well.

"Rory, I'd never hurt Evelyn," Nick began. "Doesn't matter how angry I am or if I've been drinking. Real men don't use violence. Besides, if I even thought of raising my hand, she'd kick my ass from here to next Tuesday and back."

"Well, that's true," Evelyn agreed. "Seeing we're all wide awake, why don't we go downstairs. I'll make us some warm milk."

In the kitchen, Evelyn simmered sweet cinnamon milk over the stove.

"My dad used to make this for my brother and me when we were upset or couldn't sleep," Evelyn explained to Rory. "Always worked like a charm."

She brought three mugs over to the kitchen table and set them down. Rory took a small sip, then nodded at Evelyn. "It's good."

Nick looked towards Evelyn with a smile, then reached over and took her hand. She squeezed it in return. Then Nick turned to Rory.

"When I was growing up," Nick began, "my father thought he could deal with his problems by beating the crap out of my mother and eventually us. I don't know if Paula told you what it was like."

Rory shook his head. "She doesn't really talk about your dad."

"Can't blame her," Nick replied. "I never felt safe. I was

constantly on edge, trying to avoid hidden land mines. I learned to become small so no one would notice me. Yet at the same time, I desperately wanted to protect my mother. Being unable to made me feel so powerless."

"The guys Mom brings home sometimes . . ." Rory said. "I don't know what she sees in them."

"Sometimes people are lonely and make bad choices," Nick offered. "Sometimes they don't believe they deserve better."

"But she has me."

"It's not the same," Evelyn said. "She's supposed to be taking care of you, not the other way around."

"We take care of each other," Rory replied defensively.

"Evelyn grew up very different from us," Nick explained. "Her parents loved each other and their kids. She never had to worry about where they were going to live or what they were going to eat. She never had to gauge her father's mood or worry he had one too many drinks. Have you ever seen one of those Christmas movies with Cary Grant or Jimmy Stewart? The dad is funny, the mom is kind, and by the end of the film, they had presents under the tree. Growing up, I thought that kind of family was a fairy tale–as similar to my life as Oz was to Kansas. Then I met Evelyn's dad."

"Nick was carrying me because I'd been slightly overserved," Evelyn remembered.

"And you were singing 'La Marseillaise' at the top of your voice," Nick added fondly. "Logan showed me where to put her to bed. No criticism. No threats. Just relief that she was home safe."

"My dad's the one I always went to when my world tilted off course. Life would be okay because I wasn't alone," Evelyn explained with a sad smile.

"It's brave of you wanting to protect Evelyn," Nick said.

"I didn't mean to stick my nose into things," Rory replied.

"There are things worth sticking your nose into," Nick insisted. "Especially as you get older. You have a huge heart and you're growing into an honorable man. The kind of person I am proud to know."

Rory blushed, but was flattered by the words.

"Come on," Evelyn said. "I'll show you how Dad tucked us in."

Evelyn led Rory upstairs, into his room. She held the covers up so Rory could slide into bed, then set them gently around him.

"You want the full experience?" Evelyn asked, before tucking all sides of the blanket under him so he was wrapped up tightly. " 'Snug as a bug in a rug.' "

"I don't think I can move," Rory replied.

"That's the point," Evelyn laughed. "When we were little, Dad didn't want us to accidentally fall out of bed. Felt like a long hug as I slept."

Rory nodded uncertainly.

"Just roll to one side to free yourself," Evelyn advised. "It's supposed to be a cocoon, not a prison."

"Thanks," Rory said, wriggling slightly. Evelyn turned off his light, closed his door, and headed downstairs.

Nick was waiting for her at the table. She sat down across from him.

"I'm sorry I didn't tell you about my father," Evelyn said. "Genuinely, it never occurred to me. It felt like he was separate from us."

"I'm sorry I was so upset. I don't know what got into me," Nick replied. "When Rory first showed up, it brought back a flood of memories from growing up. After my family left, I felt like there was something I missed. A clue I hadn't seen that would explain why they abandoned me. I swore I'd never let that happen again. When I found out you were still talking to your father, it felt obvious. Of course, you're in contact with him, but I had no idea. It made me wonder if there were other secrets I didn't know. If one day you'd disappear."

"Do you think I'm a good person?" Evelyn asked.

"Yes," Nick answered immediately.

"Good people don't walk out on their families," Evelyn said. "There might be parts of our past or our present that we don't discuss, or issues that we keep to ourselves. There might be times when we are so blindingly angry at each other that we can't be in the same room. What you need to know is that I am never going to leave. I will stay and fight for you. Always."

Nick pulled Evelyn into his lap and held her close. She wrapped her arm around him and he buried his face in her shoulder. With her free hand, she brushed her fingers through his hair tenderly. He looked up and kissed her.

"I don't talk about my childhood because I don't want you to see me as that broken, terrified child," Nick said. "I don't think I could handle the pity in your eyes."

"Then how about admiration for the man you've become?"

Nick kissed her again, but stopped when he did not feel her reciprocate.

"What is it?" Nick asked.

"In the interest of sharing . . . I'm broke," she said.

"I don't understand."

"I'm out of money. I have no idea how to keep Bishop Aeronautics going. Sure, I put on a good face in front of Lewis, because I won't let him see he's right. I can't tell anyone else because I don't want them to panic. I'm supposed to be in charge, with all the answers."

"You're really worried," Nick said.

"If I had to declare bankruptcy, we'd never recover. Do you know how many people would lose their jobs? I'm responsible for them. I can't be the socialite who drove a thriving company into the ground in less than a year and a half and destroyed everything my father built."

"You've hit a stretch of bad luck. If it's not the recall, it's the dead body in your construction site," Nick said. "Taffy gave me a hundred thousand for our wedding. Take it. It's yours."

"I appreciate that, but the recall is going to cost forty-five million."

Nick let out a low whistle. Taffy's gift was a fortune to him; and to her, it was a rounding error.

"The bank revoked my line of credit."

"Why?"

"I don't know," Evelyn said. "Something tells me I'm not going to like the answer."

Chapter 33

Nick sipped coffee in one of Joe Aoki's client chairs. He had stopped by the bakery on his way up and arrived with a bag of fresh pastries. Having already finished a blueberry muffin, he was contemplating going for a croissant. The one thing holding him back was the thought of adding to the already-substantial pile of crumbs. Behind his desk, Joe wrapped up an angry phone call.

"Just because I understand does not mean I have to like it. If Hanzo Takemura is not charged or freed by three-eighteen tomorrow afternoon, I'll be filing a lawsuit for civil rights violations. Am I understood?"

The other voice grumbled, using a lot of words that sounded like expletives. Joe's face remained neutral.

"I will certainly take that suggestion under advisement, but it does not change the facts. Oh, and if my client should happen to slip and injure himself, you can expect a lawsuit naming you, specifically, as the plaintiff."

There was another bout of yelling before the sudden silence of a disconnected call.

"Went well?" Nick asked.

"Think I made my point."

"Sheriff Richardson's not the most agreeable man I've ever met."

"I've seen worse," Joe said.

"I imagine you have," Nick replied. "How's Hanzo holding up in there? He doesn't strike me as a man who handles confinement well."

"He's not," Joe agreed. "I'm trying to convince him it's temporary."

"Is it?"

"I don't know. The evidence is not overwhelming. Thanks to you, we know about the threatening letters other people sent and the datebook. I'll argue that *HT* could stand for anyone."

"Harry Truman, for example."

"Sure. Why not?" Joe joked. "Not like the man has better things to do."

"Hanzo smokes, right?"

"Lucky Strikes," Joe said. "Like in the car."

"And the pocket of almost every single returning GI," Nick replied. "I'll ask the deputy if they found any fingerprints."

"Assuming they dusted the car."

"Are you questioning the acumen of Sheriff Richardson's office?" Nick asked sarcastically.

"Not going to help us much one way or the other," Joe said. "If Hanzo's prints are there, it's pretty damning. If they're not, the DA will argue he wore gloves."

"Would Hanzo think to wipe down the surfaces?" Nick asked.

Joe thought for a moment before answering, "Maybe. He's a smart guy. I wouldn't put it past him to believe he could plot a perfect crime."

"This was far from perfect. The shallow grave makes me think it wasn't premeditated."

"The fact that it's close to the Takemuras' business isn't ideal," Joe added.

"When was the restaurant bulldozed?"

Joe looked through some of his papers before finding the timeline he had composed.

"April nineteenth."

"About five days after Russell Clements went missing," Nick said. "If you wanted the land back, killing Clements was not the best way to go about it."

"No, but if you lost your temper . . ."

"Are you playing devil's advocate, or do you really think he's guilty?" Nick asked.

"Both. Neither," Joe said. "It doesn't matter what I think. I'm going to have a Japanese American client in front of what will probably be an all-white jury, many of whom either fought or lost a son in the Pacific Theater. I'm not feeling overly optimistic."

"What about other suspects?"

"Sheriff stopped looking the moment Hanzo seemed like a possibility. Richardson's always had it out for him," Joe explained.

"What's your next move?"

"Eventually I'll have to bring on a real defense attorney," Joe replied. "This isn't my specialty."

"And attorneys cost money."

"Quite a bit," Joe agreed. "You really want to help out?"

"I really want to discover who killed Russell Clements."

"What if it is Hanzo?"

"I'll come to you first," Nick promised.

"I was hoping you were going to say you'd bury the evidence," Joe replied with a sly smile. "But I suppose that's as good as I'll get."

"It would be useful to find the man who impersonated Hanzo and the others to sell the land for Clements," Nick suggested.

"Evelyn thinks it's someone from our community," Joe said. "If people found out he swindled them, he'd be ostracized."

"Think that'd matter to him?" Nick asked. "Seems like he's only out for himself."

"Everyone needs their own people. There's a freedom when you don't have to explain yourself to others because they already understand your culture. If this imposter is discovered, it won't just be Los Angeles that's closed to him. Maybe before the war he could have headed east, but now many of us have close connections in other cities. Word travels fast."

"Protecting that secret sounds like a pretty good reason to kill someone," Nick said.

"It would be in my top ten," Joe replied.

"Maybe a former soldier who developed a taste for Gauloises cigarettes in France?" Nick suggested. "Can't be too many places around here that sell them."

"I'll ask around," Joe said. "Maybe have Billy keep an eye out. We're also looking for anyone who came into money since the war. Don't see that happening often."

Joe turned back to his work and Nick decided it was time he and Evelyn went house hunting at one of the C & W communities.

Chapter 34

Despite her appointment and the long history Bishop Aeronautics had with Security First National Bank, Evelyn had to go through four people before the bank president agreed to see her. At first, the receptionist insisted there had been a mistake. Clearly, she was not the owner of Bishop Aeronautics. They were expecting Evelyn Bishop, pronounced the British way with a hard "E" at the beginning, denoting it was a man. Then one of the bankers informed Evelyn that she could not take out a loan without her husband's approval. After all, what if she ran up a large bill while clothes shopping? When Evelyn told him she needed thirty million dollars to go with the fifteen she already had in reserve, he blanched and sent her onward. The president's secretary suggested Evelyn wait in the lobby until the head of Bishop Aeronautics arrived. When Evelyn politely told her the reality of the situation, it took several minutes before the woman believed her.

Finally she was allowed into the hallowed presence of a tall man whose gray hair was clipped short in a healthy acceptance of his own impending baldness. He introduced himself as Albert Langstrom. He wore a three-piece suit that was expensive enough to fit his station, but not so pricey as to make people think him extravagant. His office was exactly what Evelyn expected. The room was paneled in dark wood, with portraits of old men; Evelyn presumed they were former bank presidents. A Persian rug lay on the floor. The desk was monstrously large, and empty aside from a pen inscribed with the bank's name.

"Sorry for all of the confusion," Langstrom said, ushering her to a chair. "You're not what we expected."

"I get that a lot," Evelyn replied. "I'm glad we have the chance to meet. I believe your primary contact has been Lewis Bryson."

"Yes. Wonderful man. We attended Loyola together as boys," Langstrom said as he took a seat behind his desk. "How can I help you today?"

"I recently discovered your institution has revoked our line of credit."

"That is true."

"I never received notice."

"An oversight, I'm sure," Langstrom replied. "We regularly review our business relationships and yours gave us pause regarding long-term stability."

"Why?"

Langstrom looked deeply uncomfortable. He cleared his throat awkwardly before saying, "Leadership capability."

"Because I'm new or because I'm a woman?"

"We feel that a certain type of experience would be beneficial."

"Do you tell all of your customers how to run their companies?" Evelyn asked. Her tone was polite, but it did not disguise her anger.

"Of course not," Langstrom said.

"What about my father?"

"He was the founder."

"Did you know him personally?"

"We had a very cordial relationship," Langstrom said. "I was surprised to hear he retired. It was sudden, was it not?"

"It was," Evelyn replied, offering no more explanation.

"I heard there might have been conflicts that arose from certain transgressions during the war."

Her father's treason was not common knowledge. Evelyn wondered where Langstrom got his information.

"We are in good standing with the government," Evelyn replied confidently. "It's our largest client and I spoke with General Clay three days ago. I'd encourage you to call him if you have any concerns."

"It is not only that," Langstrom said. "There's the issue of the recall."

"Which is why I'm in your office. These are the situations for which lines of credit were invented."

"You already have significant debt, including an outsized loan for the construction of a new factory."

"The loan is not outsized. It's appropriate for a project this large and is backed with more than enough collateral," Evelyn replied. "More to the point, you were aware of this at our last credit review."

"Yes, yes. With Lewis Bryson."

"Over drinks at the Jonathan Club, where you are both members."

"There are quite a few businessmen who are members."

"But no women," Evelyn noted.

"They are very traditional," Langstrom confirmed.

"How many women-led companies do you lend money to?"

"I resent that implication."

"Is that your way of saying none?"

"Mrs. Bishop, our decision is final. If your situation changes, we can always revisit this arrangement."

"So, basically, what you're saying is that when we no

longer need money, you would be happy to let us borrow some," Evelyn clarified.

"No, that's not—" Langstrom began.

"Do you know how much we expect to pay in interest on our current loans?" Evelyn asked. "It's over two million dollars, this year alone. That's not insubstantial. My company and your bank have had a long, mutually beneficial relationship. Yet, it seems as though you're telling me this relationship is at an end."

"No! Of course not."

"Then what is it?" Evelyn asked. "If you revoke our agreement when it suits you, why should I trust you in the future?"

"There's no need to be rude," Langstrom huffed.

"I'm not. I'm asking a simple question, for which I would appreciate an answer."

Langstrom did not have one.

"I see," Evelyn said. "I believe I have all the information I need."

Evelyn stood to leave the room. At the doorway, she stopped and turned.

"By the way, do you know Juliette Wallace?"

"The wife of the chairman of the board?" Langstrom asked. "No. I haven't had the pleasure."

"She's great friends with my aunt. I'm having dinner with her and her husband next week. I'm sure we'll have a lot to discuss."

Langstrom blanched.

"This has been enlightening," Evelyn said as she swept out of the room.

In deference to the fact that it was not yet noon, Evelyn was drinking coffee, instead of whisky, on the couch in Colette Palmer's office. Outside the window, the hum of appliances making their way down the assembly line was soothing. What had once been a munitions factory now produced washers and dryers to fit every home and budget.

"If you're going to storm out, it's a pretty good line to go on," Colette remarked.

"Not that it will help. I've already called Wallace's office. He seems to have even less faith in a woman running a company than dear Mr. Langstrom," Evelyn said. "I'm not even the first woman to run an airplane company. Look at Olive Ann Beech."

"Technically, her husband is still president of Beechcraft."

"She's been running the place since 1940. She got an eighty-three-million-dollar loan for her factory expansion!" Evelyn exclaimed.

"Wasn't that because of the war?" Colette asked.

"Of course, it was, but she still got it done!"

"While her husband was technically the president of the company," Colette reminded Evelyn. "Her title was secretary. I'm not trying to discount her achievements. I'm saying what you're trying to do is harder because they have to openly acknowledge that a woman is capable of running a major company."

"It's ridiculous!"

"Do you ever wonder," Colette began, "why is your line of credit drying up now? How did Albert Langstrom know about your father and the recall?"

"My best guess is Lewis," Evelyn said. "But I can't figure out why. He's been in my office every day, sometimes twice a day, complaining about money. His yearly bonus is tied to the company's performance."

"Do you trust him?" Colette asked.

"My father did."

"It's not the same."

"I know," Evelyn replied. "I want to. He's been with the company almost twenty-five years and brought in some of our largest clients."

"There are other banks," Colette offered.

"I had Julia call them. Not a single one is willing to meet with me."

"Then they're fools," Colette said. "Do you think the recall is the right decision?"

"Yes."

"Do you believe this is the right time to build the new factory?"

"I did," Evelyn replied wryly, before becoming serious, "I do."

"At any given moment, life can turn upside down. That doesn't make you a bad businesswoman and it certainly doesn't make you a failure. You're going to figure this out. You just need to trust your instincts."

It was the one thing that had never failed her, but right now they were telling her something was very wrong.

Chapter 35

Evelyn sat in her office reading the initial reports from the recall. As predicted, the airlines did not want to ground their fleets. Most had their mechanics look at the part, and if there were no indications of stress, they continued as usual. Still, it was difficult to maintain their tight schedules while having to rotate out some planes for service.

From outside her office, Evelyn heard Julia ask someone if they had an appointment. There was a quiet, mumbled response. The gentle tone in Julia's voice alerted Evelyn to the fact that this was not a typical visitor. Shuffling the reports into a stack, Evelyn stood and opened the door to the waiting room of her office. There she found Rory, looking around uncertainly.

"Rory! What are you doing here?" Evelyn exclaimed.

"You said it would be okay to visit you at work," Rory replied nervously.

"Of course. I see you've met my incredible secretary, Julia."

Rory nodded and Julia smiled at him. He blushed slightly, looking awkward.

"Come on in," Evelyn said. She gestured for him to sit

on the couch, while she took a seat beside him. He perched on the edge, looking like a bird ready to take flight.

"I'm so sorry." He reached into his pocket, withdrew Evelyn's mother's pearls, and handed them to her.

"Thank you," she said, fastening them around her neck.

"Did you tell Uncle Nick?" Rory asked.

"No," Evelyn replied. "There's no harm done. Besides, you probably had a very good reason."

"I think I've mentioned my mom's boyfriend, Dean. He was around when I was younger; then we moved to Sacramento. Life got better. There were a few decent guys, but Mom got bored. She swears he's not the reason we moved back to Barstow, but . . ."

"You said he was living with you."

Rory gave a bitter, ironic smile. "He didn't want a kid around, so he made Mom get her own place. Then he couldn't afford his rent, so he moved in with us. Mom got a second job just to pay the bills. He doesn't cook. Doesn't clean. I have no idea what he does for work. Mostly, he takes money from Mom's purse, but every so often he comes home flush with cash."

"That sounds legal," Evelyn replied sarcastically. "Does he drink?"

"Is the pope Catholic?" Rory asked. "Mom always swore that if a man hit her, she'd leave. It was usually true, but Dean is the exception. He mostly stayed away from me until a few months ago. One night, he came home drunk. Started beating on her and I told him to stop. He didn't take it very well. Broke my arm and a couple ribs."

"Oh, Rory," Evelyn whispered.

"When we went to the hospital, I told the doctors exactly what happened. Mom said it was a car accident. I don't know whether they believed her or not. It didn't matter. Family squabbles were not their concern."

Evelyn put her arm around him.

"It's okay," Rory mumbled.

"No, it's not."

Though he didn't cry, he took a long, shuddering breath.

"It's her job to keep you safe," Evelyn insisted.

Rory let Evelyn hold him for a moment longer, before pulling away with an embarrassed smile.

"Dean has been better," Rory said. "But it's not going to last. It never does. I want to get Mom out of there. Start over somewhere new."

"Do you think she'll leave?" Evelyn asked quietly.

"I think I can convince her. We did okay in Sacramento. Or maybe we could start fresh out of state. Phoenix might be nice."

"I've heard the sunsets are beautiful," Evelyn agreed. "We'll get you the money."

"Just like that?"

"Yes."

For a moment, Rory sat in stunned silence.

"Almost a year ago, I saw the picture of you and Nick from your engagement party," Rory said eventually. "I fished the paper out of the trash, cut out the photograph, and hid it in the back of one of my books. I had always wondered what it would be like to have family around. Real family. I don't know what I was expecting when I first came here. Maybe I needed the hope of something different. You and Nick were so nice and welcoming. Then I stole from you."

"We all make mistakes," Evelyn replied. "You fixed yours. I can't imagine you doing it again."

Rory shook his head vigorously. Evelyn gestured to the phone on her desk.

"Why don't you call your mom and see what she says."

"Thank you," Rory said.

They both stood and Evelyn stepped outside to give him some privacy.

Chapter 36

Nick and Evelyn parked on the dusty, half-finished street. In the distance stood a few houses in different stages of completion. Some were stakes and string denoting the footprint, others had framed walls rising from the foundation, while still others had newly shingled roofs. They got out of the car, Evelyn's heel catching on the uneven ground. Nick offered her his arm and she gratefully took it. On the drive over, she filled him in on her conversation with Rory, leaving out the temporary theft of her necklace.

"My sister could have set him up," Nick said.

"Maybe," Evelyn agreed. "He could be lying, but I don't think he's that good of an actor. Regardless of Paula's intentions, I think he really believes this could be a second chance."

"You think I should give it to her?"

"I think we should give it to him. Rory wants to believe in his mother and I hope he's right," Evelyn said. "I'll stop by the bank on my way home today."

"No. I'll do it. My sister. My problem."

"Our family. Our problem," Evelyn countered. "You're not alone in this."

Nick stopped and enveloped Evelyn in a hug.

"Thank you," he whispered.

She pulled him closer, holding him tightly. They stood like that for a long moment until a chipper voice called out to them. A woman with bright blond hair, wearing a yellow, flower-printed dress, approached with a broad smile that was almost aggressive in its friendliness.

"Mr. and Mrs. Murphy?" she asked.

"Yes," Evelyn replied, turning toward her with an extended hand. "I'm Mrs. Charles Murphy."

"Which makes me Mr. Charles Murphy," Nick replied with a jovial laugh. In picking their cover names, they slipped back into their old routine of being different people. Evelyn was a cheerful housewife and Nick the manager at a local Chevy dealership.

"Welcome," the woman chirped. "I'm Lauren Davidson and I'll be showing you around the development. As you saw on the signs on the way in, this is a planned community from C and W Developers, which has a long and storied history."

"We can't wait," Evelyn said. "It's been such a struggle finding a place to live. All of the housing gets snapped up the minute it hits the market."

"Well, all of the housing we can afford," Nick agreed. "My wife thinks we need four bedrooms, but I think we'll be all right with two."

"Three is a nice middle ground," Lauren replied. "We have plenty of options to show you. At our prices, you might even get that fourth bedroom your wife's been wanting. Imagine, your children could each have their own room."

"Assuming we stop at three," Nick joked.

"Let's not get ahead of ourselves," Evelyn replied with a smile.

"How long have you been married?"

"Five months," Nick and Evelyn answered in unison.

They saw no reason to alter their actual wedding date to suit the plan. To most, they were still newlyweds.

"Won't be long now," Lauren responded enthusiastically.

"Fingers crossed," Nick replied, wrapping his arm tightly around Evelyn. In response, she rested her head on his shoulder.

"You two are the cutest!" Lauren exclaimed, staring pointedly at Evelyn's flat stomach.

"I feel so lucky to have found him," Evelyn said.

"That goes double for me," Nick replied with the kind of warmth that made Lauren audibly sigh.

Evelyn laced her fingers through Nick's. "Show us our new home!"

"You're going to love it," Lauren said as she led them up to a display house that would show them what to expect when they purchased their very own. The front was symmetrical with a door in the middle and large picture windows on each side. The front lawn was a lush green, with red and pink flowers edging the front of the house. The sidewalk and driveway consisted of pristine, newly poured concrete. There was even a late-model Cadillac parked in front of the garage. It was the American dream.

"This is something," Nick said as Lauren led them inside.

The foyer consisted of a hall leading back to the kitchen and a stairwell up to the second floor. To the left stood the dining room, and to the right the living room. Behind the former stood the kitchen. Rounding out the ground floor was a den in the back. A single bathroom was tucked under the stairwell. The furniture was of upper-middle-class quality. Solid, but not showy. The muted colors let a person imprint their own ideas on the space. There was even the smell of freshly baked chocolate chip cookies wafting from the kitchen.

"Oh, honey," Evelyn said. "Isn't it wonderful? Look at . . . What do you call it, around the edge of the ceiling?"

"Crown molding," Lauren offered. "It's just one of the many upgrades you can make to personalize your house. Similarly, you can choose your flooring, appliances, and types of cabinets. Even whether to have a garage or a carport. We have three different house styles, with three to four bedrooms each. Though your house might have the same footprint as your neighbors', I have faith you'll know how to make it your own."

Lauren led them out to the backyard, where a wooden play structure stood on the neatly trimmed lawn. There was a large concrete patio, decorated in wicker furniture, with a barbeque off to the side.

"Look at this giant window from the kitchen, sweetheart," Evelyn cooed.

"Can't you imagine our little guys running around out here," Nick said.

"My husband really wants a boy," Evelyn confided in Lauren.

"I only care that they're healthy. We get a little girl who looked like her mama, I'd be over the moon."

Evelyn looked at Nick. He would make a great father. Lauren sighed again, gazing at them as if they were Cinderella and Prince Charming.

"I should take a look at the kitchen, don't you think?" Evelyn asked.

"You have no idea the wonders my wife can produce in there," Nick said. He caught Evelyn's eye and she struggled not to laugh.

"Well, you know, my husband works so hard all day, the least I can do is have a delicious dinner waiting for him," Evelyn agreed.

"Your job is important, too," Nick replied encouragingly. "Without ladies like you, I don't know how this world would function."

"And don't you forget it," Evelyn teased. She wondered if they were laying it on a bit too thick, but Lauren seemed to believe wholeheartedly in their traditional roles. It was, after all, the life to which most women were told to aspire.

Lauren took them through the rest of the house, with Evelyn and Nick properly fawning over the second-story bedrooms and bathrooms.

"Would you mind if I powdered my nose?" Evelyn asked Lauren.

"Of course not, take your time," Lauren replied. "Your husband and I can talk details downstairs."

Evelyn closed the door and waited until she heard the footsteps receding down the stairs. Then she turned to the sink. Despite this being the model house, the grout around the sink yielded to Evelyn's fingernail, crumbling into small pieces. The paint on the hot water handle was chipped slightly, revealing that it would be a rusted mess within two years. In one of the bedrooms, Evelyn peeled up a corner of the carpet, revealing cheap plywood. The windows were single-paned and it did not look as if any insulation or noise-dampening material had been placed between the rooms or the floors. Evelyn made a note of the design flaws, then met Lauren and Nick in the dining room.

"It's incredible how much you can see from upstairs," Evelyn marveled. "Remind me what the distance between the houses will be."

"This is where the setup is so smart," Lauren bragged. "The driveways are on the right side of everyone's house, so there's at least ten feet between each place."

"Ten feet!" Nick exclaimed to Evelyn.

"If you're coming from an apartment building, that's gonna feel like a lot," Lauren said. "Plus, with a freestanding house like this, you won't have to worry about noisy neighbors."

"It would sure be convenient to borrow a cup of sugar," Evelyn replied.

"Or more likely a second cup of coffee," Nick teased.

"I have a friend who lives in a place like this up in Simi Valley, but it was made by a different builder," Evelyn began. "What was his name, honey?"

"Oh, you know I'm not good at remembering those kinds of things," Nick replied.

They both looked to Lauren plaintively.

"I can't say for certain, but our partners, Ashton Developers, are building communities in that area. In our brochure, you'll find the names of many of our suppliers, including options for appliance upgrades, like Whirlpool."

"Honey, look at the size of this refrigerator," Evelyn cooed. Then she turned to Lauren.

"May I take an extra brochure? My sister and her husband are looking for a larger place. It's always better to live close to family."

"Of course," Lauren said, handing over another brochure, then one more. "Here! Take two in case you think of someone else."

"I so appreciate this tour," Evelyn said.

"I look forward to getting you into the house of your dreams," Lauren said.

She was still standing in the doorway, waving at them, when they reached the sidewalk and headed back to their car.

"More like nightmares," Nick said as he put the car into gear and pulled away.

"That place was a few months old and it was already falling apart," Evelyn replied, filling Nick in on all of the issues she had found.

"The kitchen's not much better," Nick replied. "The pilot light on the stove kept going out."

"That's a quick way to burn the place to the ground."

Evelyn handed one of the brochures to Nick, then tucked the other two into her purse. "The city-planning department might find this development interesting."

"You mean your friend Alan Hunsaker?"

"Colette's friend Alan Hunsaker," Evelyn corrected. "And yes. If he can approve good projects, hopefully, he can stop bad ones."

"You're going to take down C and W Developers," Nick said.

"I'm going to protect people's life savings."

"One thing I'm curious about," Nick began. "Patrick Wilson seemed very proud of his family name and his own high standards. This certainly did not match that. How much influence do you think he had over Clements?"

"Not much. If my name was on a product so poorly made, I'd be furious," Evelyn stated.

"He did not strike me as a man who stood up to people very often," Nick said.

"But when those people snap . . ." Evelyn trailed off.

Sometimes the quietest people were the most dangerous.

Chapter 37

Evelyn, Nick, and Rory sat around the kitchen table. Rory finished his dinner in record time, while Evelyn and Nick listlessly moved their food around their plates. Usually, the wind and waves formed a calming background of white noise. Tonight, however, Nick nearly jumped out of his skin when their screen door slammed closed. Evelyn had not seen him this on edge since the war. Rory went to the stove for more food.

"Might as well take advantage of it, seeing neither of you look particularly hungry. Besides, I'm not likely to eat this well anytime soon."

He had finally acknowledged the elephant in the room. When Paula left, she would take Rory with her. Nick glanced at the fully packed duffel bag standing by the front door. It contained Rory's new clothes, as well as some of his books. The ones he already finished were on a special shelf in the living room, waiting for him to come back and reread them. They just prayed there would be a next time.

"We're going to miss you," Evelyn said. "And you know . . ."

"That I'm always welcome," Rory finished. Then he

nodded his agreement. "It depends on where we end up, but maybe we could all do Thanksgiving together."

"I'd love that," Nick said. "Turkey, gravy, stuffing, all of the sides."

"I'll buy a pie," Evelyn offered.

"You'll do no such thing," Nick scolded. "I'll make the pie."

"What do I do?" Evelyn asked.

"Sit there and look pretty," Nick joked.

Evelyn scowled in response. Just then, the doorbell rang. Rory froze with a fork halfway to his mouth. Evelyn looked to Nick, who stood and went to the door. His hand rested on the knob for a minute before he took a breath and twisted it open. Standing on their front stoop was a woman whose jet-black, dyed hair looked out of place on her weathered face. Time had not been kind to her, nor had the company she kept. The yellow and green of a faded bruise traced her cheekbone. She was of average height, with slender arms and a softly rounded belly. Nick would not have recognized her if they passed on the street.

"Paula?" he asked.

"Hey, Nick," she replied, stepping inside. "You look exactly the same."

"I still look twelve?" Nick asked.

"You know what I mean," she said.

Nick did. It was possible to trace the trajectory of the child he once was into the man he had become. He struggled to find his sister anywhere in this woman. The corners of her mouth used to rise inadvertently. Now he wondered, when was the last time she smiled?

Paula glanced at Rory. "Hey, kiddo."

For a moment, neither moved toward the other. Then, realizing Nick and Evelyn were watching, Rory stood and Paula gave him a one-armed hug.

"Had a real scare," Paula said. "Woke up one morning and you were gone. No idea how you got a bus ticket."

Nick heard the recrimination in her voice.

"I saved up," Rory confessed. "Did odd jobs here and there, then hid the money from Dean. You know he would've just spent it on booze."

"I'm your mother," Paula said. "You shoulda told me."

Nick saw the part Rory would not say aloud. He did not trust her.

"However he came," Evelyn said as she approached Paula, "we're grateful for the chance to get to know Rory. You have an incredible son."

Paula looked at her, frowning slightly. Nick put his arm around Evelyn and introduced his sister to his wife.

"You've done quite well for yourself, Nicky," she said. "Always were a charmer."

Evelyn felt Nick tense up and she intertwined her fingers with his.

"Still is," Evelyn said. "We were finishing up dinner. Are you hungry?"

"Nick's the best cook. You have to try some," Rory insisted.

"I had a sandwich on the bus."

"He made risotto," Rory enthused.

"I'm not hungry," Paula replied. Rory stepped back, shrinking into himself. For a moment, there was tense silence.

"Was it a long ride from Barstow?" Evelyn asked.

"You've never done it?"

"Can't say I've had the pleasure."

"Don't know that I'd call it a pleasure," Paula remarked. "This place is nice, right on the beach."

"Funny how we never went to the ocean much as kids. Could have been a hundred miles, for all our parents took us," Nick remembered. Then, having broached the topic, he waded deeper. "Do you still talk to them?"

"They're dead," Paula said bluntly. "Dad's heart gave out about eight years ago and Mom stepped in front of a car a short while later. They said it was an accident, but come on. She never knew what to do with herself. Living in a shithole, no one around, no money for booze? I think it all just got to her."

Nick stood in silence, contemplating the fact that he was an orphan. He was not sure if he was sad or merely unsatisfied that he would never have the chance to stand up to his father as an adult. Nor did he know what he expected from his mother. The space inside him where she was supposed to reside had been empty so long, it felt like a scar rather than an open wound.

"What about Brennan and Cassian?" Nick asked, naming their brothers.

"What about them?"

"Do you know where they are? How they're doing?"

"No clue," Paula replied. "Bren got picked up for assault and was sent to Lompoc a while ago. Cassian joined the Army the minute he turned eighteen and I never heard from him again."

"You don't know if he survived the war?" Nick wondered.

"There wasn't a telegram, or soldier's pay arriving at the house, so I'm not too bothered."

The shock at her callousness must have shown on Nick's face because Paula shrugged. "Not like we were some Norman Rockwell painting, even in the best of times. You forgot how awful it was."

Nick had not forgotten a thing. However, the hell that came after his abandonment was so much worse. At least with his family, he had a place to sleep, usually enough food, and people he believed would occasionally take care of him.

"What happened?" Nick asked. "Came home one day and everyone was gone."

"We were behind on rent," Paula explained. "Landlord kicked us out. We packed up what we could carry; then Dad borrowed a car and we drove to Tustin. Seemed as good a place to start over as any."

"What about me?" Nick hated the slight quaver in his voice.

"You kept insisting on school, instead of working," Paula replied. "Mom and Dad didn't want an extra mouth to feed."

"I was twelve," Nick stated. "I wasn't an extra mouth, I was their child."

"Wasn't my decision," Paula said.

"Did you try to stop them?" Nick asked. "What about Brennan or Cassian? Did anyone think to wait for me? Did they consider coming back?"

"Maybe it was for the best," Paula replied. "Look at you now. Good job, great life. You were always gonna make something of yourself. The smart one. That's what Mom called you. Always reading books and asking questions. I think she was proud of you, in her own way."

Nick's jaw tightened in anger. There was so much he wanted to yell, but he forced himself to remember that those with whom he was truly angry were gone.

"What about you?" Nick asked, once he had his temper under control. "It's been almost twenty-two years. How have you been?"

"Same as ever," she replied with a dry, humorless laugh. "Won't bore you with the details."

"Rory said you were looking to get out of a bad situation," Nick began.

Paula glared at her son. "You shouldn't be sharing our personal business with strangers."

"They're not strangers," Rory replied. "They're family."

"Well, they're strangers to me."

Paula moved toward Rory, reaching for his arm. Nick moved faster, inserting himself between his sister and her son.

"How much do you need to start over somewhere new?" Nick asked. "To get away from Dean or whoever did that to your face."

"Think about it, Mom," Rory pleaded. "We could go back to Sacramento or someplace new, like Phoenix. Hell, maybe we could even stay in LA near Nick."

"Los Angeles is not my home," Paula snapped. "Yours either."

"Then pick somewhere and we can make it home," Rory said. "I can get a job to help out. We'll be okay, just the two of us."

"It would be hard," Paula insisted.

"It's already hard," Rory said. "Dean makes it worse. We don't need him."

"Is this really what you want?" Paula asked.

"Yes."

There was so much longing and sadness in that single word that Evelyn's heart broke for Rory. Paula thought for a long time, weighing her decision.

"I don't know how to start from scratch," she said finally.

Nick went to a cupboard, pulled out an envelope of cash, and extended it to his sister.

"This should be enough to get you settled wherever you want. You need more, you let me know."

Paula took the envelope and looked inside. Her eyes widened.

"What's the catch?" she asked.

"Number one, no more men in the house," Nick replied. "Do whatever you want on your own time, but

Rory deserves to feel safe in his own space. Number two, Rory goes to school. He wants some spending money, he can get a job, but that money is his."

"Never been a fan of people telling me how to live my life," Paula retorted.

"Never been a fan of doing it," Nick countered. "It's not about you and it's not about me. It's about Rory. He's going to grow up and do incredible things. He's going to make you so proud."

Paula debated with herself a moment longer, before putting the money in her purse.

"Fine," she said, without an ounce of gratitude. Nick had not expected any. She gathered her things. "Come on, Rory. We gotta get moving if we're gonna catch our bus."

Nick picked up Rory's new duffel and handed it to Paula.

"What's this?" she asked.

"Rory's stuff," Nick said pointedly. "Clothes. Books. Stuff he needs."

Paula refused to take the bag. "He's big enough to carry it himself."

Evelyn gave Rory a long hug, then she slipped money into his pocket.

"So, you always have a way to come visit us," she whispered. "Plus, a little extra just in case."

Rory nodded his thanks. Then Nick enveloped him in a huge hug.

"Don't be a stranger," he said.

"Rory!" Paula called. "Let's go."

Rory grabbed his bag, then looked over his shoulder at Evelyn and Nick.

"Thanks for everything!" he called as he followed Paula out of the house, shutting the door behind them.

For a moment, Evelyn and Nick stared at the closed door.

"I feel like we've made a huge mistake," Evelyn said.

"What other choice did we have?" Nick replied.

He wrapped his arms around Evelyn. They held each other, each mentally tallying the miles and minutes that took Rory farther from their lives.

Chapter 38

Nick stood on the corner of Olympic and Sawtelle, leaning against a lamppost and reading the *Los Angeles Times*. Footsteps approached, and when he looked up, Billy Takemura was standing in front of him.

"Thanks for doing this," Nick said.

"Joe said you're trying to help," Billy grumbled as he led Nick down the street. "This is the least I can do, seeing I created this mess."

"Regardless of whether you'd come to Evelyn's groundbreaking ceremony, Clements's body would have been found. Sheriff Richardson would have arrested Hanzo and he'd be exactly where he is right now," Nick said. "We started early, so we're ahead of the game."

Billy led them to a small café. A few patrons sat at tables, chatting with friends or flipping through newspapers. In the corner, a Japanese American man read Sartre in the original French. He dressed well, wearing sharply creased pants, a starched shirt, with shoes that were polished to a high shine. However, it was possible to see the gentle fraying on the cuffs of his trousers and the slight yellowing inside his shirt collar from too many washes. The result looked to be a man who cared deeply about his appearance, without the means to indulge that concern.

"That's him," Billy said. "Daisuke Ito. Always had a passion for French culture. At one point, he tried to join Josephine Baker's band. Almost made it, too."

"A jazz fan."

"A fan of anything that got him the hell out of here. His parents are first generation *Issei* and they were very strict—early curfew, no friends allowed to visit, no school sports or clubs. They are the kind of people who only speak Japanese at home and feared their son assimilating."

"How'd they feel about Daisuke joining the 442nd?"

"Considering they applied for repatriation to Japan in 1944, I'm guessing not great."

"Did they leave?" Nick asked.

"I don't know what happened to them," Billy replied.

Billy led Nick into the café. When they arrived at Daisuke's table, he raising a single finger in a silent plea for one more moment of concentration. Billy glanced at Nick, who was perfectly content waiting. Daisuke turned the page, read to the end of the chapter, then looked up at them. It took his eyes a moment to adjust; then he shook his head in surprise.

"I though the waiter had come to take my cup and saucer," Daisuke said. "Apologies for keeping you waiting. Please sit down."

Nick and Billy took the chairs on the opposite side of the small table.

"How are you, Daisuke?" Billy asked.

"Good. Good," he said, then held up his book. "I'm trying for a translator position with the government. Just brushing up on my fluency."

"I imagine you'd do well there," Billy said.

"Thank you," he replied, before looking to Nick. "I don't believe I've had the pleasure."

Nick introduced himself and told Daisuke he was investigating the murder of Russell Clements.

"I wish you luck," Daisuke said, then checked his watch and began gathering his books. "If you'll excuse me, I'm afraid I have an appointment."

"How long did you know Russell Clements?" Nick asked.

"I don't."

"Yet, you didn't ask who he was. Most people, when finding out a person was killed, have a natural curiosity about the victim and the circumstances."

"I saw enough death during the war not to have a prurient interest in random people," Daisuke replied.

"But he's not random, is he? Your Gauloises were in his car's ashtray," Nick said.

"You smoked them during the war," Billy remembered. "Picked up a taste for them in Paris."

"A lot of people smoke Gauloises," Daisuke retorted. "Are you speaking with all of them?"

"Only the ones listed in Russell Clements's calendar," Nick said. It was not the whole truth, but it was close enough. "You saw him the day he died."

Daisuke hesitated a moment, then knowing the jig was up, he pulled out his Gauloises and lit one. He offered the pack to Nick and Billy, but they both refused. Daisuke took a deep inhale, then exhaled slowly. He tapped the ash from the end of his cigarette and finally looked at them.

"What do you want to know?" he asked.

"How could you do it?" Billy demanded.

"I'm afraid you'll have to be more specific," Daisuke replied.

"You pretended to be Hanzo and sold our land illegally," Billy hissed.

Daisuke sighed, then took another long drag from his cigarette. He did not respond to Billy's accusation.

"This kind of fraud can put you in prison for years," Billy continued.

"Wouldn't be the first time I was locked up," Daisuke said dryly.

"You betrayed us. You betrayed our whole community!" Billy insisted.

"Because our community did so much for us," Daisuke countered. "Tell me, Billy. Where did you go when you returned to Los Angeles?"

"My family got a house about a mile from here."

"Right," Daisuke said. "And they stayed in Manzanar until the bitter end?"

"No, they met up with Hanzo in Chicago," Billy replied. "You know all of this."

"I do," he agreed. "But you never wondered what happened to my family?"

"I knew they wanted to go back to Japan and . . ." Billy trailed off, as if too embarrassed for Daisuke to continue.

"They were miserable. Like everyone else, my parents were kicked out of their home in 1942 with only what they could carry," Daisuke began. "My father tried to work at Manzanar, but the pay was laughably low. The camp slowly emptied of people heading east, but they had nowhere to go. No money to travel or rent an apartment. There was not a single person who helped them start over. For all that people talk about solidarity, my parents were completely alone."

"I didn't know," Billy said.

"Of course not, it was easier not to ask," Daisuke replied. "Mom and Dad stayed in that camp until the bitter end, because at least they had a roof, such as it was, over their heads and three meals a day. The war ended and suddenly they were 'free,' whatever that meant. They came home to find that Little Tokyo was now Bronzeville. New people were living in their old apartment. It was impossible to find a place they could afford. They were homeless, so the government put them back in camps. Sure, at Winona, you were mostly free to come and go as you pleased, but the barracks were even worse than at Santa Ana. In a matter of months, they became squalid, filthy places, where you wouldn't send a dog to beg its dinner. It was violent, with gangs roaming through it. My mother was terrified to step outside at night and my father panhandled on the streets, desperate to find any type of work. When I came home from the war, I found them there. For whatever reason, my Army pay never reached them. Bureaucratic error. Trying to get it sorted would take months. One day, I saw a flyer in the camp, advertising the need for a young Japanese man. I didn't know what the job was, but it paid decent and I didn't ask any other questions."

"And when you discovered you'd be cheating people out of their land?" Billy asked.

"I asked for ten percent," Daisuke replied coldly. "Like I said. Not a single person in our community offered to help us. I did what I had to in order to get my parents out of that hellhole and into somewhere safe. My father worked his whole life as a gardener. My mother spent her days on her hands and knees scrubbing other people's floors. They deserve to spend their later years in peace, not pain."

"Don't you feel even a little bit guilty?" Billy said.

Daisuke thought for a moment before replying, "No."

Billy gaped at him.

"However, I would rather people don't know," Daisuke continued. "This community is important to my parents. If my actions came to light, they'd be ostracized and my girl would break up with me."

"Do you love her?" Nick asked.

For the first time, a smile crossed Daisuke's face. It was warm and Nick understood how a woman could fall for him.

"Yes," he said. "I'm trying to get a job that will support us, so I can finally propose. Hence the studying."

"Why should you get your happy ending when you ruined my family's business?" Billy asked. "I could talk to a reporter and it would be all over *Rafu Shimpo*."

"My money's gone," Daisuke replied. "I'm sorry you lost your land, but it's not my fault. Blame the government who kicked us out of our homes. Blame the businessmen who profited from our absence. Blame the judges who keep siding with unscrupulous land seizures."

"Did you ever want out?" Nick wondered. "Maybe your parents wondered where all of that money came from?"

"They didn't ask questions. In fact, I think it's the first time they were proud of me."

"How so?" Nick asked.

"As I'm sure Billy can attest to, it's not easy being a second son. My older brother died before I was born and it's impossible to live up to a ghost. My parents imagined the perfect child and I always fell short. I try to ensure they have everything they need, but they've made it clear I am not one of those things."

"What about your girlfriend?" Nick wondered.

Daisuke's face softened. "She makes me want to be a better person. When I met her, I asked Clements to let me go. Instead, he threatened to expose me as the fraud."

"What did you do?"

"I threatened him right back. If he took me down, I wasn't going alone. I mimeographed copies of all of the paperwork to protect myself. There were two sets, the real one and the one he filed with the county."

"So, you have the records from the sale of my family's restaurant?" Billy asked.

"Potentially," Daisuke dangled. "Of course, if someone else were to discover my little secret, I might forget where I put them."

"Did you try to end it any other time?" Nick asked.

"Sure. Especially when it was people I knew personally," Daisuke said. "Yes, Billy. Even your family. Clements always held the threat of exposure over my head."

"Seems like a good reason to want him gone," Nick commented.

"If he fell into a pit of vipers," Daisuke said, "I'd pull up a chair and watch the show, but I wouldn't be the one to push him. I have too much to live for right now."

"Did Clements ever threaten your girlfriend?" Nick asked.

"What?"

"He had a wandering eye and a way with women. Turning his attention on her might cause you to give him that shove," Nick suggested.

"I'm done here," Daisuke replied.

He grabbed his things, pushed past Billy's chair, and stormed out of the café. Nick watched him hurry down the street.

"You think he did it?" Billy asked.

"He didn't say no," Nick replied. "Right now, the name of the game is finding other people with a strong desire to see Clements dead. Joe doesn't have to prove Hanzo is innocent. He needs to create a reasonable doubt that someone else could have done it. Of course, all of Daisuke's documents would be subpoenaed, which means they'd be in the public record."

"Which we could access in an attempt to get our land back," Billy said, putting the pieces together.

"Or, at least sue C and W for repayment," Nick agreed.

Billy was officially on his side again.

Chapter 39

Lewis knocked sharply on Evelyn's closed door, calling her name. He was the last person she wanted to see, but there was no other exit and the window was too high above the ground to use as an escape.

"Come in."

"I told you Albert Langstrom would be of no help," Lewis said as he entered and took a seat across from her desk. "Especially when you threaten him."

"I did no such thing. I simply inquired about a social connection," Evelyn replied. "My question is, why would he sever our relationship, then reach out to you?"

"Let's not be hasty," Lewis said. "We've been banking there since the twenties. This is just a little hiccup."

"I don't like working with people I can't rely on," Evelyn said.

"I'll talk to him again," Lewis offered. "He's an old friend."

"I wonder if that will still be true when we pay back our loans and take our business elsewhere."

"Now, Evelyn, you're being dramatic," Lewis said.

"For the amount we pay them every year for the privilege of borrowing money, I expect better service. If we had a supplier that only fulfilled our orders when they felt like it, I would find a new supplier. This is no different."

"It's complicated. There are issues you don't understand."

"So, explain them to me."

Lewis did not have a response.

"Langstrom knew a lot about the internal workings of our company," Evelyn said. "Information that is not public knowledge. Like the reason for my father's departure."

"Are you accusing me of something?"

"Should I be?"

"I have been here almost twenty-five years," Lewis stated. "The better part of my life has been devoted to this company. If you think I'd put that in jeopardy, you're crazy. I love this place more than you can imagine."

"So, what brought you to my office?" Evelyn asked. "And please don't tell me about how we're almost bankrupt, unless you have a solution to fix it."

"I do," Lewis said. Evelyn sat up in her chair. "But you're not going to like it."

"Try me."

"We bring on investors. I have five businessmen lined up, all willing to put in enough capital to partially fund the expansion, pay for the recall, and keep us afloat for at least another year."

"You're right. I don't like it. Bishop Aeronautics is a family company."

"In case you haven't looked around recently," Lewis said, "you don't have a lot of family left . . . Unless, of course, you're pregnant."

"You think a baby in swaddling blankets is going to take over in nine months? Or would we appoint a regent for it, like in medieval France?" Evelyn retorted.

"No, of course. I just meant . . ." Lewis stammered.

"My uterus is not relevant to this conversation."

Lewis blushed, but pressed onward. "I'm just asking, who are you saving this for?"

"Did you ask Dad that question after Matthew died?" Evelyn asked.

"No, but he knew what he was doing," Lewis said. "A board of directors could help you make difficult decisions. They could give you guidance."

"And who would be on this board?"

"Our five investors, me, maybe Hank, and you, of course."

"Of course," Evelyn replied dryly.

"Bishop Aeronautics gets bigger every year. It's a lot for anyone to manage. The people I'd bring in have years of business experience and they care about making this place the best it can be," Lewis explained. "Let me set up a meeting to get more information."

"And if I say no?" Evelyn asked.

"Then I'd suggest you have another source of money lined up."

"It sounds an awful lot like you're giving me an ultimatum."

"This structure and their resources will set up the company for generations."

Evelyn stood up, walked to the door, and held it open. Lewis grudgingly stepped into the lobby of her office, insisting she let Julia find a time. Julia looked to Evelyn for guidance. For a long moment, Evelyn considered Lewis; then she looked out onto the factory floor, where production was going full tilt. She knew every single worker's name. Finally she gave the barest of nods. Triumphant, Lewis hurried down the stairs. Evelyn felt dirty, as if just agreeing to the meeting was a betrayal of her father. Then she looked around her office and saw Willa standing near Julia's desk, her natural buoyancy dimmed.

"Willa," Evelyn said. There was more exhaustion in her voice than she intended. "What's wrong? Is it the recall?"

"No, uh, no," Willa stammered. "I don't want to bother you."

"You're not," Evelyn promised.

Willa started to turn away, but Julia grabbed her arm. "Tell her."

"No. It's okay. I can handle it myself," Willa replied before fleeing down the stairs.

"What's going on?" Evelyn asked Julia.

Julia looked torn. "It has nothing to do with work, but . . ."

"Her PhD program?"

Julia shook her head. "I was told in confidence."

"How can I help?"

"I don't know," Julia said. "It has to do with Ben. He's not who you think he is."

"His name keeps coming up recently."

"He's a bad guy with a bad temper."

"I can believe that," Evelyn replied. "What does it have to do with Willa?"

"You should talk to her."

"I'll go now."

"No," Julia insisted. "Wait until tomorrow morning. She's usually in early."

"Are you sure you can't tell me what's going on?" Evelyn asked again.

Julia nodded. Evelyn hated delay and loathed uncertainty, but for the moment, there was nothing more to do.

Chapter 40

The main office of Ashton Developers was located at the intersection of Flower Street and Sixth, downtown. When Nick arrived, he was told that TJ Ashton, the head of the company, never spent any time there. He worked out of a trailer that moved from site to site. The secretary called to confirm Ashton would see Nick, then handed him the address written on the edge of a brochure for a middle-class housing community.

It took Nick over an hour to drive to Simi Valley. Every time he thought he had gone too far, he checked his *Thomas Guide* to see there were still a few more miles. Like Clements's development, this consisted of former farmland. It was plotted to within an inch of its life, with curving streets ending in cul-de-sacs, and houses that looked exactly like their neighbors. Though the brochure might advertise the ways in which people could customize their homes, it was clear conformity would reign. The central street was bordered by neat sidewalks. A few cars were parked in the driveways and there were enough American flags to confirm that VA Loans paid for most of these houses. Nick drove on another mile before the houses slowly shifted from finished, to nearly there, to newly poured foundations. A few trailers dotted the scene. Nick parked his car, then got out and knocked on one whose sign read: OFFICE.

A young man in khaki pants and a chambray shirt opened the door. "You must be Nick Gallagher," he said. "I'm Gus Headly."

Gus turned back in the office long enough to tell someone where he was going; then he led Nick through the unpaved streets.

"You been working here long?" Nick asked.

"About two years now."

"You like it?"

"Yeah, TJ's a good guy. Treats us fair," Gus said.

"Between us," Nick began, dropping his voice conspiratorially, "would you want to live here?"

"Already do. My wife and I moved in six months ago. Ashton gave us a great deal. Otherwise, it might've been years before we could afford our own place."

They approached a man in his mid-fifties who wore jeans, a T-shirt, and a sweat-stained baseball cap. His face was weathered, open, and friendly.

"A pleasure," Ashton said, extending his hand to Nick. "Downtown office said you were coming, but didn't say why."

"I'm looking into the death of Russell Clements," Nick said.

Ashton looked to Gus. "Do me a favor. Get Victor Kelly to come round this afternoon. I found some sloppy pipework in one of the houses on Washington Street. I want him to fix it and check the rest from that new crew."

"Of course, Mr. Ashton!"

Having been dismissed, Gus trotted back to the office trailer. Ashton turned to Nick.

"I heard about Clements," Ashton said noncommittally.

"You guys work together?" Nick asked.

"Hell no," Ashton replied. "I'm in the process of suing the ever-living shit out of him. Forgive my language."

Nick handed Ashton a brochure from the C&W's housing development. "Your name's still on it."

"That son of a—!" Ashton swore under his breath. "Mind if I keep this?"

"Be my guest," Nick replied.

Ashton tucked it into his back pocket. "That's another thing I'll be adding to the complaint. I have a reputation to uphold."

"And C and W does not live up to it?"

"You been out to see their places?" Ashton asked. Nick nodded. "Then come take a tour of mine."

Ashton led Nick to a house in the process of being built. Even without a professional's eye, Nick saw the difference. The support beams were close together with a steady, uniform quality. The floors were thick planks of pressure-treated hardwood, and the bathroom floor consisted of tiny, tessellated tiles. The faucets showed no sign of peeling or rusting, and the appliances were all brand names.

"What do you think?" Ashton asked.

"I could see a family making a life here and passing it down to their kids," Nick replied, knowing it was what Ashton wanted to hear. It was also the truth.

"Would you say the same about the other development?"

"No."

"Theirs cost more than ours. Granted the real estate is closer to the city, but for what they're charging, those houses should last the next hundred years. I doubt they'll make it through the end of Truman's presidency. I'd ask where all of the money went, but I'm pretty sure the answer is Russell Clements's pocket."

"Be my guess, too," Nick agreed.

"When I first met Clements, he seemed a decent enough guy. Maybe not someone I'd want to spend much time with, but he came with good references. He wanted to partner up because he needed additional investors. He said he appreciated the expertise I developed over the years. He showed me some of his work and it looked solid. However, when I saw that first home . . ."

"Not what you were expecting?" Nick suggested.

"If I had used the same words back in grade school, Sister Mary Teresa would have beaten my knuckles bloody. I like to pride myself on managing my temper, but that day . . ." Ashton trailed off with a shake of his head.

"Never feels good to be cheated," Nick offered.

"It's more than that. I'm proud of the work we do. I'd never sell a house I wouldn't live in. I meet each family who buys one and I like to walk the neighborhoods and see their kids grow up. For a lot of people, buying their first home is a financial stretch, but it's usually a good investment. It's a place where you make the memories that form a worthwhile life. Except in Clements's houses, they might not make it a year before the refrigerator conks out. Or the stove needs to be replaced. Or the wiring shorts. Maybe the homeowner curses himself for not spending extra for the 'upgrade'—when, really, decent appliances should come standard. Now this guy has his mortgage, his taxes, and unexpected bills on top of that. His budget no longer works and he's stressed every night about how he and his family are going to keep a roof, which might be leaking, over their heads. Scamming me is bad enough, but don't you dare do it to those people who are just trying to achieve the dream this great country has promised."

"You feel strongly about this," Nick observed.

"Is this where you point out I've got a pretty good reason to kill the man?" Ashton said.

"It is."

"You're not wrong, and, believe me, I fantasized about it once or twice. At first, I fought Clements to gain control and make those places decent. When that failed, I fought to get my money back. Lawsuits take forever, and in the meantime, people are getting fleeced and blaming me. If he hadn't died, I would have enjoyed seeing that man go bankrupt." Ashton smiled to himself, before continuing, "So, no. I didn't kill him, but I'm not sorry he's gone."

"That seems to be a fairly common sentiment," Nick replied. "I have to ask, where were you the night of April fourteenth?"

"That was right around Easter, wasn't it?" Ashton asked. "In that case, we were down in San Diego at my sister-in-law's house. Spent a whole month there in the span of a week."

"You sound so pleased about it," Nick laughed.

"We're very different people," Ashton said, diplomatically. "But it means a lot to my wife."

"Out of curiosity," Nick continued, "you have any dealings with Patrick Wilson?"

"Knew him back in the thirties when we were both struggling. Hired him for a few jobs. Good guy. He's why I took the meeting with Clements in the first place. When I saw him recently, he was a different person."

"How so?" Nick asked.

"Struck me as a man who got in over his head. Clements was a bulldozer, just like Wilson's dad. Seemed to mistake bluster for strength, only realizing the difference when it was too late. Don't think Wilson much liked Clements, but he seemed to appreciate the money he generated and the lifestyle that came with it."

"That's not unusual."

"Maybe, but it's sure as hell not practical. You ever notice his shoes? That's forty dollars down the drain the moment you show up on site. His car? His watch? Don't get me wrong. I make enough to support my family, and then some. I believe in buying a watch you can pass down to your son. End of the day, though, I come home covered in dirt, my hands callused, and near-constantly sunburned. There's little room for luxury on this job."

"You think Wilson would be capable of hitting someone over the head hard enough to crack their skull?"

"That what happened? I'd always imagined a gun—" Ashton said, breaking off. "Probably not helping my case."

"Points for honesty," Nick replied.

"Don't know that Wilson has cold-blooded murder in him, but I certainly do believe he could shove someone hard enough for them to lose their balance and have it turn into a horrible mistake."

"You think of anyone else?" Nick asked. "The name Ben Strover keeps coming up."

Ashton thought about it for a minute. "I'm not Strover's biggest fan, but he does decent work. Will get the job done. At one point or another, Clements probably reached out to every contractor in the county."

"Why don't you like him?" Nick asked.

"He could charm the spots off a snake, but he gets a bit ahead of himself. Doesn't have a realistic perception of his own virtues," Ashton replied.

"Care to elaborate?" Nick asked.

"Let's just say I wouldn't let him near the plans for my construction site and I wouldn't let him near my family."

"Is he dangerous?"

"Suppose that depends on who's asking. If you're wondering whether he killed Clements, it's doubtful. He's an arrogant bastard, but it's mostly bluster. Seems like a very specific thing to kill a man. Imagine a lot of people might think about it, but it's hard to find someone who would actually do it," Ashton said.

While Nick appreciated the sentiment, he was not sure he agreed.

Chapter 41

Evelyn rested her head in her hands. The numbers were swimming before her eyes and she knew she should go home. Still, it felt like she was missing something. Some answer that eluded her or a deeper question she did not know how to ask. Her instincts were screaming that there was a solution beyond taking on investors, but the company's financial problems felt like a giant wall around which she could not see.

There was a knock on the door and Evelyn looked up to see Hank holding a bottle of scotch.

"How did you know that's exactly what I need right now?"

"Because I need it, too," Hank said as he stepped into her office. He set two glasses on the coffee table and Evelyn moved to sit beside him on the couch. Hank poured them both a large slug and handed one to Evelyn. She chimed hers against his.

"*Saluté,*" Evelyn said before drinking. Hank took a long sip as well, then set his on the table.

"You want to go first, or shall I?" he asked.

"By all means," Evelyn replied.

"I'm concerned about Willa," Hank said. "She hasn't been herself lately."

"She was in my office earlier today looking more nervous than a treed cat. Julia swears it's not the recall, but I'm worried."

"Julia say any more?"

"Only that Willa swore her to silence," Evelyn said. "I'm going to come in early tomorrow morning and see if I can catch her alone. Maybe she'll be more willing to talk about whatever's bothering her."

"Oh, thank God. I was going to ask, but I appreciate not having to beat around the bush," Hank admitted. "Willa's been coming in late and leaving early. Usually, the opposite is true. Not that I think she's slacking. It's clear she's been working at home. Every morning, she has brilliant ideas and well-thought-out plans."

"Does she have family? Is her mother nearby? Maybe she's sick?"

"Last I heard, her mother was working at a casino in Vegas," Hank said.

"What did Willa say when you talked to her?"

"I messed it up, royally. Started by saying that I'd noticed she wasn't in the office as much. She apologized and said it wouldn't happen again. Then she asked if her work was not up to par and, of course, I said no. She promised that she would keep up with everything here, while also attending her PhD program. I was never worried about that. By the end, I felt like I had scolded her, without intending to, and I didn't know how to ask any other questions."

"Well done," Evelyn joked.

"Doesn't help that I handled the news of the recall badly," Hank added. "I'm glad Willa found it, but I was also furious at myself for not catching it sooner."

"This isn't your fault. We did all of the testing we knew how to do at the time. It seemed fine. Now we know better."

"Ordering the recall was the right decision," Hank said. "I also know it was a hard one."

"Mind saying that to Lewis? He's still on my case about it."

"Lewis is . . ." Hank hesitated. "Well, I have a lot of thoughts about Lewis. Let's leave it at that."

"How have you worked with him all of these years?" Evelyn asked. "It's been barely a year and I . . . struggle. He won't stop reminding me that I'm not my father."

"Nonsense. You're the best parts of him," Hank replied.

"I wish I could get Lewis's voice out of my head."

"Only way to do that is to stop believing him."

"What if he's right?" Evelyn asked quietly.

"He's not. What you lack in experience, you make up for in intelligence and good judgment. Lewis never had a talent for separating his opinion from fact."

"The numbers aren't adding up. We'll make payroll this month, but after that? We're hemorrhaging money."

"Let me guess, Lewis suggested investors," Hank said.

Evelyn stared at him.

"Yeah, he did that to your father once. Logan told him if he ever brought it up again, he'd be out on his ass."

"So, how did Dad manage when money was tight?"

"Lines of credit." Hank grimaced. "Curious how those suddenly disappeared."

"Does everyone know?" Evelyn asked.

"Not everyone," Hank replied. "But enough."

"Is it on the factory floor?"

"There are rumors."

"Goddamn it!" Evelyn said, slamming her hand on the table hard enough to make the glasses jump. "The last thing people need to worry about is losing their jobs. I won't let that happen even if I have to take on a whole flotilla of investors. I'll keep them safe."

"I know you will," Hank replied calmly. "That's what I've told everyone who's asked. I've assured them that you're a Bishop in every way that matters. Your father's so proud of you."

"What else does he say?"

"That he misses you and—" Hank broke off, realizing Evelyn caught him in a trap. Neither was supposed to know where he was or have any way of contacting him.

"I'm glad you talk to him," Evelyn said. "He sounds lonely."

"For a man who never stopped moving, he has too much time on his hands. He worries you hate him."

"I could never hate him. He was always this grand hero in my mind and now . . ."

"You've been forced to realize he's just a man," Hank said. "It's never easy when children begin to see their parents' flaws, but it's also something every single one of us does eventually."

"I don't know how to stop being angry," Evelyn admitted. "I was over there. I knew a lot of guys who flew in those planes. Dozens took off, but when you counted the returns? One parent's desire to keep their child alive is not an excuse to let others mourn."

"No. Not an excuse, but also maybe not as unforgivable as you might think. A parent's love isn't logical or rational. There's a primal need to protect your child. Logan struggles to live with what he's done, but it would have killed him to give up on Matthew."

They sat in silence for a moment, letting their shared history rest between them. It was comfortable and easy, which Evelyn rarely found at work. It's hard to have a true friendship with the person signing the paychecks.

"I'm scared and I feel so lost," Evelyn confessed. "What am I going to do?"

"You'll figure it out," Hank said with supreme confidence. "You are one of the smartest, most stubborn people I've ever met."

"Do you think I should take on investors?"

"Hell no. This is your company."

"If only I could get the sheriff to release the crime scene. It wouldn't necessarily help in the short term, but at least I would feel like something is on track."

"Don't suppose you could bribe him," Hank suggested.

"Already tried."

Hank raised his eyebrows in surprise. "Richardson struck me as a man who excels at lining his pockets."

"I have no idea what he's getting from keeping the site closed. Doubt there's much else to find at the crime scene."

"Well, if you don't like the game, change the rules," Hank said with a wry smile.

Evelyn thought on that for a minute, before a smile grew on her face.

"You are brilliant!" she exclaimed.

Evelyn exuberantly kissed him on the top of the head, grabbed her purse, and ran out of the office. Hank sipped his drink, seeing no point in wasting good scotch.

Chapter 42

The door of the giant mansion in Beverly Hills swung open to the marble foyer.

“Had a feeling you’d be darkening my doorstep,” Cheryl Clements said as she stepped back to let Nick enter.

Today she was dressed in a thin, bubble-gum-pink cashmere sweater, and neatly ironed navy wool slacks. Her hair was pulled back into a ponytail and her makeup was minimal.

“I’m sorry for your loss,” Nick said.

“Please don’t ask me to start sobbing about how Russell was the love of my life.”

“I wouldn’t dare.”

“The cops who showed up at my house seemed to expect it. Felt like I had to perform or be called a suspect,” Cheryl said. “Do you think I’m a suspect?”

“Should I?”

“If I was going to kill him, I would have done it long ago,” Cheryl replied. “Maybe the first or second time he cheated on me. By now, my ego hurts more than my heart.”

“Even so . . .” Nick prompted. “Last time I saw you, you were still waiting for him to come home.”

Cheryl sighed. "I don't know how to feel. Part of me always thought the man I fell in love with would eventually return. Then again, maybe I should be relieved that all of those betrayals are finally over."

"You're still standing, which is a good start," Nick offered.

Cheryl gave him a small smile as she led him into the pristine living room and they each took a chair. "I'd offer you a drink, but I'm afraid if I start, I won't know how to stop."

"Wise choice."

"Tell me why you're here," she said.

"Covering my bases. Wanted to see if you knew of anyone who might want to kill your husband."

"It would take days to compile that list."

"Funny," Nick replied. "I keep getting that answer and it's not especially helpful."

Cheryl thought for a long moment, then said, "As I told you before, I stayed out of his business. Patrick would be the one who could help you on that side."

"What about personal grudges?"

"We had our social circle through his work and the people at the club. They aren't what I would necessarily call friends. Not a single person has stopped by with flowers or a casserole. No one's even called to check on me. You can bet once Russell's in the ground, they'll expect life to go back to normal."

"Normal doesn't exist anymore," Nick said.

"At least someone understands," Cheryl agreed. "I don't know that Russell got on with the men at the club any more than I did with the women. There might have been a couple of angry confrontations, but I don't remember the details."

"When was this?" Nick asked.

"The first one was about ten years ago. Something about Russell going back on an agreement? I didn't really pay attention. I think the most recent was about five months ago."

"What happened?" Nick asked.

"Russell's tastes ran the gamut from showgirls to high-society wives. He liked variety. I was never sure who would pique his interest. Some were a single night, some were several months. He wasn't subtle in his pursuits and that may have left some angry husbands."

"That must have been awkward," Nick said.

"You hear stuff through the grapevine. Certain women love being the bearer of bad news, if only to add your reaction to the story. Took less time for gossip to make it from the tennis courts to the dining room than it did to finish a par three," Cheryl said. "Perhaps it's time to let the club membership lapse."

"What about your paramours?" Nick asked. "Jealousy can make people do crazy things."

"There's only one," Cheryl replied. "He's not the 'go stab someone in the chest' type."

"You mean 'hit over the head,' " Nick clarified.

"Is that how Russell was killed? The police didn't tell me and I didn't think to ask. Does that look bad? Should I have been more curious?"

Nick shrugged. "I don't know what grief is supposed to look like. I only know how it feels."

"I'm not sleeping. Not really eating. Most days, I just feel numb—like I'm going through the motions. Then every so often, part of me cracks open and I cry so hard, it feels like I'm trying to dredge out the pain," Cheryl said. "How long does this go on for?"

"Everyone is different," Nick replied. "It does get easier. You learn to live with it."

A few tears slipped from Cheryl's eyes. Nick offered her his handkerchief, but she ignored it, letting tears carve tracks down her cheeks.

"I'm sad, but I'm also angry. Damn him for making this so difficult!" After a minute, she withdrew a mascara-stained tissue from her pocket and dabbed at her eyes. "Knew I shouldn't have bothered with makeup this morning."

Nick took her ability to joke as a good sign.

"What are you going to do with the business?" he asked.

"Sell it as soon as humanly possible," she replied definitively. "Russell took me to a construction site once. I've never seen a house so poorly built. Santa Anas roll in and there's no guarantee they'll be standing the next morning. The pipes won't last five years, the Sheetrock is too thin, and the wood framing hasn't been properly treated. The floors are pine and will warp in humidity," Cheryl said.

Nick looked at her sideways.

"People always forget that my father was a handyman. Taught me everything he knew."

"You ever mention these problems to Russell?"

"Didn't want to hear it. Thought he could outrun the lawsuits forever."

"And when they hit?" Nick asked.

"I'm hoping to be far, far away," Cheryl said. "I could start over and become Cheryl Newberg again."

Nick saw a hint of excitement flash behind her eyes.

"I'm afraid I don't know any more," Cheryl said as she rose to walk him to the door. Nick doubted that was true, but he also did not think pushing would help.

"I appreciate your time, Mrs. Clements."

As she reached the front door, it opened, revealing Patrick Wilson. His tie was loose and his suit jacket tossed casually over his arm. He held the front-door keys in his hand. Looking between Nick and Cheryl, his face was first confused, then very, very angry.

"What the hell are you doing here?" Wilson demanded of Nick as he stormed into the room, dropping his briefcase and jacket onto the floor.

"He's investigating Russell's death," Cheryl replied calmly.

"No, he's trying to dig up dirt, see if he can grab our land to give to those—"

"Is it stealing if you're just taking back what was taken from you?" Nick asked.

"Russell wouldn't steal land!" Wilson replied. "Right, Cheryl?"

"I wasn't aware of the details," Cheryl said. Nick realized this would be her defense if the lawsuits finally reached her: a helpless woman, in the dark when it came to her husband's many betrayals, having no idea whether there was money and where he hid it.

"You shouldn't be talking to this guy," Wilson insisted to Cheryl. "He's going to help people put together a case against us."

"That would be unfortunate," Cheryl agreed. The tone in her voice made Nick realize she already had an exit strategy in place.

"Which people?" Nick asked. "The Japanese Americans who lost their land? The poor saps who bought your cardboard boxes disguised as houses? Or men like TJ Ashton, who invested specifically because of you. Once upon a time, the Wilson name meant something."

"Get out," Wilson said.

"It must sting to have Russell Clements use your reputation to build absolute shit. Tell me, were you in on it from the beginning, or did you think the development would be a dream community? Maybe the money was too good to pass up. What happened when you saw the lawsuit from your old friend Ashton? Is that when you realized how badly business was going? Did you know that you'd end up with nothing?"

"I begged Russell to make improvements," Wilson said. "To build homes we could be proud of, but he wouldn't listen."

"Bet that was frustrating," Nick replied. "This is half your company. Couldn't you force the issue?"

"I poured more money into the project, but somehow it never showed up in construction. I have no idea where the money went, but I've barely seen any profits."

"Did Russell reinvest as well?" Nick asked.

"He said he did, but the books don't show it."

Nick shot a glance toward Cheryl, who wore a studied innocence. He would wager all he had that somewhere in the Midwest was a sizable bank account in the name of Cheryl Newberg.

"What's going to happen to your company when your name is synonymous with houses that fall apart?" Nick asked. "That thought would make me scared . . . and really angry."

"Get the hell out or I will throw you out myself," Wilson declared.

"Last time I checked, this wasn't your house," Nick replied. "Out of curiosity, how long has this been going on?"

Wilson answered, "None of your fucking business." At the same moment, Cheryl said, "Two years."

"That's a while."

"I've been married over twenty years," Cheryl said, before testing out the new words. "Was married."

"Is this where you two ride off into the sunset?" Nick suggested. "Wedding bells after a proper mourning period?"

They both looked to Wilson, for whom the answer was clearly yes.

"Was it hard waiting?" Nick asked him. "Seeing a man

you hated with the woman you love? Knowing she would never be yours?"

"You're leaving on your feet or unconscious, I don't care which," Wilson threatened.

"Do the initials *DI* or *BS* or *HT* mean anything to you?" Nick asked Cheryl, ignoring Wilson completely.

"Not that I can think of," Cheryl replied. "Why?"

"They were entries in Russell's datebook for the day he went missing."

Wilson took a swing at Nick, catching him by surprise in the stomach. Nick let out a soft "Oof," though he managed to stay upright. Wilson swung again, but Nick grabbed his arm. Wilson struggled to get free, then tried to kick Nick in the shin.

"Stop," Nick said. Wilson threw another wild punch, followed by yet another. Nick stepped out of range with a sigh. He did not want to hurt the man, but words did not seem to have an effect. After Wilson charged at him, Nick sidestepped, then slapped Wilson's face with an open hand. The sting of it took some wind out of his sails. He faced Nick with his fists up, but did not advance.

"Funny," Nick said. "There was also a *PW* in the book and I'm beginning to suspect who it is."

"Are you accusing me of murder?" Wilson asked, his hands still in fists near his face.

"I haven't decided yet," Nick replied. He nodded toward Cheryl, then headed out the door.

Chapter 43

Evelyn drove to Carl's house. After parking haphazardly, near-ish the curb, she jumped out and ran to the door. His was a small Spanish-style house with white stucco, a blue door, and terra-cotta tiles on the roof and the walkways. A thick garden of native plants blocked most of the view from the road. Evelyn knocked loudly and heard someone moving inside.

"Carl!" she yelled. "Carl, I know you're in there."

She leaned over to look through the living-room window. The curtains were billowing slightly in the wind, and through their gauzy film, she saw Carl. He was shirtless, lying on the couch, kissing Billy. For a moment, he looked confused as if he did not understand the interruption; then he locked eyes with Evelyn. She pulled back, startled. She did not know what to do—stay or leave? She had already interrupted them and did not want to make it worse. She also did not want Carl to think she was running away from him. He opened the door, now wearing a white T-shirt, slightly askew. Billy stood behind him, fastening up the buttons on his oxford.

"I'm so sorry," Evelyn said. "I should have called, but I didn't think you would answer."

"Fair assumption."

"I didn't mean to interrupt you."

"Clearly, you did," Carl replied dryly. "Even if it was just from an evening's peace."

"I can go," Evelyn offered.

"You're here now," Carl said, stepping back to usher her inside. "Feels like there are some things we should discuss."

"I'm going to head home," Billy said.

"Please, not on my account," Evelyn insisted.

He gave her a sardonic look, then kissed Carl goodbye. At the threshold, he stopped and turned back to Evelyn.

"My family is very conservative. With my mother sick and—"

"Your secret is safe," Evelyn promised.

Billy glanced at Carl to see if he could trust her. Carl gave a slight nod; then Billy headed out into the night. Carl closed the door and turned to Evelyn.

"So, now you know," Carl said.

"Looks like we've both been keeping secrets."

Carl led her into the kitchen, where a small table sat at the far end of the room. Carl set down two juice glasses, unstoppered a bottle of whisky, and poured them both an inch. They drank. There was a long pause, where neither knew what to say. Evelyn finally gave him a lopsided smile.

"So, that's why you didn't bring a date to my wedding."

Carl let out a short, staccato laugh. "Yes. That's the takeaway from all of this."

"I'm sorry I didn't tell you I was still talking to my father," Evelyn said. "I thought it would be better if no one else knew."

"Better for you or him?" Carl asked.

"Better for everyone. I never wanted to put you in a position where you had to lie," Evelyn replied.

"Been there, done that."

"It must be so hard feeling like you have to keep this huge part of yourself hidden," Evelyn said.

Carl shrugged. For a moment, Evelyn worried that was all the response she would get.

"Wasn't easy growing up in the Church. Fiery torment, damnation, and all of that. Always felt like there was something wrong with me."

"There's not, you know."

"California Penal Code 288a would disagree with you . . . as would most Americans."

"Most Americans think sex outside marriage is wrong . . . and many do it anyway. How many times have you heard of a rushed wedding and a baby born 'three months early'?"

"Once or twice."

"God knows Nick and I didn't wait for a certificate from the state. Do you think I'm going to hell?" Evelyn asked.

"Do you believe in hell?"

"No, which makes my life easier."

"I know you're not religious," Carl began, "but my faith has always been important to me. I prayed every single day during the war. Even when I was so hungover I couldn't see straight, I dragged myself to Mass. For a long time, I thought I could put that part of my life in a box and try not to think about it too much. Then I met Andrew . . ."

"Your buddy from the Army Rangers? You brought him around to the pub sometimes," Evelyn remembered. "He was a good guy."

"He was more than that. He was funny and kind. Sometimes we'd stay up all night talking. He rescued dogs and cats that were homeless after the bombing raids and found their owners. It's seemingly simple, but to a child who's lost everything, he gave them back hope," Carl remembered fondly. "He gave me hope. For the first time in my life, I felt like someone really knew me and accepted me for exactly who I am. I'd never been loved like that before.

He made me think that I wouldn't have to spend the rest of my life alone. But then, there was D-Day . . ."

"Oh, Carl," Evelyn said. "I knew his death was hard on you, but I didn't know how hard."

"I still miss him. Every day."

Carl broke down in tears. Evelyn put her arm around his shoulders and drew him into a hug. He wept for several minutes, and she rubbed his back like her mother had always done for her as a child. Finally his sobs slowed to ragged breaths and he raised his head to look at Evelyn.

"I finally found love and he was taken away," Carl said. "What kind of God does that?"

Evelyn did not have an answer. Not being a religious person, she could only imagine the emptiness the loss of faith would create. It would make grief that much more difficult to bear.

"I'm so sorry you had to go through that on your own," Evelyn said.

"The worst is the regret. I wish I could have given him more, but I didn't know how to reconcile those two sides of myself."

"I have news for you," Evelyn began. "The people you love, know you love them. It's not about saying the words, it's in the way you show up for us every single time we need you. Andrew knew how you felt."

"I hope so," Carl said. "We had plans for after the war. Move to Los Angeles. Maybe New York or DC. Bigger cities are easier. Can't live in the same house, of course. It's too suspicious, but maybe apartments in the same building. I was going to try for the FBI, and he thought he'd be happy working as an accountant. It was simple and he liked numbers."

"That sounds nice," Evelyn replied, her heart breaking for a future that would never exist.

"He always believed there might be a world one day

where we could live together, like any other couple. Get married. Have a dog. Crazy, right?"

"No. Not crazy at all."

"Some days, I feel so tired from all of the secrets."

"Well, this is one less you have to carry with me. I love you, and nothing in this world will ever change that fact. I'm glad I got to find out about this part of your life. It's important. The people we love shape who we are," Evelyn said. "Even if this might not have been the way you chose to tell me."

"I wouldn't have told you at all," Carl said.

"I'll respect however you want to deal with this, even if it's pretending the last half hour never happened," Evelyn offered.

Carl sighed. "Might be nice having someone to talk to, besides a priest."

"Did they have helpful advice?"

"Some sent me away with a few Hail Marys. Some were more fire and brimstone. All of them agreed this was a moral failing I needed to rise above. Andrew taught me that was impossible. He helped me discover the very best parts of myself. The bible tells us to care for one another, be selfless, and have faith. It was a struggle until I met Andrew and my world expanded in ways I could never have anticipated. Everything I felt with him, was what I had been looking for in church."

"And now?" Evelyn asked.

"I don't know. I want to believe in God and it means a lot to my father to go with him on Sunday, but their teachings . . ." Carl trailed off. "Billy is the first person I've dated since Andrew."

"Is it serious?" Evelyn asked.

"I don't know, but I'd like the chance to find out. During the war, we had a brief fling in Italy. I was still mourning Andrew and not in a great place. We ran into each other five months ago and the spark was still there. It's rare that I meet someone with whom I really connect. I know he seems brash and angry, but that's because he cares intensely. He has a strong belief in right and wrong."

"You have that in common," Evelyn replied.

Carl smiled slightly. "He has this dry sense of humor that cracks me up. Plus, he understands what it was like during the war. I feel like I can be myself around him."

"That's everything," Evelyn agreed. "I want you to be happy. That's it. Full stop. I don't know if that's possible without being your whole self. You deserve to be in love without hiding it."

"I'm not ready to tell Nick."

"Won't change the way he feels about you," Evelyn said.

"Probably, but I don't want to risk it. If there's even the slightest chance he might not understand . . ."

"My lips are sealed," Evelyn promised.

Carl nodded and took a deep, ragged breath.

"I'm sorry I got so upset about your father. Regardless of how I feel, I shouldn't have shut you out like that."

"Thank you," Evelyn replied.

"It was one more secret than I could handle. Nor did I like that you were keeping secrets from me. Ironic, isn't it?"

"But also, very human."

"It occurs to me that you came over for a reason."

"I need a favor . . ." Evelyn began.

"Of course, you do," Carl sighed. "All right, tell me what it is."

With that, Evelyn spilled all of her troubles across Carl's kitchen table.

Chapter 44

As the sun rose, the first rays began to peek through the windows as Nick watched Evelyn sleep. A shaft of light landed on her bare arm thrown out from under the covers. Her dark waves were tangled across her pillow, and in sleep, he still saw the girl who first walked into his office at the OSS.

Nick sat on the edge of the bed, contemplating his wife and feeling, not for the first time, he had been blessed. Maybe it was repayment for his horrible childhood, but he was more inclined to believe that somehow he had won the cosmic lottery. Nick gently traced his fingers along Evelyn's arm. A small smile formed in her sleep. He then stroked her cheek and down her neck. As his hand moved lower, the small catch in her breath told him she was awake, but not yet ready to open her eyes. Nick leaned down and kissed her, feeling her smile grow below his lips. He pushed aside the covers and traced the curve of her waist. She hummed softly in approval of his exploration. He was about to slide his hands under her nightgown when they heard frantic banging at their front door. Both sat upright.

Nick was first downstairs, with Evelyn close behind,

knotting the sash of her robe. They opened the door to find Rory, his clothes torn and bloodied. His lip was split and a bruise covered his left eye.

"Jesus," Nick said, staring at his nephew.

Evelyn pushed Nick aside and gathered Rory in a hug. He winced slightly at the pressure.

"Come in," she said.

"I'm sorry," he pleaded. "I didn't know, you have to believe me."

Evelyn steered him to the kitchen table and sat him down. Grabbing a towel, she ran it under the water, then dabbed at the blood near his mouth. Noticing that Nick had not sat down, Evelyn glanced back him. His knuckles were white with the effort it took for him not to put his fist through a wall. His eyes were circles of rage.

"Whatever's going on, we're going to help you," Evelyn assured Rory. "I promise."

Rory met her eye, saw the truth in her words, and started crying. His were the great gasping sobs of a person who had endured far more than their capacity. Nick slowly released his fists and blinked a few times. He took a deep breath and sat down at the table beside Rory. He put his hand on the young man's back, patting it gently, and waited until the storm passed. When Rory finally looked up, he said again, "I'm so sorry."

"What happened?" Nick asked.

"I really did come here wanting to find family," Rory began. "I just . . ."

"I believe you," Nick assured him.

Rory took a shaky breath, then another. And another. Finally he gathered himself together.

"It wasn't my idea to ask you for money to start over, it was Mom's. When she found out I was here, she said she was sick of Dean pushing her around and we needed to get out of Barstow. Told me I should steal something we could pawn, then promised a fresh start. I thought she really meant it. I thought this time would be different. When we got back home, I was expecting her to hide the money, but she handed it over to Dean."

"What happened here?" Evelyn asked, gently tracing his eye.

"Dean was pissed I saved money for a bus ticket, instead of giving it to him," Rory said. "Apparently, he missed the logic that if I didn't take that bus ride, he wouldn't currently be flush with cash."

"Never the brightest bulb in the box," Nick agreed.

"You're safe now," Evelyn said.

"No one's ever safe with Dean around," Rory said. "They know you're rich. They're going to come after you."

"How?" Nick asked.

"Dean says he saw you kill a guy."

"That's crazy," Evelyn said; then she saw the expression on Nick's face. "Isn't it?"

Nick didn't answer.

"Nick?" Evelyn asked again.

Nick sat silent for a long moment, looking down at his hands. Evelyn watched him, but he could not meet her gaze. Finally, he began to speak in a voice that cracked with pain and memory.

"When I was thirteen, I'd been rummaging through a garbage bin behind a local restaurant. I hadn't eaten in a few days and I was so hungry. I found a burger that only had a few bites out of it. I scarfed it down, then looked for more. I was so intent, I didn't even hear his footsteps. This guy grabbed me from behind and pulled down my pants all at the same time. He tried to . . . But I fought as hard as I could. It was all instinct and fear. He threw me to the ground. I grabbed a bottle and hit him. It broke, but didn't slow him down. Pissed him off, though. He started whaling on me—broke my ribs, my nose. Thought he was going to kill me. I reached out again, grasping around, finally grabbing a shard of glass. I swung wildly. Caught him in the neck. Blood was everywhere. I only realized what I'd done when I had to roll his limp body off me."

"Oh, Nick," Evelyn said quietly, reaching for his hand.

"Dean used to tease me on the streets," Nick said. "Said things that made me think he'd seen what happened. Told me he could put me in prison whenever he wanted. I never took the threat seriously. How much worse could prison be?"

"It was self-defense," Evelyn insisted.

"Everyone knew the guy was a letch," Nick said. "Paid kids for sex. Some agreed. Some he forced. He was a rich movie producer, slumming it down by the docks. His watch and his wallet were missing, so the cops thought it was a mugging gone wrong."

"It's been over twenty years," Evelyn said.

"No statute of limitations on murder," Nick replied.

"Who's going to believe him?" Evelyn asked. "It's your word versus his."

"Dean says he's going to go to the press," Rory said quietly. "Doesn't really matter if you're arrested, but how would it look for Evelyn to be married to a murderer? He thinks you'll pay to protect her reputation."

Nick's eyes flared. It was one thing to threaten him, but he would never put Evelyn in danger.

"*Nick,*" Evelyn said, her tone a warning.

"You know I'll never let him hurt you."

"It doesn't matter. Who's going to listen to him?" Evelyn pleaded.

"Enough people," Nick replied.

"I don't care about them. I care about you."

"The fact that you love me still feels like a miracle," Nick said. "I'm not going to make it worse for you."

"I'll be fine," she promised. "We'll be fine."

"I'll handle it," Nick said. "Do you know when they're coming?"

"Tonight," Rory replied in a small voice. "Mom told him your address."

"Nick, what are you going to do?" Evelyn asked

He turned to her. "It will be alright. I promise."

"Not if I lose you. They're not going to put you in prison for killing that man," Evelyn said. "So don't give them any other reason."

"Trust me. I'm not the same man I was when we met," Nick replied. He took her face gently in his hands and kissed her.

Nick drove across town to his old police station. Brushing past the clerk at the front desk, he headed upstairs to his old captain's office. He knocked on the open door and Wharton looked up to see him. His expression wasn't quite a scowl, but it wasn't a smile, either.

"What did you do now?" Wharton asked.

"Can I close the door?"

Wharton's eyebrows rose, but he nodded. Nick shut the door, then sat in front of the desk. He took a deep breath, surprised to hear it quaver. It was difficult to start. Wharton watched him, bewildered.

"Let me tell you a story," Nick began. "There was once a young police officer, who had just made detective."

"Oh, God. Please don't tell me this is going to be some fairy tale with you as the reluctant hero," Wharton groaned.

"Not me. You."

Wharton frowned.

"It was twenty-one years ago. You wore a blue suit that looked like it had been bought at a three-for-one sale, black shoes, and a pink tie that had small pineapples. It was a gift from your mother-in-law. You hated it, but she was in town visiting, so your wife made you put it on."

"How do you know that?" Wharton asked.

"You told me. It was the day we met," Nick said. "You'd been transferred to Long Beach a few weeks before and you caught a murder case. Hollywood type got his throat slit down by the docks."

"Wallet and watch stolen," Wharton remembered. "They ruled it a robbery."

"You knew better. On the side stood a thirteen-year-old boy, his face beaten to a pulp. He was a bit too curious," Nick said. "You wanted to help him. Asked him where his parents were. Asked him who beat him. And eventually you took him to get a hot dog because he would not speak."

"I took him to get a hot dog because the poor kid looked like he was starving," Wharton corrected. "That was you?"

Nick nodded. "You talked to me about all kinds of random stuff, just to make me relax. When the senior detective came over, you told them I might be a witness. Always had the feeling you knew better."

"I asked around a bit. The guy deserved what he got," Wharton said.

"He did," Nick agreed. "It was self-defense, but you could slap me in cuffs and finally close the case."

"That's not the reason you showed up here this morning."

"I'm here because you're a man of integrity who I trust," Nick said. "And if you were going to arrest me, you would have done it already."

"Many times over," Wharton sighed.

"Unfortunately, you're not the only person who knows that story," Nick said.

"And all of that time you worked for me . . . ?" Wharton asked.

“I knew who you were. I was grateful to you, not only for that day, but for all of the chances you gave me. Wish I could have pulled myself out of that hole sooner.”

“Well, you’re out now,” Wharton said with something akin to approval. “Tell me what you need.”

Nick explained his plan and crossed his fingers that Wharton would agree to help.

Chapter 45

It was still early when Evelyn and Rory arrived at Bishop Aeronautics. There were few cars in the parking lot and only the emergency lights illuminated the main floor. Evelyn asked Rory to wait in her office with a promise of breakfast to come, then she headed to engineering. From the hallway outside the drafting room, she heard voices.

"You're just a little tease, aren't you?" said a male voice.

"It was a mistake," replied Willa.

"Don't be like that," the voice said. "We start to have a little fun, and then you shut it down. You should be nicer to me."

"I am nice," Willa responded. Evelyn could hear her fear. "But, I . . . I have work to do."

"It can wait."

Willa cried out as Evelyn heard the sound of table legs scraping the floor. Evelyn entered the room to find Willa, her back against a drafting table. Ben stood too close, one hand on the table, the other on her arm, trapping her.

"You're here early," Evelyn said loudly.

Ben whipped his head around, surprised. He still held Willa's arm.

"As are you," Ben said. "Wasn't expecting you in until later."

"With the construction site shut down, I wasn't expecting you at all," Evelyn replied.

"Ah, yes, well, Willa offered to show me the specs for the jet engines so I can make sure the crossbeams can withstand the load."

"Funny," Evelyn said. "I thought that was why you were here last week."

Ben gave an abrupt, humorless laugh.

"And what brought you in?" Ben asked.

Evelyn felt as if he was waiting for her to leave, but she would be damned if she surrendered ground in her own factory.

"I'm the president of the company."

"Of course, I just meant . . ." Ben trailed off. His eyes hardened as he glared at her, then he slowly released Willa's arm. His fingers left red marks on her skin. "It's fine. I was on my way to meet Lewis anyway."

With a glance back at Willa, Ben sauntered out of the room. Once his footsteps receded, Willa's shoulders dropped and she exhaled.

"You okay?" Evelyn asked.

"Yeah, no . . . I'm fine," Willa said, unable to meet Evelyn's eyes.

"Very convincing."

"I can handle it," Willa insisted.

"You don't have to," Evelyn said. "Not here."

Finally Willa looked up. "I know how this goes. I tell someone and they tell someone else and eventually it makes its way up to you or to the personnel department. Suddenly I'm the problem. The girl who couldn't keep her knees together and lured a happily married man away from his home. I'm a slut who's bad for morale and needs to be replaced."

"If I tried to replace you, Hank would start a rebellion, complete with banners and flags," Evelyn said. "He'd probably come up with a surprisingly catchy chant."

That got a small smile from Willa.

"Tell me what happened," Evelyn continued. "Your job is safe and I promise not to judge."

Willa stared at her hands as she started speaking.

"Ben's the kind of guy who likes to flirt with women. It was kind of fun, at first, but it didn't mean anything. At least I didn't think so. It was just a break from . . . everything else"

There was a sight hitch in her voice that caught Evelyn's attention.

"What else?"

"When I first started here, I wanted to be accepted . . . but that wasn't in the cards. I'm the only woman in the department. There were pranks that weren't funny and insults disguised as jokes. Ask me how many times I've had to get coffee for a meeting."

"Hank know about this?"

Willa shook her head. "They were good at hiding it and I didn't want to be a tattletale."

"How bad did it get?" Evelyn asked.

Willa shrugged, but the expression on her face told the truth. Evelyn felt ashamed for not considering this before. When she took over as president, scores of men quit because they did not want to work for a woman. The rest might grumble behind her back, but they had to treat her with a modicum of respect. She held their careers in her hands. How much worse it would have been if they thought they could team up and force her out?

"I'm so sorry," Evelyn said. "I should have done better."

"I can't expect special accommodations."

"Being accepted by your coworkers is not special accommodations," Evelyn replied. "Nor is feeling safe at your job. Tell me about Ben."

"One night, a bunch of people went out for drinks. They invited me and I finally felt like I was making some headway. It was a big group; Julia came, too. Her boyfriend, Gabe, met us there. Ben's good at making you feel special. Unique and smart and beautiful. The whole kit and caboodle. I usually don't drink much, but fresh gin and tonics kept arriving. Eventually he kissed me. It took me a minute to realize what was happening. Then another minute to remember he was married. I stopped it, but probably not as quickly as I should have.

"Ben didn't get the hint. First he wanted to come back to my place. I said no, of course. Then he offered to get us a hotel. That's when I found Julia and asked her and Gabe to take me home. That kiss was clearly a mistake, which is what I told him when he came to find me the next morning. And the one after that. And the one after that. He's been here every day and sometimes at night. I started coming into the office later to avoid him, but then Hank—"

"He's worried about you," Evelyn assured her. "That's all."

Willa looked relieved. "I thought—"

"You're still his favorite. Hank can build an engine like nobody else, but he's not always great with words."

"This is where I've been happiest in my entire life. I never, ever thought I'd get to do this job. Now, with UCLA on the horizon, it's a dream come true," Willa said. "But Ben won't leave me alone. He kept calling me a tease and getting too close. I tried to push him away, but he'd back me into a corner. He kept talking about . . ."

"Sex?" Evelyn asked.

Willa nodded, blushing deeply. "It was really graphic. Sometimes it was compliments and propositions. Sometimes it felt like threats. I'd never want to quit, but—"

"Don't you dare," Evelyn said. "I'll tell Hank about what's happening and—"

"Please, no. I don't want anyone else to find out."

"This isn't your fault," Evelyn said.

Willa did not look convinced. "Maybe, but I don't think it matters. Reputation is everything."

"I'll protect yours," Evelyn promised. "For what it's worth, I thought you were going to tell me you saw him kill a guy."

"The body outside?"

Evelyn nodded.

"He told me about his family trip to Hawaii a week before they started prepping the construction site," Willa said. "Seems like it would be right around that same time."

"Funny how he wouldn't deign to give me that answer himself," Evelyn replied. "You know my door's always open—for good news, bad news, and everything in the middle. You can talk to me."

Willa nodded, but Evelyn doubted she would take her up on the offer.

After promising Willa Ben would not harass her again, Evelyn made her way across the factory floor. People were beginning to trickle in for their shifts. She greeted them by name, before heading upstairs to her office, where she found Julia sitting with Rory, who was eating one of Evelyn's emergency chocolate bars.

"I just spoke with Willa," Evelyn said.

Julia snapped to attention. "And . . . ?"

"Why don't you take her out for breakfast? She could use someone to talk to and she's not comfortable enough with me," Evelyn said. Julia nodded and began to gather her purse. Evelyn handed her cash to cover the tab. "I'm realizing a lot happens here that I don't know about. People don't really talk to me."

"You're their boss," Julia pointed out.

"Will you help me stay up-to-date?" Evelyn asked. "You're good with people. They trust you. Ruth knew everything that happened here. I think I took that for granted."

"Of course," Julia said. "For what it's worth, you're a really good boss. Not just to me. It's what people say on the floor. They trust you."

"Thank you," Evelyn replied, knowing those two words could not encompass her gratitude for the reassurance.

Julia nodded, then headed down to get Willa.

"I'm sorry," Evelyn said to Rory. "I'm almost done here. I know this isn't the morning you expected."

"This hasn't been the week I expected," Rory replied dryly.

Evelyn couldn't help but laugh.

"One more call, then breakfast," Evelyn promised.

She went into her office, picked up the phone, and dialed Colette.

"Can you set up a meeting for me?" Evelyn asked.

"Of course," Colette replied. "With whom?"

After Evelyn explained the situation, Colette's voice rose an octave. She loved gossip when it had nothing to do with her.

"Can I be a fly on the wall?" she asked.

"No," Evelyn replied.

"Fine," Colette said with a sigh. "I'll set it up."

Chapter 46

Evelyn and Rory arrived at the long, low office building. It was two stories, with windows on the top half. Men in suits walked past them, their shirts starched and their shoes polished to a high shine. Some of them did not appear to notice Evelyn and Rory. Others gave a long stare as if memorizing their faces. None would detour to talk with them.

"Not exactly friendly, are they?" Rory asked.

Evelyn looked over to see him slightly discomforted.

"I think they're in the habit of seeing the world as suspicious. Unless, of course, you're secretly a spy," Evelyn teased. "Now would be the time to tell me."

"Yes," Rory replied. "That's my deep, dark secret. Everyone knows Barstow Junior High is a hotbed of Russian activity."

"Rory Gallagher, did you just make a joke?" Evelyn asked, delighted.

Rory smiled, slightly embarrassed, but also proud of himself. Nick approached, looking wrung out. Evelyn raised her eyebrows.

"Everything's set," Nick replied.

"For my mom?" Rory asked.

"For Dean," Nick said, then looked at Evelyn. "I thought we agreed it would be good for Rory to spend a couple of days with Taffy?"

"We can't surprise Taffy before eleven a.m. It's not civilized," Evelyn replied. Then, turning toward Rory, she confidentially explained, "She has a whole morning routine. It's better if you don't know the details."

"You're afraid I'm going to out her to the Soviets, aren't you?" Rory asked.

"Well, they do need all of the beauty secrets they can get up in Siberia," Evelyn replied.

"Let's not use the *S* word around here," Carl said, coming up beside them. "Even as a joke."

" 'Siberia' or 'Soviet'?" Evelyn asked.

"Either. Both," Carl replied.

"You guys are talking again!" Nick exclaimed.

"Told you he couldn't stay mad at me forever," Evelyn crowed.

"You are annoyingly persistent," Carl said.

"And that's why you love me."

"This is my nephew Rory," Nick said, introducing them. Carl's eyes traveled over Rory's injuries and a hard expression flashed across his face. Then his mouth formed his usual warm smile.

"It's a pleasure. I've heard good things," Carl said as he shook Rory's hand. "Shall we get on with it?"

Carl led them to the door. The gold lettering on it said FBI and several American flags greeted them as they stepped inside. A portrait of Harry Truman and another of J. Edgar Hoover hung prominently on the wall. Evelyn noted that they were of equal size and stature, as if both men held the same rank. After signing in with the guard at the front, Carl led them upstairs, to a large bullpen. Desks were lined up, two by two, in a long grid. The men looked anonymous in their conformity. Carl led Evelyn, Nick, and

Rory down a row to a desk tucked into a windowless corner. A man in his mid-thirties, with straight blond hair, looked up with a smile. Carl introduced him as Scott Goldberg.

"Why don't we go somewhere quieter?" Scott said as he opened a desk drawer and pulled out a notebook. Then he led them to an empty conference room.

"Carl's filled me in on most of the information," Scott began, once everyone was settled. "Because your company is a federal contractor and this deals with the Japanese internment, I think we have standing to step in."

"You're a ten-thousand-pound gorilla," Nick said. "Don't you step wherever you want?"

"Yes," Scott agreed. "But my boss will be fielding angry calls from the sheriff's office, so I like to give him some kind of justification."

Scott returned to his notes. "Russell Clements, who by all accounts was a horrible person, died. No loss there. Hanzo Takemura was released last night from police custody, but it's not looking great. The sheriff in this case sounds like he couldn't find an actual clue if it showed up in his breakfast cereal. Am I missing anything?"

"Patrick Wilson," Nick said. "Clements's business partner. Doesn't seem like there's much love lost. They build middle-class communities on the cheap."

"Sounds like a license to print money," Scott replied.

"Patrick Wilson values his family name and Clements left it in tatters," Nick continued. "Plus, Clements hid his earnings. He could bankrupt the company and walk away just fine, while Wilson would be left with nothing."

"Other than lawsuits," Evelyn added.

"And Wilson is sleeping with Clements's wife," Nick said.

"The plot thickens," Scott replied, writing that down as well.

"Hanzo's initials were in Clements's datebook for the day he disappeared," Nick noted. "But so were Wilson's."

"He's a strong suspect who was never investigated," Carl said.

"I'll look at all of the evidence," Scott promised.

"When do you think you'll be able to release my construction site?" Evelyn asked, trying, and failing, to keep the eagerness out of her voice.

"I'll need to do some paperwork here to make this official," Scott said. "Why don't I meet you there in a couple of hours?"

A smile of relief spread across Evelyn's face. "Thank you."

"Don't thank me yet," Scott replied. "All I've promised is that I will pursue this case to the best of my abilities. There are no guarantees."

"There never are," Evelyn agreed, but hope still lit up her face.

Chapter 47

Evelyn and Rory pulled up to Taffy's home in Beverly Hills. Most of it was hidden from the street by a large hedge. Evelyn used her key to unlock the front gate; then she and Rory walked up the driveway. The house was Tudor style, with a gabled roof. The left side of the house was shaped like the tower of a castle, complete with a two-story turret. Behind the right side, there was a large backyard, which included a swimming pool and a tennis court. Evelyn rang the bell and Clara, the housekeeper, opened the door and ushered them inside.

"Welcome," she said brightly. "Mrs. Foster did not tell me to expect you."

"Taffy loves surprises," Evelyn joked.

"She seems the type," Clara replied sarcastically.

Evelyn laughed. "You know her well."

"Clara is exceptional at her job," Taffy said as she swept into the room, giving Evelyn a kiss on each cheek. Then she looked to Rory, taking in the sight of his bruised face. She gently cupped his cheek, looking at his injuries. Rory started at her touch. He did not pull away, nor did he meet her eyes. His expression was something akin to shame. Then she nodded to herself.

"Young man, you look like you could use a cinnamon roll. Clara made a fresh batch this morning."

Rory's shoulders relaxed and he glanced at Evelyn, who nodded with a smile. He followed Clara into the kitchen, leaving Taffy and Evelyn alone.

"What the hell happened?" Taffy asked, her anger fierce.

Quietly Evelyn explained the situation and the fact that Paula was expected that evening.

"At the end of the day, she's still Rory's mom. He loves her and wants to believe in her," Evelyn said. "It's better if he's not there when she arrives."

"He can stay with me for as long as he wants," Taffy said. "Livens up the place."

"Thank you."

Taffy studied her niece closely. "There's something else."

"It's only work," Evelyn said, trying to brush off her anxiety.

"'Work' is when you don't sleep and have too much coffee in the morning," Taffy admonished. "This is more."

Evelyn hesitated for a moment, before confessing her troubles. "With the new factory, I knew money would be tight, but the recall put us over the edge. The way we're going, I might have to file for bankruptcy."

"Nonsense," Taffy replied. "You have plenty of money, it's just invested elsewhere. I'm sure you've called in all outstanding debts."

"Lewis said he would, but nothing's come in."

"What about other banks?" Taffy asked. "Get a different line of credit."

"I tried that. All of them told me—" Evelyn broke off. "They told me they already discussed this with Lewis."

"I'm sensing a common theme," Taffy said. "You said he was the one who wanted to bring in investors. Ever wonder who would be the chairman of the board?"

Evelyn always assumed she would retain control of the

company. She could barely imagine selling ten percent, never mind over fifty. However, Taffy's words made sense.

"I'm an idiot," Evelyn said. "I trusted Lewis because my father did. I trusted him because I've known him almost my whole life."

"When William first started at his father's company, he invented a new system to secure the lumber to the truck," Taffy said. "A friend of his offered to engineer a prototype. William believed in him . . . right until the moment he patented it in his own name. The man made a fortune and William was left empty-handed. When his father discovered what happened, all he said was 'I bet you'll never make that mistake again.' And he didn't. Part of William's success was learning from his errors. The other part was knowing every single detail of the business."

"I thought I did," Evelyn replied.

"You know your company," Taffy agreed. "You know your airplanes, your suppliers, your customers. The hard part is knowing the people who work for you."

"How do you trust them?" Evelyn asked.

"You can't," Taffy said. "Not a hundred percent. You might get to ninety-nine, but you have to keep your mind open to the possibility that you could be wrong."

Evelyn thought about that for a long minute. "Do you know how much I hate that you're always right? Now I know how Nick feels and it's annoying as hell."

Taffy laughed. "Not always, but often."

"Mind if I use your phone?" Evelyn asked. "I need to give Julia a quick call."

When Evelyn returned to her office, it was filled with Bankers Boxes that were neatly labeled as the financial records for the past five years. A slender man in his late twenties, with thick black hair, was standing beside them.

He looked slightly uncertain, not knowing why he was there.

"Andy Begay!" Evelyn greeted him. "I don't think I've seen you in at least two months. Has your nephew been born yet?"

"Three weeks ago. We were a little worried because he came early, but he's growing like a weed. Every time I see him, I swear he's doubled in size."

"You have to bring me a picture," Evelyn replied, then called Julia into her office and closed the door behind her. "Before we start, I have one request. I need you to keep what we're doing a secret from Lewis. Andy, I know he's your direct supervisor and I understand if you don't feel comfortable."

"My loyalty is to this company. Not Lewis," Andy stated. He motioned toward the boxes. "What are we looking for?"

"Money. It's time to turn over the couch cushions," Evelyn said. "How much has the shutdown of the construction site cost us so far?"

"Nothing."

"I'm sorry, what?" Evelyn asked. "Lewis has been in my office every day with dire warnings."

"When we made the budget for this project, we factored in three months' overrun. We're nowhere near that yet. It might be an issue toward the end, but hopefully by then, we're on better financial footing," Andy said.

"We will be," Evelyn promised. "So that leaves the recall."

"We're expecting it to cost about forty-five million," Julia said. "Assuming it all goes according to plan."

"When has it not?" Evelyn joked. "We're smooth sailing around here."

"Always," Julia replied wryly. "Fifteen million is coming out of our reserves . . . which is basically the last cash on hand."

"So, we need to find another thirty million," Evelyn said.

"You think we can find it in the budget?" Andy asked.

"At least part of it," Evelyn said. "Let's start with low-hanging fruit. Who has outstanding balances?"

Andy turned to the Bankers Boxes and pulled out a folder. Quickly he scanned the documents inside.

"TWA has paid the deposit on the six planes we delivered last year, but has not made final payment."

"Okay," Evelyn said, picking up a pencil. "So that's three million right there."

"Yeah, but how are you going to get them to write that check?" Andy asked.

"Two ways. The first is that we're going to start charging five percent interest on any balance more than three months overdue. Next we're going to make this recall work for us. Let's prioritize service for the airlines that are up-to-date on their payments."

"The carrot and the stick," Julia said.

"Whatever works," Evelyn agreed.

"If Lewis was here . . ." Andy began.

"He would tell me that this will cause bad feelings," Evelyn said. "And I would tell him other people's feelings do not pay my bills. We are a business. Unless they're letting people buy plane tickets on layaway, there's no reason they can't pay promptly."

Andy nodded and made a notation.

"Though, I'll make those calls instead of sending letters," Evelyn clarified.

"I'm sure they'll appreciate it," Julia said.

"Who else?" Evelyn asked.

Together they went through a long list of their customers, realizing most were in arrears. When they were done, they had found almost 12 million dollars. It was a good start.

"Where else do you think we should look?" Evelyn asked Julia and Andy.

"Trade conferences," he replied immediately. "They're giant extravaganzas we put on for our clients. We pay for their flights to Houston. Pay for their hotel suites. Pay for all of their meals and throw a giant party."

"How much business did we get out of the last one?" Evelyn asked.

"About a hundred planes," Andy said.

"That's a decent amount," Julia offered.

"Now ask me how many of those people were going to put in orders anyway?" Andy continued.

"Don't tell me," Evelyn said. "At least half?"

"About a hundred," Andy replied. "Lewis told me to wait until after the conference to record the total. He said it was because he wanted it to be final, but he came back bragging about his work there."

"How drunk did he get?" Evelyn asked.

The corner of Andy's mouth quirked upward. "Enough to put a lesser man in the hospital. From what I've seen, which is admittedly very little, these events cement relationships with our old customers without bringing in new ones."

"My father always said real business happens when you put two people together who can seal the deal with a handshake," Evelyn replied. "Let's cut it. That gives us an extra hundred thousand. Add another 213,000 in savings. I won't be taking a salary this year."

Julia looked at her sharply. "Will there be general pay cuts?"

"No," Evelyn said. "Everyone on the floor relies on their salary and budgets for their yearly raise and bonus. They stay the same."

"I hate suggesting this, but I would be remiss in not mentioning it," Andy began. "There's about ten million in the pension fund. We could borrow it."

"It's not my money," Evelyn said. "I won't risk it."

Julia pulled out another folder. "I have some ideas about our advertising budget."

Andy grabbed a different one. "I think we can save on transportation costs."

Together they went through the boxes, adding up the small cuts that would not cause too much pain and the larger ones they could live with. It was an arduous, hours-long process, but by the time they finished, they had found another 10 million to put towards the recall.

"So, we only need another eight," Evelyn said, looking at the others from where she sat on the floor. Her shirtsleeves were rolled up, her stocking feet tucked under her, and her hair had pulled free of the morning's neat chignon.

"Easy," Andy joked.

They looked up at a knock at the door. Hank opened it, then seeing all of them together with files and scratch paper everywhere, he stepped inside and closed the door behind him.

"Looks like a tornado hit this place," Hank noted.

"A twenty-two-million-dollar storm," Evelyn agreed. "What can I do for you?"

Hank tapped his watch. "The investor meeting? It was supposed to start fifteen minutes ago."

"I totally forgot," Evelyn said, her eyes widening in surprise. Then she looked down at her wrinkled skirt and ink-stained fingers. "Guess this is the best they get."

Evelyn got to her feet, then wandered around, looking for her shoes. Andy found them tucked in a corner, under the lid of a Bankers Box.

"You're not actually going to take on investors, are you?" Andy asked.

"We're still eight million short," Evelyn replied. "Besides, they might have good ideas."

"And unicorns might be real," Hank snorted.

"What if we called the banks again?" Julia wondered. "We'd be asking for a much lower amount."

"We could also go to smaller banks," Andy offered. "Ask for a quarter or a half million instead of the whole amount."

"I like it," Evelyn said. "Just don't go to Security First National. Once we have repaid our current loan, our business relationship is over."

Andy raised his eyebrows, but did not question her.

"I'll start making the calls," Julia said.

"No," Evelyn replied. "I'd like Andy to do it. Tell them specifically you're calling from Lewis's office."

"If they ask questions like why I'm calling instead of him?" Andy wondered.

"The company is undergoing restructuring," Evelyn replied. "Leave it vague."

Andy nodded.

"If you have any questions, come find me," Evelyn said. "I don't think this meeting is going to take long."

She stepped out of her office, to see Lewis, Ben, and the five investors sitting at the conference table.

Evelyn looked back into her office and quietly instructed Julia to call security.

"They don't need to come into the meeting, but I'd like them up here just in case."

Unflappable as always, Julia went to her desk and picked up the phone.

Chapter 48

Walking into the conference room, Evelyn found Ben, Lewis, and his five investors on one side of the table. The lopsided configuration might seem intimidating, if only those men could stop squirming to find a comfortable position on the small, hard stools. Silently she thanked her father's foresight. She looked at the single stool they had left for her, looked at Hank, then went outside to grab one of the more comfortable chairs from the waiting room. Hank did the same.

"You're late," Lewis snapped as Evelyn settled into her chair.

"Apologies, gentlemen," Evelyn said easily. "I was in the middle of something important."

"This is important," Lewis said. "And you come in here looking like—" He gestured to her disheveled appearance. "And I don't understand why Hank is here. This isn't his business."

"The same could be said for Ben," Evelyn replied.

"He knows these gentlemen and I believe he'll be an asset," Lewis said.

Evelyn glanced around the room, her eyes landing on each man in turn. Their ages ranged from Ben, who looked the youngest at forty, to a septuagenarian, whose cane rested beside him. Lewis introduced each man in turn, but halfway through his recitation of their credentials, Evelyn realized she had already forgotten their names and did not care enough to ask again. Lewis informed her how they were graciously willing to put money into Bishop Aeronautics, though they did need to see some concessions, of course. Hank glanced at her, but Evelyn just sat back in her chair and motioned for them to continue. It took another twenty minutes of them congratulating themselves on their experience before they finally came around to practical recommendations for her company.

"As we see it, there is room for cost cutting in the interior of the plane," one of the investors said. "For example, you are using wool carpet. We think you could go for rayon, instead. Or—"

"We use wool carpet because it's easier to clean and repels stains," Evelyn informed them. "Plus, the airlines paid a premium for this material. We'd be breaking our contract."

"We should also consider cutting back on the insulation. It seems excessive and they can always crank up the heat," a second man suggested.

"That might work for lower altitudes," Hank responded. "But at twenty thousand feet, where most of our advanced commercial planes fly, it's minus twelve degrees outside."

"Have you ever flown in a minimally insulated plane?" Evelyn asked. "They were common during the war."

The men looked among themselves. The answer was clearly no.

Evelyn nodded to herself. "Continue."

A third man jumped in. "We should expand our client base. Right now, you make one of the most expensive planes on the market, which is fine for TWA and Pan Am, but to be competitive, we could create another brand that has fewer bells and whistles. The kind you might expect for a budget airline."

"We already service smaller carriers with our Bishop Clipper," Evelyn responded.

"Yes, but if they were cheaper, those airlines could buy more," the fourth man added.

"Do they need more?" Evelyn asked. "When I spoke with Nick Bez from West Coast, he said that they're just starting to turn a profit. They only offer a few flights daily so they're not running half-empty planes. Especially seeing fuel is their largest operating cost."

"The real issue is company culture," the last man began.

" 'Company culture'?" Hank asked tersely.

"You offer unlimited sick time!" the man exclaimed.

"You want the whole factory to be out with the flu?" Evelyn wondered.

The man ignored her, intent upon his rant. "Three weeks' vacation. Maternity leave! That wouldn't be necessary if you didn't have so many damned women on the floor."

"Plus, you're giving them free lunches!" the third man insisted.

"Well, technically, there is no such thing as a free lunch," Evelyn retorted.

"The cafeteria does not charge!" the third man continued. "Think about all that lost revenue."

"We are not a restaurant, nor are we in the habit of profiting from our workers' purchases. We provide food because a well-fed workforce is a safer, more productive one. These lunches are not free, they are part of our employees' compensation. Besides, if we got rid of the cafeteria, I'd have to start packing my own lunches and I'm way too busy for that."

"This is what we're talking about," the second man replied. "You're not seeing this as a bottom-line business."

"No. You're the one being shortsighted," Evelyn corrected. "Skilled workers are difficult to find. They're even more expensive to train. I want the people here to be happy. Part of that is because I feel a responsibility toward them, but it's also good for your so-called bottom line. If we had high job turnover, it would be infinitely more expensive than offering decent wages and good benefits. I know the name of every single person on that floor, as well as the ones who work in the cafeteria. Do you know what they tell me? The names of their most qualified friends. I already have a stack of applications for when we open the new factory. These are people who will require little training, because many are coming from car companies or other airplane manufacturers and they already know the equipment. Quite a few of our employees stay until they retire, taking ownership over the quality of their work. They invest their energy into building the best-possible planes because they feel valued."

"Don't even get me started on the recall," said the fourth man.

"No, please do," Evelyn requested. "Tell me how much a reputation is worth. I don't know a way to buy it back once it's been squandered. Do you? People purchase our airplanes because they trust us. The military buys from us because we're honest. This respect wasn't given to me because of my father's name or my wartime service—and yes, gentlemen, unlike you, I did serve. People trust us because we've earned it. What have you earned, other than money?"

The room was silent and Evelyn felt the thrum of these men's anger. Finally Lewis cleared his throat.

"Now, Evelyn," he began. "You're jumping to unfair conclusions."

"As far as I can see, everything Evelyn said is correct," Hank offered.

"When your father ran this company, we never had these financial issues," Lewis said. The rank paternalism in his voice did not cover his irritation. "Now I wonder about the longevity of a place to which I've devoted my life."

"Luckily, your life's not over," Evelyn replied. "Out of curiosity. How would this work?"

"We'd each take ten percent," the first man said.

"I have an engineering degree from UCLA," Evelyn reminded them. "I'm pretty good at math. What you're describing is highway robbery."

"There are, of course, other considerations besides the numbers," the fifth man replied, an undercurrent of spite in his voice.

"Like what?" Evelyn asked.

"You're newly married. You're going to be a mother soon. This isn't where you belong."

Evelyn looked to Hank. "I'm going to be a mother soon? This is news to me. "

"It's human nature," the second man explained as if it was obvious.

"So, you're asking for fifty percent of my company," Evelyn said.

"Sixty," the first man corrected. "You'd keep forty percent. The other ten would go to Lewis. We'd be more comfortable with him in charge."

"He has more experience," the fourth man added.

"He's less . . . emotional," the third man agreed.

"What about Hank?" Evelyn asked. "He's worked here even longer than Lewis."

"We believe Hank should receive other types of remuneration," Lewis said.

"Just because you use big words does not make you any less of an asshole," Hank stated.

"You know things are different since Logan left," Lewis spat.

"True," Hank agreed. "There's no way you would've pulled this shit when he was here."

"Where would I fit into this new configuration?" Evelyn asked.

"You'd be a minority stakeholder," Lewis said.

"The company would still carry your name," the fourth man offered.

"That's because you know no one would buy so much as a wing box without it," Evelyn replied. "Don't act like you're doing me a favor." The fact that they believed this deal might have a chance of success meant they either thought her stupid or desperate. Probably both.

"Lewis," Evelyn began. "Why do you think my father left me in charge of this company?"

"It was a rash decision. He was running from—" Lewis broke off, glancing at the investors. "He was grooming Matthew for this job; then your brother went and got himself killed."

"Would you care to rephrase that?" Evelyn asked.

"You know what I mean," Lewis said with a dramatic sigh. "Logan panicked and didn't have time to put a real plan in place. You're nothing but a socialite pretending to be president, and frankly, it's irresponsible of you to continue. You're going to drive a once-great company into the ground."

"My company," Evelyn reminded him.

"Frankly, you don't have a choice in this," Lewis stated. "I already had the lawyers draw up the paperwork."

"I don't have a choice?" Evelyn responded.

"That's right," Lewis said.

Evelyn looked to the assembled investors, then stood up, walked to the door, and held it open. "This meeting has been enlightening, gentlemen. It is now over, please get out."

They didn't move.

"Evelyn—" Lewis began.

"I don't think you're going to want them to see what comes next, but it's up to you," Evelyn warned.

Lewis stared at her, trying to discern what she had in mind. Clearly, the look in her eye warned him not to push too hard. He turned to his guests, apologizing. "It will only take a minute to get this sorted."

Grudgingly they stood and exited to the waiting room. As Ben stood up to leave, Evelyn looked at him. "Not you."

Ben sat back down. Evelyn closed the door behind the investors, then turned to study Lewis, as if trying to figure out the pieces of a puzzle.

"Whatever happened to those caramels you kept in your office?" Evelyn asked.

"What?" Lewis replied, confused at the turn of the conversation.

"It was such a kind gesture. It always made Matthew and me like you. Funny how little it takes to win the affection of a child."

"They're outside waiting," Lewis grumbled impatiently.

"Let them," Evelyn said. "You worked with my father for as long as I can remember. Joined us for Thanksgiving dinners and all of our birthday parties. I always thought of you and Hank almost like uncles. You were family."

"This is business," Lewis instructed.

"It is," Evelyn agreed. "So, as a businessperson, I have to ask if you think I'm insane enough to give up sixty percent of this company for pennies on the dollar."

"Perhaps we can negotiate the details if you'd be willing

to accept a board of directors," Lewis offered. "Things here need to change."

"What was it that man said? 'Company culture'?" Evelyn asked.

"It's a good place to start," Lewis allowed.

"I agree," Evelyn said. "Ben, you're fired."

"What the hell do you think you're doing?" Lewis exploded.

"You . . . you can't do that," Ben stammered.

"I can. Plus, I'm firing you for cause, so do not expect the rest of your contract to be paid out," Evelyn said, then turned to Lewis. "See? I can save money."

"I don't know what that little bitch told you, but—" Ben began as he stood up.

"I'm going to stop you there, because whatever else you have to say is not going to end well for you," Evelyn informed him.

"Willa's a tease," Ben argued. "It's not my fault. She was throwing herself at me."

"You can't fire our contractor because some little girl didn't know how to behave," Lewis agreed. "She should be flattered by the attention."

"It's not about Willa," Evelyn said. "Everyone who works here should be able to do so without feeling awkward, uncomfortable, or unsafe."

"It's really not a big deal," Ben argued.

"To you," Evelyn replied. "It is to her. And it is to me."

"That's because you're a woman. You don't understand," Lewis said.

"Are you listening to yourself?" Hank asked incredulously.

"You're really going to throw away this whole project because of some girl?" Ben challenged.

"Do you have any idea how long it would take to find

another contractor? How much this delay will cost?" Lewis asked.

"This is all a misunderstanding," Ben said, switching his tone to ingratiating. "You want me to stay away from Willa, I'd be happy to. She isn't my type anyway."

"Your wife must be so glad to hear that," Hank drawled.

"Go to hell," Ben snapped as he took a swing at Hank. The older man stepped out of his way. Ben brought his hand back again, but Evelyn grabbed him by the wrist and twisted his arm, forcing him to cry out in pain as his shoulder over rotated and he fell to his knees. Then she turned to Hank.

"Sal and Marcus are outside. Would you please ask them to come in?"

Hank did and two security guards entered. They went to Ben, each grabbing one arm and hauled him to his feet.

"You can't do this!" Ben yelled. "I'll make sure everyone knows you're a psychotic bitch. No one will work with you ever again."

"Yes, well, that's a problem for another day," Evelyn said. The security guards dragged Ben out of the room, past the stunned investors waiting in the lobby, their mouths agape.

"What the fuck do you think you're doing?" Lewis asked. "Once you sign those papers, I'm just going to hire him back. If he'll even come and—"

"I won't be signing those papers."

"This company will go bankrupt," Lewis threatened. "There isn't a single bank that will loan you money!"

"What did you do?" Hank asked, incredulous.

"What I had to, to ensure the longevity of this company," Lewis stated before turning to Evelyn. "You shouldn't be president. You have no idea what you're doing. Logan was a fool to leave you in charge and if he could see you now, he would be ashamed."

"Actually, I don't think he's ever been prouder," Evelyn replied. "Now, if you'll excuse me, I have an infinitely more important meeting."

Evelyn and Hank stopped by Julia's desk and picked up a thin manila envelope and a pen. As they headed downstairs, she heard Lewis reassuring the investors he could handle her.

Chapter 49

Evelyn and Hank walked toward the construction site. Excavators, dump trucks, and cranes all sat silently. Wooden police barricades stretched the entirety of the land, rendering it off-limits.

"What are you going to do about Lewis?" Hank asked.

"He backed me into a corner." Evelyn replied. "It's strange to think I've known him my whole life, but I never really saw him until recently. It's a surprisingly painful lesson."

"You can't blame yourself," Hank said.

"If I blame others, I'll never improve."

They arrived at the barricade and looked into the distance, where Nick and Scott huddled near the crime scene. Angry footsteps stomped up behind them.

"Do you have any idea how long it took me to put that meeting together?" Lewis demanded.

"No, but I'm certainly curious," Evelyn replied dryly.

"You went in there, without a thought for everything I've—" Lewis broke off, staring at the field. "What the hell are they doing! They can't be there! Do they have any idea what Sheriff Richardson will do when he gets here?"

"How will he know?" Evelyn asked. "Unless, of course, you instructed our security guards to call him?"

"This is an active crime scene!"

Sirens sounded in the distance and they saw flashing light speeding down the road toward them. Evelyn looked to Hank, who shook his head.

"Lewis, I gotta give you credit," Evelyn began. "You've never been one to waste an opportunity. A closed construction site was useful in pressuring me to worry about money. Tell me, did you include the bribes you paid Richardson on your expense report, or were those out of your own pocket?"

"How dare you!" Lewis exclaimed

"Tell me I'm wrong," Evelyn said.

"I won't even dignify that with a response."

The police cars screeched to a halt in front of them. The sheriff was yelling before he had fully exited the car. "I will have you thrown in jail!"

"For what?" Evelyn asked. "I haven't crossed the perimeter."

Deputy Polansky carried himself with a resigned frustration as he approached.

"You arrest her and it'll be more trouble than it's worth," Polansky said. "She looks like a woman with good lawyers."

The sheriff did not hear him, yelling, "You let those people go through!"

"I did not 'let' anyone do anything," Evelyn replied. Then she dropped her voice to a whisper and leaned toward Hank. "Though I may have invited them . . ."

The sheriff directed his ire at Scott and Nick. "Hey! You! Get over here! The minute I grab hold of you, I'm tossing you both into prison."

Not exactly the words to make a person hurry. Nick

and Scott knelt to examine one more thing before they stood and casually walked over.

"It's a crime to cross this barrier without permission!" the sheriff roared. "I'll have you thrown in jail so quickly you—"

"That only applies to persons unauthorized to be in a closed emergency area," Scott replied.

"I will have you know that I—" The sheriff wound himself up for a long speech, but Scott held up his hand.

"This case is mine," Scott said as he pulled out his FBI badge.

"That doesn't mean shit," the sheriff countered. "You've got no juris—"

"Actually, this request from the governor says I do," Scott replied, handing Sheriff Richardson the papers. "So, what's going to happen now is that I'm going to get into my car and follow you to the station, where you're going to hand over all the evidence you've found so far. Something tells me it won't be a lot. Then, after I've had a chance to do my own investigation, I'll decide whether to reach out to the attorney general regarding my suspicions that you've been accepting bribes. How's that sound?"

The sheriff did not answer. Instead, he turned on his heel and stormed back to his car. Evelyn glanced at Deputy Polansky, who barely hid a smile, as he followed his boss. Evelyn would not be surprised if he had documents of his own to give to the FBI.

"What did you find?" Evelyn asked Scott and Nick.

"Exactly what I expected. Nothing," Scott replied.

"So, you're releasing the crime scene?" Evelyn asked.

"I am," Scott said. "Go, build with my blessing."

Unable to help herself, Evelyn threw her arms around him and gave him a hug. Scott looked uncomfortable.

"Just doing my job," he assured her as he stepped back and headed to his car.

Evelyn turned to look at Hank and Lewis.

"That was fun," Nick said with a smile.

"It doesn't mean diddly-squat if we don't have a contractor," Lewis muttered.

"Fortunately, that won't be an issue," Evelyn informed him. "I hired Charlie Morgan this morning. He did the retrofit of the Palmer Factory. Brought it in early and under budget. Talked with Percy Winnett, too. He was thrilled with Charlie's work on the new Bullock's store in Pasadena. Charlie even knows a lot of Ben's crew, so the transition should be seamless."

Lewis stared at her, agog.

"Careful," Nick said. "That's a good way to catch flies."

Lewis's jaw snapped shut. "Well, it seems you've thought of everything."

"There's always going to be surprises," Evelyn replied. "You've taught me some important lessons, and for that, I thank you."

"You're welcome," Lewis said.

"I also want to thank you for your many years of service to this company," Evelyn continued. "I know how hard you worked to find clients, set up the deals, and make this place profitable. You were the one who convinced the military to take that initial meeting with my father. You were the one who laid the groundwork for our partnership with TWA and Pan Am. Bishop Aeronautics would not be what it is without you."

For a moment, Lewis looked surprised; then he nodded, as if these compliments were the least of what he was owed. "That is true. I appreciate you acknowledging that fact."

"This past year has been difficult for you. There's been a lot of changes," Evelyn said. "Which is why I think it's time for you to go enjoy your retirement."

"W-what?" Lewis stammered.

"You have a generous pension and other benefits. We'll also be giving you a bonus in gratitude for all your hard work. Of course, that money comes with strings," Evelyn noted.

"Meaning?" Lewis asked.

"If you want the bonus—and trust me, it is generous—you cannot talk badly about the company, or take our trade secrets to another airplane manufacturer."

"You're never going to build the new factory without me," Lewis said. "How are you going to pay for the recall?"

"Fortunately, that's no longer your concern," Evelyn replied. "My decision is final. The only question is whether we can count on your continued support of Bishop Aeronautics."

"You're kidding, right? Lockheed or Douglas will hire me in a heartbeat. You can't kick me to the curb and expect me not to talk about it," Lewis stated.

"That's exactly what I expect," Evelyn said. "I was trying to be kind and let you believe it was a choice. Unfortunately, it's not. You should have read your most recent contract more closely. It states that your pension will be forfeited if you choose to work at another airline company within the next five years. It will also be forfeited if you speak ill of the company, those who work here, or share trade secrets at any time. Now, do you want that bonus or not?"

Evelyn held out an exit agreement to Lewis. He stared at her incredulously for a moment, then grabbed the pen and signed.

"I know you think I fell into this job because my father fled the country," Evelyn began, "but those transfer papers were drawn up long before he left. My father put me in charge of his company because he believed I was the best one to run it. Took me a while, but I finally agree with him."

"You'll regret this," Lewis promised as he turned on his heel and stormed away. Evelyn watched him with both sadness and relief.

Hank turned to Evelyn, frowning. "You know, I did read my contract and I don't remember any of those clauses in there."

"They're not," Evelyn replied. "His either. Lewis has a lot of friends in this town and in DC. I needed to keep him silent. Hopefully, he'll take the money and jet off to a tropical island."

"Maybe not Cuba," Nick joked.

Evelyn and Hank laughed. It was one place Lewis would not receive a warm welcome.

Chapter 50

Evelyn and Nick's day had already felt like a year, and the worst was still to come. They sat silently at the kitchen table, too anxious to eat. There were no dishes in the sink nor a cup out of place. Evelyn put her hand over Nick's. His fingers curled around hers, grateful for the support. Finally the doorbell rang, followed in quick succession by a series of ferocious knocks.

"That's a bit excessive," Evelyn said as they both stood, the tension evident in their bodies.

Nick gave Evelyn a grim smile, then went to open the door. A man with greasy blond hair pushed past Nick into the room. Once upon a time, he was probably fit, but his physique faded into softness. He wore a short-sleeved brown button-down with three parallel stripes running vertical. Below were matching brown pants. The outfit would be stylish on a man like Sinatra, but on him, it made a mockery of good taste. His internal vision of himself did not match reality. He glanced around the room, assessing everything, stopping only when he landed on Evelyn. She could feel his appraisal. Once, it would have made her uncomfortable, but that was a lifetime ago. Paula followed him in, her bravado trying to match his and failing.

"Hello, Dean," Nick said. "Paula."

"Nice place you got here," Dean said. "Must've cost a pretty penny to be this close to the water."

Neither Nick nor Evelyn answered.

"You don't seem surprised to see us," Dean continued.

"Had a feeling this is where my son disappeared to this morning," Paula said.

"Worthless little shit," Dean replied. "Next time I catch him, I'm gonna—"

Paula put her hand on his arm, silencing him. Evelyn got the impression this was for her and Nick's benefit. She suspected Paula rarely stayed Dean's hand at home.

"Speaking of, where is my delightful child?" Paula asked.

"We didn't think he should be here for this," Evelyn said.

"Ah! The princess speaks!" Dean exclaimed. "Just because you were raised in a fancy house and fancy schools, you think you're better than us." Then, getting inches from Evelyn's face, he spat out the words, "Don't you?"

Nick handed her his handkerchief and Evelyn calmly wiped off Dean's saliva.

"What?" Paula mocked. "You're not going to protect your wife? What kind of a man are you?"

Dean jumped at Evelyn, pushing his face into hers, trying to get her to step back in fear. Instead, the blade of her right hand shot straight into his windpipe. It was almost too fast to see. They might not have known anything happened, had Dean not fallen to the floor gasping for air.

"What the hell did you do to him?" Paula demanded, rushing to his side.

Evelyn shrugged. "Reflex."

The corner of Nick's mouth tipped upward in appreciation. "I'm the kind of man who knows my wife can handle herself."

Dean slowly found his breath, then got to his feet.

"Fucking bitch," he muttered, standing a few feet away, his bravado lessened. "You're going to pay for that."

"Let's get on with it," Nick said.

Dean stared at Nick for a long moment, before saying, "You've done good for yourself. Real good. Much different from that kid I once knew on the street."

"He's still in there," Nick warned.

"You were so soft when we left," Paula said. "I honestly didn't know if you were gonna make it. Told Dean to keep an eye out for you."

"Which I did," Dean agreed. "In my own way."

"Yes," Nick drawled sarcastically. "I remember all of your kindness."

"Never suspected you had it in you to take out that old pervert. It was an impressive amount of blood."

"You saw this man attack Nick and you didn't try to stop it?" Evelyn asked.

"Maybe Nick likes it rough," Dean sneered. "Who am I to get in the middle of a tryst?"

"So, what now?" Nick said.

"Now? I go to the papers. Maybe even the police. I'll line up a group of people who swore they saw you attack that guy out of nowhere. I'll let it be known you were happy to sell yourself for money," Dean continued. Then, looking at Evelyn, "Perhaps you still are. How's it going to look when your perfect wife is shown to be married to a monster? That will keep the gossip pages busy for a while."

"Other people's opinions are not my concern," Evelyn replied.

"Bet you'll change your tune if Nick ends up in prison," Paula said. There was a certain glee in her voice. Nick studied her, as if trying to figure out a puzzle.

"Why do you hate me so much?" Nick asked.

Paula stared at him as if it were obvious. "You were always the smart one. Even as a kid, I knew you were going places I could only dream about. I didn't have brains like you. People didn't like me the way they like you."

"That's not true," Nick replied. "Growing up, you created these incredible worlds. You made me believe there was a future."

"And there was. For you. If it was me on the street, not a single soul would have stepped up to help. You had Hildy and that guy Dan, who let you sleep in the back of his bar. I had no one."

"You had our parents," Nick replied.

"Fat lotta good that did me," Paula said. "You're living this fairy-tale life, giving away your wife's money. A couple grand and you don't even miss it."

"Which makes me think you have more to give," Dean added. "We can start with twenty grand to keep you out of prison, then a regular maintenance fee. Your wife can put me on the payroll to keep it all aboveboard."

"You caught me on a bad day," Evelyn replied. "I've been firing people. Not hiring them. Might have to wait for the dust to settle."

"This isn't a joke," Dean barked. "You're going to give me that money."

"No," Evelyn said.

"You'd let your husband be arrested?" Paula asked.

"No," Evelyn replied again. They waited for Evelyn to elaborate, but she did not.

"Don't test me, little girl," Dean threatened. "After the press, I'll go straight to the police."

"So, let me get this straight," Evelyn clarified. "In order for you to stay silent about Nick defending himself against a rapist, you're demanding we give you money."

"You're finally getting it," Dean said.

"I think we did," Nick agreed. "Captain Wharton, is that enough?"

Captain Wharton stepped out from behind the staircase, where he was waiting with two other police officers.

"Certainly is," Wharton replied. "Dean Haynes, these gentlemen are arresting you for attempted blackmail."

One of the officers reached for Dean's arm, to put on handcuffs. Dean punched him in the jaw. Nick hit Dean hard with a right cross, followed by several sharp jabs to his abdomen. Dean doubled over in pain as Nick finished him off with a left hook. This time, the officer was able to get the cuffs on him without a fight. He hauled Dean to his feet and dragged him out of the house.

"I was just helping to subdue someone resisting arrest," Nick said to Wharton.

"Of course," Wharton replied. Then he looked to Paula. "What about her?"

Nick struggled with an answer. How could he balance his anger and pain with wanting to do what was right for Rory?

"How long is the statute of limitations for attempted blackmail?" Evelyn asked.

"Five years," Wharton replied.

"And we could file charges at any time?" Nick continued.

Wharton nodded.

"Rory would be eighteen. His own person," Evelyn offered. "Perhaps Paula might find her maternal instinct with Dean gone and the threat of prison hanging over her head."

"You want me to become some model mother, straight out of Good Housekeeping magazine," Paula said. "That's never going to happen."

"Do you have any idea how much he loves you? How much he believes in you?" Evelyn asked.

Paula's face softened briefly. Then she shook her head. "You have no idea what it's like. I've busted my ass putting a roof over our heads and food on the table. It never ends."

"That's not Rory's fault. He didn't ask to be born," Nick insisted.

"Well, I sure as hell didn't ask for that either," Paula said. "I am so goddamned tired. It's about time he starts pulling his weight."

Nick studied the broken woman before him. Then thought back to how desperately he needed someone to care for him growing up. Thirteen might look mature, but Rory deserved a few more years to grow into manhood. Nick looked to Evelyn, who nodded in agreement to the words he had not said aloud. He was reminded, once again, why he loved her.

"We'll take him," Nick said. "We'll give Rory a home on one condition. You sign a document making Evelyn and me Rory's legal guardians. You can see him as often as you'd like, but we get to make decisions for him, without you meddling or trying to get more for yourself. In exchange, you keep the money we gave you and never ask for more."

Paula thought for a moment. "Fine." Then she turned to Wharton. "Can I go now?"

"You're not even going to say goodbye to Rory?" Evelyn asked, horrified.

"He doesn't care," she said.

"Trust me," Nick replied. "He does. You will leave him with something to hold on to. Tell him you love him and that you've made mistakes. Tell him you're doing this for his sake. Make him believe he has value and that you'll miss him. If you leave before you do that, I will track you down and bring you back."

"Fine," Paula relented.

"The Sand Dollar Hotel is a half mile down the beach," Nick said. He reached into his pocket and pulled out twenty dollars. "This will cover it, and then some. I'll pick you up at nine tomorrow morning."

Paula took the money and left. Nick turned to Captain Wharton, who ran his hand through his hair. "Meeting your family explains so much, Gallagher."

"Don't know if that's good," Nick said.

"Me neither," Wharton replied. He held his hand out to Nick. "Know I didn't give you much credit, but coming from where you started . . ."

"You almost sound proud," Nick joked as he shook Wharton's hand.

"Let's not get carried away," the police captain warned. He turned to Evelyn and gave her a kiss on the cheek. "Always a pleasure."

"You as well," she said. "Thank you."

Wharton grumbled a reply, then left the house, quietly shutting the door behind him. For a moment, Evelyn and Nick just stared at each other.

"Wine?" she asked.

"Whisky," he answered.

He got the glasses and she got the bottle. They sat down at the table and Evelyn poured them both hefty servings. They drank, refilled, then drank again.

"I'm sorry I pushed you to tell me about your childhood," Evelyn said. "I don't think I realized . . ."

"How could you? We've seen the worst of humanity, but somehow, when it's on a personal level, the cruelty has more resonance."

"We'll give Rory something better. More my family than yours," Evelyn said.

"It's going to be hard. Between your work and mine and . . ."

"My father believed that if kids feel safe and they know they're loved, they're going to be okay. At the absolute bare minimum, we can do that for Rory," Evelyn promised.

Nick nodded and tears began to flow down his cheeks. Evelyn slid closer and pulled him into her arms. He was not a man who cried often, but his body shook with heaving sobs. Evelyn knew she could not fix all that ailed him, but she would always be beside him.

Chapter 51

Evelyn and Nick slept fitfully, with Nick waking up from one nightmare after the other. Finally, he gave up and held Evelyn close, feeling the length of her body curled against his. The rise and fall of her breath calmed his own. They lay like that until the sky began to turn from black to blue. She rolled over to face him. Nick rarely found it easy to hold another's gaze, but with Evelyn, it felt like coming home. She kissed him and he pulled her closer. They broke their embrace only long enough to lift Evelyn's nightgown over her head. The comfort and familiarity of being together did not dim the pleasure they found in each other. When they finished, sweat slicked and tangled in sheets, their shared anxiety subsided slightly. These moments were the only time Nick's mind would let the world slip away.

Through the open window, they watched the sun creep across the sand until its light touched the Pacific. That was their sign to begin the day. After coffee and showers, they got in the car and drove to the Sand Dollar Hotel. Neither really expected Paula to be there, but when they knocked on the door, she opened it in her slip, with yesterday's makeup caked on her cheeks. Evelyn wondered if she had been crying.

Paula grunted a greeting, telling them she needed ten minutes. It was closer to thirty before she emerged from her room.

"Let's go," she said, walking past them to the car.

"First things first," Nick said. He withdrew guardianship papers from a manila envelope and set them on the car's hood. Evelyn had called her lawyer after Paula left. As a favor to a life-long client, he expedited the documents and sent them over at midnight. Nick handed Paula a pen. "Sign."

A small smile on Paula's lips. "And if I don't?"

"I'm not doing this with you," Nick said. Fearing the worst of his sister, he had planned for this eventuality. He pulled a thousand dollars from his pocket. He saw the calculations in her head, wondering if she could get more. "My final offer."

"You still want Rory," Paula said.

"I want to take care of Rory," Nick said. "There's a difference. Deep down, you know this is the best for him."

Paula grabbed the pen and signed where Nick indicated. Then he handed her the money and slipped the papers back in their envelope. They got in the car to drive to Taffy's house. It was several miles before Paula broke the silence.

"I've known Dean over thirty years," she said quietly. "Don't really remember life without him. Could be a real bastard, but he took care of me."

"What about Rory?" Nick demanded.

"What about him?" Paula said.

"Is Dean his father?" Evelyn asked. It was not the question Nick meant, but wanting Paula to choose her son over this particular man was a fruitless pursuit.

"No. I met a guy. Decent sort. Said he was gonna save

me." Paula laughed humorlessly. "Who knows? If I'd told him I was pregnant, he probably would've stepped up, but what kind of life is that?"

"A stable one for your son," Nick answered.

"Wouldn't have lasted. Seems I always go back to Dean," Paula said.

"Do you love him?" Evelyn asked.

"What is love?" Paula replied.

Evelyn looked over to Nick and intertwined their fingers.

Though it was early, Taffy answered the door, fully dressed, her hair and makeup perfect. She wore her large diamond wedding ring and a long strand of pearls, each the size of an olive. Sometimes Evelyn forgot that Taffy could be a truly imposing figure, but today she left no doubt.

"You must be Paula," Taffy said as she stepped aside to let the other woman enter. There was no warmth in her voice.

Paula looked around the house covetously. "Never knew people lived like this."

Taffy did not deign to reply. Finally Paula's eyes landed on her son. For a long moment, they stared at each other, trying to gauge the state of their relationship. Rory ventured towards his mother.

"Dean's going to prison because of you," Paula told him.

Rory stopped, finding himself second, once again, to a man he loathed. Pain flashed across his face, then he straightened his shoulders.

"Good," Rory replied. "I hope they lock him up and throw away the key."

Paula slapped her son. Rory saw it coming, but did not bother to dodge the blow.

"Are you leaving?" Rory asked.

"Yes," Paula replied flatly.

"Where will you go?"

"I don't know?" Paula said.

"Will you be back?"

"I don't know," Paula repeated. There was a slight tremor in her voice. "Nick will take good care of you. It's for the best."

Rory nodded. There was so much to say, but Nick understood those questions would leave him too vulnerable. Rory bit his lip, unable to trust his voice.

Paula's face softened as she stepped toward Rory. "I love you."

Rory looked surprised. "Do you?"

"Of course," Paula said. "How can you ask me that?"

"Because you never once put me first," Rory replied.

For a moment, Paula looked like she wanted to embrace her son, then realized it might not be welcome. Instead, she walked to the door, threw it open, and disappeared down the driveway. When they could no longer see her, Rory took a deep, shuddering breath. Nick put his arm around him. Right now, this felt like an end. Nick hoped with time, it would also be a beginning.

Chapter 52

Evelyn always appreciated the chance to wear her Wellington boots. There was rarely enough rain in Los Angeles to justify it and that day was no different. However, she and Charlie Morgan, her new contractor, were walking the construction site together and the soft earth was hell on heels. Looking at the plans, he had several questions and that could be best addressed at the actual location. Plus, it gave her the chance to meet him in person. Bright blue eyes shone from his tanned face and his mouth formed an easy smile. Everything about him, from his relaxed posture to the shirtsleeves rolled up to his elbows, radiated kindness and an easy confidence. He seemed a man at peace with himself.

"I can't tell you how much I appreciate you stepping in on such short notice," Evelyn said.

"Colette Palmer is a hard woman to refuse," Charlie replied. "Besides, she told me why you fired your last contractor. Not many people would, and I admire that."

They walked to the far corner of the field. Around the edges, the crew was starting to arrive, balancing thermoses of coffee on the edges of the construction trucks. Under a tent stood a large drafting table, with Hank, Willa, and Julia standing around it. Evelyn introduced Charlie.

"Looking over the plans," Charlie began, "I feel like these beams are being retrofitted before they've even been fitted. I called over this morning and got another set of the architect's original plans. It was hard to see over all of these additions."

He rolled out two sets of blueprints. They were similar, but one had edits crowding out the original measurements.

"Those were Ben's changes," Willa said.

"Ben?" Charlie asked.

"The former contractor," Julia clarified.

"People always get into trouble when contractors make changes," Charlie said. "I'm gonna admit right now, calculus is not my strong suit."

"Ben kept saying the support beams weren't strong enough," Willa replied.

"Well," Charlie said, "I'd love to talk to someone in engineering and figure out what kind of weight load to expect. We'll have the architect figure out new numbers if needed."

"I brought my best," Hank said, nodding to Willa.

"Looking forward to working with you." Charlie reached out to shake her hand. Then he turned to Julia. "You look like the person who keeps this place running."

"Yep," Julia agreed with a sly smile towards Evelyn.

"Let's expand beyond engineering," Charlie said. "Can you arrange for me to speak with the head of every department? I'm sure you went over this with the architect, but I want to make sure this building will still be a good fit fifty years from now."

"Never hurts to have a second look," Evelyn agreed, feeling the tension loosen in her shoulders.

"In the meantime, I'm going to continue digging the foundation. Don't want to let any time go to waste."

"We'll get you whatever you need," Evelyn replied.

"I'm going to have a word with the foreman; then I'll meet you inside."

Charlie walked toward an older man and offered his hand. Evelyn could not hear what was said, but she saw the smile on the foreman's face and heard the loud guffaw of laughter. A few other men drifted nearer and Charlie greeted each of them in turn. Hank and Julia led the way across the field, while Willa hung back to talk with Evelyn.

"Thank you," Willa said.

"You have nothing to thank me for," Evelyn replied. "In fact, it looks like you've done me a favor. I'm feeling good about our new contractor."

"Certainly sounds like he knows his stuff," Willa agreed.

"How are you holding up?"

"I think people know Ben was fired because of me."

"No. He was fired because he behaved inappropriately in a professional setting," Evelyn assured her. "Plus, he was an asshole."

"I'm probably going to get a lot of the same crap in my PhD program," Willa guessed.

"Maybe," Evelyn said. "But because of you, that door's going to open just a little wider to the women who follow you. By the time you and I end our careers, I hope women in these jobs are so normal, it's not even worth mentioning."

"Well, now, that's my hope, too," Willa answered.

Evelyn stopped. A flash of gold in the dirt caught her eye.

"You okay?" Willa asked.

"Yeah, you go ahead."

Willa lengthened her stride to catch up to Hank and Julia. Evelyn knelt and brushed the dirt away from a small metal tube. Picking it up, she looked at the writing: Tangee Red Majesty lipstick.

Mary Takemura's favorite shade.

Chapter 53

Evelyn called Nick. First she tried their home, then his office, and finally Taffy's house, where she had left them several hours ago. Clara answered the phone and Evelyn was surprised to learn they were still there. Nick and Taffy had a grudging respect for one another, but nothing she considered closeness. It was a few minutes before Nick came on the line, a smile in his voice. After that morning, she would not have thought it possible.

"Can you believe Rory doesn't know how to swim?" Nick asked, incredulous. "We're practicing in Taffy's pool before we throw him in the ocean."

"Walk before you run," Evelyn agreed.

Nick heard the tone in her voice. "What is it?"

Evelyn told Nick about finding the lipstick in the field.

"It's a common color," Nick offered.

"How many women have been on that site?" Evelyn asked.

"Fair, but Mary Takemura? Really?" Nick replied.

"Think about it. She stopped wearing the lipstick because she lost it."

"Which she could have easily replaced."

"I think it was a sign of bigger problems. Russell Clements was killed two months ago, around the same time she called off her engagement with Joe Aoki. I think she's a good person, who doesn't know how to deal with the guilt."

Nick considered that for a moment. "She was especially upset when Hanzo was the main suspect."

"He kept warning her to keep silent," Evelyn said. "We assumed the *HT* in Clements's calendar was Hanzo Takemura, but it could have been Himari Takemura."

"Her Japanese name. What would killing Clements accomplish?"

"Probably nothing, but what if it was an accident? Or she lost her temper?"

"It's not a lot to go on," Nick replied. "You think we should take it to Scott Goldberg?"

"No," Evelyn said. "I think we should take it to Carl."

"Carl? Why Carl?" Nick asked.

"He's friends with Billy," Evelyn replied. "Might have some insight."

A half hour later, Evelyn, Nick, and Carl sat in a broom closet masquerading as an FBI conference room.

"Mary? Really?" Carl asked.

"It's possible," Nick said. "I was skeptical at first, but the more I think about it . . ."

Carl looked torn.

"You let my father go," Evelyn began. "It's possible I never found this lipstick. Russell Clements was a terrible man, who won't be mourned. The Takemuras already had so much taken from them and I highly doubt Mary's a threat to anyone else."

"Morals aren't morals if they only exist when it's convenient," Carl replied after a long minute.

"Give the information to Scott Goldberg and let him sort it out," Nick said. "I know Billy's your friend, but don't understand why this is so difficult."

"Because I'm falling in love with him." It wasn't how Carl planned to tell Nick, but he needed all of the cards on the table. Hiding them required more energy than he currently possessed.

"Oh," Nick agreed. "That does make it more complicated."

"That's all you have to say?" Carl asked. When Nick looked confused, Carl clarified, "I'm homosexual."

"Yeah, I got that," Nick answered. "Appreciate you telling me."

Carl stared at him for a minute, then nodded once. They were good.

"We'll support whatever you want to do about Mary," Evelyn offered.

Carl looked agonized. Finally he picked up the lipstick and walked out into the hall. Evelyn and Nick followed him to Scott Goldberg's desk.

"Tell him what you told me," Carl instructed. "I'm going to find Billy."

"I'll get Joe," Evelyn said. "He should be there, too."

They left together while Nick informed Scott of the new developments.

Evelyn and Joe were the first to arrive at the Takemuras' house. Hanzo answered the door with a confused look.

"What now?" he asked, ushering them inside.

Maiko sat in the front room, resting, with her feet up on an ottoman. Mary entered carrying a tea tray.

"Why didn't you tell me the truth about Russell Clements?" Joe asked.

"You don't know what the hell—" Hanzo began angrily.

"Your lipstick, Tangee Red Majesty," Joe said. "It was found near the crime scene. I've seen you put it on a thousand times."

"That doesn't mean anything," Hanzo retorted.

"Enough," Mary said wearily. She set down the tray, carefully poured a cup, and handed it to Maiko. "I wanted to find peace for my mother before she died. After Hanzo went to see Donald, we realized he never sold us out. The land was stolen. In fact, we could make the case it was still ours. For the briefest moment, we thought we could reopen the restaurant. Both of us tried calling Clements's office, but couldn't get through. Hanzo wrote letters, with no response; meanwhile, Mama got sicker. Finally I went to the C and W office. The girl at the front desk mocked me, but I waited. Funny, how when Clements saw me in person, he was willing to chat. I pleaded my case and he actually listened to me. Or I thought he did. We made plans to go to the restaurant. If I could show him how good the food was, and how much this place meant to us, then maybe he'd give it back."

"Oh, Mary, what did you do?" Maiko asked quietly. "That man had no kindness in him."

"I know that now," Mary replied. "I brought all of our supplies from home. Pots, pans, even our *gyuto* and *honesuki* knives. You have no idea the feast I made. I'd gone down to the market that morning to pick up fresh fish for the *sakana no nitsuke*. I made *okonomiyaki* and *tonkatsu*. It almost felt like Christmas when Mama would cook for all of us."

She glanced at Hanzo, who returned a sad smile.

"Clements didn't touch it. He was only interested in me. I told him I was engaged, but he said it wasn't a problem. He offered that perhaps we could make an 'arrangement.' God help me, I considered it for the briefest moment." Mary turned to Joe and took his hand. "I'm so sorry."

Joe did not know how to respond.

"When Clements finally understood I had no intention of . . . he began to laugh," Mary continued. "Somehow, all of this was funny to him. He told me the land was sold years ago. I felt like such a fool. He told me to grow up and join the real world, instead of hiding away in some pathetic backward culture. He said . . . he said my father deserved to die because he was too weak to protect his family."

Maiko inhaled sharply, but made no comment.

"I don't know what came over me," Mary said. "I was so angry. It wasn't entirely about him, it was every indignity we had to face: Being forced into camp, losing Dad, and having our family torn apart. Then coming home to find the restaurant, a place we worked so hard for, gone. Something inside me broke.

"I grabbed a pan off the stove and swung it. I just needed him to stop laughing."

Mary started to cry and Hanzo took over the story.

"Himari called me. Clements was dead. We panicked. I didn't want to move his car with him in it, in case we were pulled over and they found the body. The land next to the restaurant was vacant for a long time. I hoped it would stay that way until the world forgot about that awful man. We each grabbed a leg and dragged him across the field. When we couldn't pull him any longer, we began to dig."

"We didn't have shovels, so we used my mother's pans," Mary said shamefully.

"It was slow going," Hanzo continued. "Finally the hole seemed deep enough that he would be covered. I rolled him in and pushed the dirt back on top. Himari went to clean up the restaurant."

"We didn't know what else to do," Mary said. "So Hanzo got rid of the car and I came home."

"With the pans?" Joe asked.

Mary nodded.

"My pans in the cupboard?" Maiko clarified.

"I cleaned them thoroughly," Mary promised. "I didn't want you to know they were missing. Not only did I fail to get the restaurant back, but I also . . ."

Mary could not bring herself to say it.

"Why didn't you tell me?" Joe asked. "You could have trusted me."

"It wasn't that," Hanzo began. "It was—"

"I was ashamed," Mary admitted.

"Then you could have come to me as your lawyer," Joe continued, looking at Hanzo this time. "I could have tried to protect you. Both of you."

"And you could have told me so I didn't bring in outsiders," Billy said angrily from the doorway. No one had heard it open. Carl was standing behind him, looking miserable and out of place.

"We told you to leave it alone," Hanzo replied.

"Do you think losing the restaurant only affected you? Do you think losing Dad and now—" Billy broke off, looking at his mother, but unable to finish his sentence. "Do you think you're the only ones who miss him? We all wanted to make this right."

"I didn't know if we could trust you," Hanzo said. "I wasn't sure if you were our brother or the government's soldier."

"Stop!" Maiko commanded. "Enough with the squabbling. You need each other more than ever."

Maiko began to cough and Billy rushed to her side. Mary helped her take a sip of tea.

"It's not a good case," Carl offered. They looked at him.

"Why are you here?" Hanzo asked.

"Explain," Joe demanded at the same time.

"They have the lipstick," Carl said. "And motive. Opportunity in the form of his scheduled appointment, though initials alone seem hardly enough. Clements was a known womanizer. You might be able to convince a jury of self-defense. Even better, Joe might be able to convince the prosecutor not to file charges. They tend to like easy cases and this isn't one of them."

"That's a lot of 'mights,'" Billy said angrily. "The evidence 'might' have disappeared."

"I couldn't do that," Carl replied.

"Yes, you could," Billy insisted. "You could have protected my family, but I guess we weren't important enough."

"Billy, please—"

"Get out!" Billy ordered. "Stay the hell away from me and my family."

Evelyn looked to Carl, whose face was a map of pain.

"I'm sorry," he said before walking out the door.

"So, what happens next?" Hanzo asked.

"We get you a defense attorney," Joe said. "A real one."

"How do we pay for that?" Mary wondered.

"Russell Clements's estate," Evelyn replied, not missing the irony. "Sue him for the money you should have received from the sale of the land. Nick's investigation dug up more than enough evidence."

"We're never getting our restaurant back, are we?" Billy asked.

"Do we really want it?" Hanzo replied. "After all that's happened?"

"Everything has a season," Maiko agreed. "And that one has passed."

There was a knock on the open door frame. Scott Goldberg and a few other FBI agents entered.

"Mary Takemura?" he began. "I'm going to need to bring you down to the office for questioning regarding the death of Russell Clements."

Mary turned to face Scott; Joe put a hand on her shoulder.

"Keep silent until I'm with you. Not one word," Joe instructed. He grabbed a sheet of paper, wrote down a number, and handed it to Hanzo. "Andrew Carlson. Best defense attorney I know. Tell him to meet us down there."

Hanzo took it and went to make the call. Scott pulled out a search warrant and handed it to Joe. He read it quickly, then nodded.

"They're going to have to take a look around," Joe told the Takemuras. "Best thing to do is stay out of their way."

"Gentlemen," Scott addressed the agents, "you know the parameters of our search. Let's keep this as civilized as possible."

The men fanned out through the house. From the bedroom, they heard drawers opening and closing. From the kitchen, the sound of pots and pans. Scott took Mary's arm and led her outside. Joe was close on their heels. Evelyn quietly followed them.

Carl was standing on the sidewalk with Nick. He looked up to the house to see Billy glance toward him, then close the front door.

Chapter 54

Evelyn looked through the front window of her house to see Nick and Rory in the kitchen. Each held a small paring knife as they shelled and deveined shrimp for dinner. Evelyn and Carl were supposed to be shucking corn, but they mostly sat on the porch, drinking wine as the sun set. She picked up the bottle of pinot noir and refilled both their glasses.

"How are you holding up?" Evelyn asked.

Carl shrugged. "Maybe if we'd been together longer, Billy and I could have found a way to weather this. Maybe not."

"Breakups are hard," Evelyn agreed.

"Feels like I'm going to be alone forever," Carl said.

"You're not alone," Evelyn replied. "More importantly, you're one of the smartest, strongest, kindest men I've ever met. You're going to find someone."

"From your mouth to God's ears," Carl replied.

"I have a whole vision in my head of you, me, Nick, and the love of your life traveling through Italy when we retire," Evelyn said.

"And like today, Nick will appreciate the food, while we drink the wine."

"Cheers to that," Evelyn agreed.

She looked through the window again, where Nick stood shoulder to shoulder with Rory, laughing over a private joke. This was a side of Nick she instinctively knew was there, but until now, she had rarely seen outside their relationship. It was warm, unguarded, and protective all at the same time.

"How's Rory settling in?" Carl asked.

"He seems happy. It's only been a few weeks, but we've got him enrolled to start school in the fall. He still has nightmares. Nick tries to remind him he's safe. I think he wants to believe it, but he's not there yet. There's a lot he hasn't told us."

"What about his mom?"

"We haven't heard from Paula, and Rory never mentions her. Hopefully, with time and space, he'll realize her issues had nothing to do with him. He's such a good kid."

"Kid?" Carl asked. "I think he's grown two inches since he arrived."

"Calling him 'young man' feels too formal, 'teenager' sounds too clinical, and a 'good guy' feels like a buddy from the bar," Evelyn said. "There should be more words for this age. What does your father call you?"

"*Hijo*. Son."

"Which is lovely, and not helpful in this situation. I'm gonna stick with 'kid,' " Evelyn decided. "Did Nick tell you he's helping Joe Aoki gather documents to sue C and W Developers?"

"Any word on Mary?"

"The prosecutor is still debating whether to press charges. With her mother dying, they don't consider her a flight risk," Evelyn said. She waited for Carl to ask about Billy, but he resisted. Instead, he asked her about work.

"I'm trying to figure out how to replace Lewis. Andy's young, but he can handle the math. As for the rest of it,

I've set more meetings with our clients. Too many of those relationships were left to Lewis . . . which was easy to do," Evelyn stated. "Almost all of those men are super awkward around me until they've had a few drinks. Thank God I can hold my liquor."

"I find the professional qualifications for your job curious."

"You and me both."

"I left the FBI," Carl said. "Resigned yesterday. Just couldn't do it anymore."

"Congratulations," Evelyn replied. "Is that the right term?"

"Maybe? I think so." Carl considered it for a moment. "Do you know, I've worked for the government one way or another my whole life? Did ROTC in college. Joined the Army. Then the OSS. LAPD. FBI."

"You need a job without acronyms."

Carl laughed. "Can't believe I'm saying this, but I'm gonna try working with Nick. Assuming the offer's still open."

"You kidding? He'll throw you a ticker tape parade," Evelyn replied as she spotted him heading toward them.

"That's it?" Nick asked, stepping out onto the porch and looking down at the half-shucked corn.

"We've been engaged in other important work," Evelyn said, toasting him with her wineglass.

"You are both a disappointment," Nick joked, then called out to Rory, "Come show them how it's done!"

Rory appeared in the doorway, a bright smile on his face.

"You mean we have to do the shrimp and the corn?" he asked. "What are you two bringing to the table?"

Carl looked at the near-empty bottle. "We already drank it."

"Well, at least I can help with that," Taffy chimed in as she stepped onto the porch. She had a Sacher torte in one hand and a bottle of Bordeaux in the other. Nick relieved her of the first and Carl helped with the second as they headed inside. Rory quickly shucked the rest of the corn and followed them back into the kitchen.

Evelyn was left alone. In the house, lights shone warmly. Laughter drifted out on the night air that was just beginning to replace the day's heat with the chill of sunset. Evelyn watched the sun sink lower, turning the whole sky orange, then purple, and eventually blue. The first stars of twilight winked awake, guarding against the darkness. Evelyn took a deep breath, feeling happiness well up inside her. Then she went to join her family.

Author's Note

In 1942, shortly after Pearl Harbor, the Roosevelt administration designated all people of Japanese descent, residing in the United States, as enemy aliens. Those on the West Coast were uprooted from their lives and forced to leave their homes, businesses and communities. Approximately two-thirds of these people were *Nisei,* American citizens born in the United States. The last third, *Issei,* were people born in Japan who had immigrated to the United States. They were denied citizenship because of the Immigration Act of 1924, which also made it illegal for them to hold property. It was common practice to put everything into the name of the eldest son. In March 1942, over a hundred and twenty thousand people on the West Coast were rounded up, taken from their homes, and incarcerated in concentration camps. They were only allowed to bring what they could carry, which usually meant clothes, bedding, and a few personal effects. Some found neighbors, friends or clergy who were willing to store their belongings or continue their businesses. Others were forced to sell heirlooms at a fraction of their worth. Still others had their possessions looted from their homes or storage spaces.

People were forced into staging areas like the Santa Anita Racetrack where whole families were forced to sleep in unclean stalls that had recently been vacated by horses. From there, they were taken to camps such as Manzanar, Poston, Topaz, Heart Mountain, and others. These camps were formed quickly and did not have basic necessities like proper sanitation. The shacks set up as housing provided little protection against the weather, leaving people freezing in the winter and roasting in the summer. The wages for work done at the camp or at nearby farms and factories were significantly lower than the prevailing rate and payment could be delayed for months. Additionally, there were incidents of young men being shot by guards during unrest.

Eventually, the camps opened up and allowed people who signed a loyalty pledge to move farther inland until the end of the war. Some young men joined the 442nd Regimental Combat Team, which was made up entirely of *Nisei* soldiers. They were one of the most highly decorated units during the Second World War, renowned for their bravery. After the war, many people returned to find strangers living in their homes. They had to start over, still reeling from their country's betrayal, and without the resources they had spent their lives building.

With few exceptions, none of the Japanese Americans incarcerated were ever tried in a court of law, nor found guilty of any crime. Habeus corpus was suspended because of fear and racism. It is one of the darkest chapters in American History.

The books I read include, *They Called Us Enemy* by George Takei; *Infamy: The Shocking Story of the Japanese American Internment in World War II*: by Richard Reeves; *Farewell to Manzanar: A True Story of Japanese American Experience During and After the World War II Internment* by Jeanne Watasuki Houston and James D Houston; *Life after Manzanar* by Naomi Hirahara and Heather C. Lindquist. I also found Ms. Hirahara's novels *Clark and Division* and *Evergreen* both wonderfully informative, as well as being great mysteries.

After World War Two, the white middle-class expanded

rapidly in the United States. Mass-produced housing, such as Levittown in New York, sprung up all over the country. It is important to note, the majority of these communities were segregated to exclude black families. Additionally, the benefits of the GI Bill and VA Loans which helped white veterans go to college and obtain mortgages, were often denied to black veterans. If you wish to learn more, I recommend *Half American: The Epic Story of African Americans Fighting World War II at Home and Abroad* by Matthew F. Delmont, as well as *The Warmth of Other Suns* and *Caste* by Isabel Wilkerson.

Lastly, many LBGTQIA+ people hid their authentic selves during the 1940s. Not only was being queer considered unacceptable in mainstream society, there were also anti-sodomy laws in every state that allowed the police to arrest gay men and women. It was not until January 1st, 1962, that Illinois became the first state to decriminalize homosexuality. It took another forty-one years until Lawrence v. Texas, in 2003, for the Supreme Court to strike down anti-sodomy laws as unconstitutional. Carl's dream of marrying a man he loved would not be realized until June 26, 2015, with Obergefell v Hodges mandating that same-sex marriage be recognized at the federal level. Carl would have been almost a hundred years old.

This story takes place in 1949, shortly before The Lavendar Scare, which forced gay men and women out of positions in government, deeming them deviants and security risks. Like those swept up in Joseph McCarthy's Red Scare, people were encouraged to point fingers at others in order to save themselves. While they might escape going to prison, they were commonly fired from their jobs with a record that could make it difficult to find other work. I highly recommend *The Lavender Scare* by David K. Johnson, which shines a light on the hypocrisy and fear of this time.

Acknowledgments

Thank you, as always, to my incredible agent Kathy Green. I can't tell you how much I appreciate your wisdom, faith and support. John Scognamiglio, I am so grateful to you for taking a chance on Evelyn and Nick. I love getting to share their stories with the world. You've shown me such kindness and patience when I most needed it. It's meant a lot.

To the amazing team at Kensington, including Madeleine Brown, Alexandra Nicolajsen and Robin Cook, you do such a brilliant job at getting these books made and into readers' hands. I have no idea how you work your magic, but I am always impressed. To Stephanie Finnegan, I try my best to be historically accurate, and yet, things always fall through the cracks. Thank you for catching my mistakes.

Dave Ihlenfeld, you are an incredible reader and an even better friend. I'm so glad you hired me a half a lifetime ago, so you could have someone to boss around. Leif Lillehaugen, working with you gives me faith in the future, even when things feel upside down. Tracey Nyberg West, I so appreciate you standing up beside me and asking all the good questions.

Jessica Ellicott, you have been the most incredible mentor. Without your brilliant advice and you holding me accountable, I'd probably still be stuck on chapter twenty-two.

No writing exists in a vacuum and this has been one of the hardest projects I've ever done. While I was outlining this book, both my parents got sick with cancer. I wrote while sitting at their bedsides in hospitals, listening to the sound of respirators. My mother died the day after my first book was published and my father passed away twenty-three days later. Dealing with this kind of loss feels impossible, but I did not have to do it alone. My grief group at The Cancer Support Community of San Gabriel Valley helped me to function on the days I did not want to get out of bed. To protect their privacy, I won't mention them by name, but I hope they know how much they mean to me. This book would not be possible without them.

I am forever indebted to those who showed up for me at the worst possible time . . . and many other occasions: Neda Laiteerapong, Missy Stamler, Ken and Judy Freedman, Marcia Adelman, Madeline Woodward, Richard Fischoff, Carol Anne Been, Lois Glick and Pat Beneson. You will never know the depth of my gratitude.

To CeCe Pleasants Adams, Jessica Yarkin, Jessica Pratt, Burke Marksity, Ezra Siegel, Jessica Stebbins Bina, Alex Dueben, Tucker Hughes, and Danielle Lindemann. You are there through the good, the bad, and the ugly. I can't imagine life without you.

I am so grateful for my son's teachers. My work is only possible because I know Akiva is safe, loved, and learning so much that it's hard to keep up with him. I am so lucky to have such incredible partners in helping him grow into a kind, confident person. Thank you, also, to Paris Austin who is there when I do not have the capacity to juggle everything . . . or even somethings. You help keep life in balance.

And to Jason and Akiva. You are my heart and my home. I love you more than all the stars . . .

Book Club Questions:

1. What made you want to read this book? Did it live up to your expectations? *Echoes of Infamy* fits into a lot of different genres such as historical fiction, mystery and noir. Do any of those specifically appeal to you and why?

2. If you read *Under The Paper Moon* and/or *An Unquiet Peace*, the first two books in the series, how does this compare? Which themes continued and which changed? Do you have a favorite part?

3. This is the third book in a series. Do you think you need to have read the first two books to appreciate this one? Do you ever start book series in the middle or do you feel like you have to start from the beginning?

4. In the first book of this series *Under the Paper Moon*, Evelyn and Nick fall in love. In this book, we see them dealing with issues in their marriage. Which type of story do you prefer? Which do you think is more romantic, the beginning of a relationship or when it's more established?

5. One of the main stories in this book deals with Japanese Americans who were unjustly incarcerated during World War Two, because of the government's fear that

they might be spies. Has fear ever caused you to do something you regret? If so, how did you make amends?

6. Many of the characters in this book find themselves having to start their lives over with few resources and little support. What do you think is the hardest part for them? Some characters take desperate measures. Do you think their actions are justified? Have you ever had to start over from scratch?

7. Both Evelyn and Carl have big secrets that are revealed in this book. Do you think they wish they could have kept this information private? Have you ever felt the need to hide something from your friends or family? How did it make you feel? What happened when you told them?

8. One of the women Nick interviews stays in a marriage when she knows her husband is unfaithful. Are her reasons for staying understandable? Would you make a different choice if you were in her situation?

9. One of Evelyn's employees is uncomfortable with her coworkers and struggles with how to handle it. Can you understand her hesitance to bring the issue to her boss? Have you ever had similar problems? If so, how did you deal with them? Who did you turn to for support?

10. A situation arises where Evelyn worries that she is not good enough at her job. She also gets a lot of contradicting opinions from different people. Do you think she handles these challenges well? Have you ever worried that you were not qualified for something?

11. At one point in the story, Evelyn's best friend gets angry and does not speak to her. Do you think she should have respected his space or do you think she should have tried harder to apologize? How do you handle conflicts with friends?

12. Near the end of the book Carl is given a difficult choice of helping a friend or following the rules. Do you think he made the right decision? What would you have done?

13. This series deals a lot with the concept of family—the ones we are born into and the ones we choose. For both Evelyn and Nick, how are they supported or let down by their relatives? In what ways do their friends become family? To your mind, what defines a family? Do you think the ties of friendship can ever be as strong as a family of origin?

14. How much do you think the title and cover of this book represents the story?

15. Where do you think Evelyn and Nick will be in fifty years?